THE
FIRE
TRAIL

CHRISTINE SUNDERLAND

eLectio Publishing
Little Elm, TX

The Fire Trail
By Christine Sunderland

Copyright 2016 by Christine Sunderland. All rights reserved.
Cover Design by eLectio Publishing. © 2016. All rights reserved.

ISBN-13: 978-1-63213-284-0
Published by eLectio Publishing, LLC
Little Elm, Texas
http://www.eLectioPublishing.com

Printed in the United States of America

5 4 3 2 1   eLP   21 20 19 18 17 16

The eLectio Publishing editing team is comprised of: Christine LePorte, Lori Draft, Sheldon James, Court Dudek, and Jim Eccles.

Without limiting the rights under copyright reserved above, no part of this publication may be reproduced, stored in or introduced into a retrieval system, or transmitted, in any form, or by any means (electronic, mechanical, photocopying, recording, or otherwise), without the prior written permission of both the copyright owner and the above publisher of this book.

If you purchased this book without a cover, you should be aware that this book is stolen property. It was reported as "unsold and destroyed" to the publisher and neither the author nor the publisher has received any payment for the "stripped book."

The scanning, uploading, and distribution of this book via the Internet or via any other means without the permission of the publisher is illegal and punishable by law. Please purchase only authorized electronic editions, and do not participate in or encourage electronic piracy of copyrighted materials. Your support of the author's rights is appreciated.

Quotations from *With Hearts of Oak, The story of the Sisters of the Presentation of the Blessed Virgin Mary in California 1854-1907*, by Sister Mary Rose Forest, PBVM, used with the kind permission of the Sisters of the Presentation.

Quotation from UT History, used with the kind permission of Dianne Walker, Berkeley.

Publisher's Note
The publisher does not have any control over and does not assume any responsibility for author or third-party websites or their content.

This is a work of fiction. Names, characters, places, and incidents either are the product of the author's imagination or are used fictitiously, and any resemblance to actual persons, living or dead, business establishments, events, or locales is entirely coincidental.

Acknowledgments

I wish to acknowledge with thanksgiving:

The many friends, family, and clergy who read early and late drafts and encouraged me in the writing of this work, especially those who attended the University of California, Berkeley, and those who have lived in Berkeley.

The lovely ladies of Curves, Walnut Creek, for their listening to me chat about my latest novel as we exercise together, and for their encouragement and friendship.

The Sisters of the Presentation for their assistance with this project.

Dianne Walker for her excellent online history of University Terrace in Berkeley.

Kathie Johnson, contributor to *Touchstone*, who welcomed me into her bright and colorful children's library in her Berkeley home.

Christopher Dixon and Jesse Greever of eLectio Publishing who have made the publication of *The Fire Trail* a reality.

Editor Margaret Lucke who once again has given me invaluable suggestions in the creation of characters, the development of plot, changes in phrasing, punctuation, and grammar.

My dear husband Harry who reads my many drafts, cheering me on through the ups and downs of life and love, providing me safety and sanity, our own fire trail.

"Stand ye in the ways, and see, and ask for the old paths, where is the good way, and walk therein, and ye shall find rest for your souls."

Jeremiah 6:16, KJV

"Congress shall make no law respecting an establishment of religion, or prohibiting the free exercise thereof; or abridging the freedom of speech, or of the press; or the right of the people peaceably to assemble, and to petition the Government for a redress of grievances."

First Amendment to the Constitution
of the United States of America, 1791

"Liberty cannot be established without morality, nor morality without faith . . . . When the past no longer illuminates the future, the spirit walks in darkness."

Alexis de Tocqueville,
Democracy in America, 1831

"There are two freedoms — the false, where a man is free to do what he likes; the true, where he is free to do what he ought."

Charles Kingsley (1819-1875)

"The barbarians are those who in principle refuse to recognize a normative ethic or the reality of public virtue."

Richard John Neuhaus,
The Naked Public Square, 1984

THE
FIRE
TRAIL

One

Jessica

Jessica Thierry paused on the edge of the Fire Trail and gazed at San Francisco Bay spread before her. She had made the right decision, she thought, to walk alone this Wednesday afternoon, even though her roommate could not come. She fingered the lipstick-sized pepper spray in her pocket. She was nearly back at the trailhead and perfectly safe. She removed her glasses, wiped them carefully on her blouse, slipped them on, and looked out toward the wide water, the Golden Gate, the city, and the fog. She sighed, her shoulders relaxing.

San Francisco lay like a bride awaiting her lover, the bank of mist caressing her northern shoulder, slipping slowly in and over her bay. Spanning the gateway, the bridge was disappearing beneath the fog that rolled toward Berkeley's hills. The sweet rounded crest of Marin's headland rose, aloof. Pale blue sky crowned the city and the fog and the land, anointing them. Jessica inhaled the moist air, filling her lungs, and once again was touched with awe. She exhaled.

She was not winded, for she was a walker, not a runner, on this Berkeley trail that looped high into the forest of plane and pine, bay and eucalyptus, but she was thirsty. She pulled out a bottle of water, twisted the top, and sipped. Sitting down on the gravelly edge of the path, she wrapped her arms, protected by long sleeves, around her knees, her hands feeling the rough denim of her jeans. She leaned forward, studying the scene, drinking it in. The fog would lap these East Bay hills, fingering the shallow valleys, but the San Francisco skyline with its highs and lows might soon be buried, along with the bridge's rust-colored spires. Five o'clock was drawing near and ocean breezes were pushing the fog through the gate on schedule, this third day of September 2014.

Jessica loved September in these hills. She had only recently discovered the Fire Trail. In all of her twenty-two years growing up in neighboring Oakland, she had never hiked it. It wasn't until she was a student at Cal that she explored the easy wide path that protected Berkeley from uncontrolled brush fires in the surrounding hills. The firebreak passed through dappled light and sudden shadow, under canopies of old limbs, offering leafy windows that opened to patches of blue, with vistas beckoning around corners. Hiking the trail soon became part of her routine, and then part of her, but always it was new, changed by time and season, old growth and new growth as the living replaced the dead.

She loosed her honey-blonde hair from its white cotton band and wiped her forehead. As the sun warmed her skin, she considered she should have used sunscreen on her light complexion. Now, she feared, more freckles would appear. She stood and placed the empty water bottle in a corner of her pack, then slipped the canvas strap over her shoulder. She re-tied her hair, this time higher.

As she pulled the thick plait through the elastic and formed a bun, she heard a scream, shrill and terribly human. A girl's scream.

It came from the glen farther down the path, toward the trailhead. Jessica knew that the trail parted a grove of dense brush and pines, a dark shady stretch on the way to the parking lot. She summoned her courage, forcing herself to follow the cry, to help if needed. *No man is an island . . .* the words came unbidden. An intuition told her to stay where she was. She ignored it. As she entered the glen, a tall tense figure darted from the bushes, blocking her way. Unmoving, he stared at her. She stared back, her fingers tightening around the pepper spray in her pocket.

His eyes were wild and empty, his weathered face thin and haggard, his nose crooked as though once broken, his cheeks hollow. An angry red welt ran from ear to mouth. His straight black hair, limp with oil, brushed his neck. He raised a bloody hand as though to strike her, then withdrew it and hitched up his pants. He turned and loped down the trail toward town.

2

Trembling, Jessica watched him go. She pulled herself together and stepped toward the bushes, fearing what she might find, wanting to flee. She saw protruding feet, running shoes. She parted the brambles.

The girl's throat had been slashed and her head lay in a pool of blood soaking into the leafy soil. Her open eyes stared. She was young, probably a student, her only clothing a tight-fitting purple top.

Feeling sick, Jessica turned away and heaved. She wrapped her arms around herself to stop shaking. Finally her body quieted, and she staggered to the path. She glanced down the trail. No sign of him. She lowered herself to the ground, landing on a bed of pine needles and leaves. She reached for her phone and tapped 911 with quivering fingers.

* * *

Jessica waited, guarding the body.

She heard the siren first, wailing from the parking lot and screeching to a stop, then footsteps, followed by a hoarse female voice: "Here she is." Two officers approached, a man and a woman. "I'm Officer Moreno," the woman said gently.

A comforting face, framed by dark hair pulled into a police cap, peered at her, a mole near the upper lip. She evaluated Jessica, her hands on her hips. "What's your name, Miss?" She helped Jessica up and guided her away from the crime scene.

"Jessica Thierry."

"Jessica, let's go down to the station."

"Okay." Jessica glanced back at the body of the girl. The second officer was taping off the area.

"My partner will take over." Officer Moreno tapped her phone, spoke quickly, and slipped it into her pocket. "Detective Gan will meet us at the station. Can you tell me what happened?"

3

Jessica began haltingly, each word hunted down and trapped. "I was walking when I . . . heard a scream. I saw a man . . . come onto the trail. He ran away . . . I found the girl. Blood." Slowly, trying to tamp the panic, she described the horrific minutes that collapsed into a grave of open wounds in her memory; somehow the words formed sentences. "I . . . closed her eyes. I called you. I waited."

Jessica's eyes filled. Her throat constricted and she choked. She sat on the gravel and covered her face with her hands and sobbed. A dam had burst.

Officer Moreno sat alongside and slipped an arm around her shoulders. "It's okay, let it out." She pulled a tissue from her pocket. "Here you go. Let's wipe those eyes. It's over. You're safe now."

* * *

Detective Eddie Gan exuded an air of assurance, as though no problem were unsolvable: he merely needed to tackle it. He was a tightly built man of Asian descent, medium height, with short black hair and kind eyes in a wide face. He could have been a wrestler, Jessica thought. His muscled arms strained at the sleeves. A pencil rested behind one ear.

Jessica sat at a table with the detective. He asked and she answered. He made notes as she spoke. He looked up and nodded. He shook his head. He tapped the table and chewed the pencil. Officer Moreno brought them black tea in plastic cups, sweetener packets, wooden stir sticks, and creamers in mini-tubs.

"Do you think you could identify him?" Detective Gan leaned forward with such earnestness that Jessica wanted to say yes.

"I might." She sipped her tea with a shaky hand.

"We'll do a sketch and show it around. We'll get this guy."

Jessica nodded. The entire interview seemed outside her, running parallel, remote. The tight structure of the conversation was comforting, but she wanted to go home.

4

"I'll drive you back to your car," Officer Moreno said, touching her lightly on the shoulder. "Will you be okay tonight? Do you want to call anybody? You've had a shock."

"I'm okay." Who would she call? Who could she possibly pull into this heartache? The body flashed before her. "Who was the girl?"

"We're finding out," Officer Moreno said.

Detective Gan gave her his card and held open the front door. "We'll contact you when we have a sketch, and you can go over it with our artist. Is that okay?"

"Fine." Jessica shifted her pack and allowed Officer Moreno to drive her to her car.

Two
Graves

Jessica carried in her mind the girl and the blood and the horror as she drove to meet her mother the next day for their monthly visit. The images imprisoned her thoughts with unexpected waves of fear—panicky, prickly fear.

The fear had trailed her throughout the previous evening, ambushing her and clouding her concentration. She had kept the detective's card in her jeans pocket, fingering it from time to time for reassurance. She had made a sandwich and called her mother to confirm their meeting at the cemetery, but said nothing of the murder. The burden was too great to share, something that might tilt her mother even more toward the edge.

Queen of Heaven Cemetery in suburban Lafayette nestled in a quiet valley, thirty minutes east of Berkeley. Jessica followed Highway 24 to Pleasant Hill Road and soon entered the cemetery's open gates. She parked near a towering sculpture of the risen Christ, locked her car and, slipping her pack over her shoulder, headed up the path. Pink and yellow flowers splotched sweeping lawns crisscrossed with marble headstones etched with names and dates, some stones flat, some upright. Sunlight glanced off the polished slabs like diamonds.

Her mother sat in her usual place, head in hands, on a stone bench amidst the flowery graves, just as she had the first Thursday of every month for three years. Her hair had turned white, a public witness to grief. Jessica wondered how long she had been sitting there. It was ten o'clock, their appointed time.

"Hi, Mom." Jessica sat down beside her, slipping her arm around her mother's delicate hunched shoulders.

Carrie turned toward her youngest, forcing a smile. "I didn't see you come. I was afraid you weren't coming." She checked her watch. "You're late."

"I'm here, Mom. I said I was coming. I called, remember? Your watch is fast." Jessica tried to hide her irritation at the scolding; she could see her mother had been crying again. She had once been beautiful—an English beauty, some said—but today her face was pinched, her eyes bloodshot, her lids puffy.

They sat without speaking, as they often did, honoring her father's grave.

"Your father," Carrie began, wiping her cheek with a finger, "I miss him. It's been nearly three years . . . I thought it would get better, but it hasn't. Closure! Ha! What does anyone know about closure!"

Jessica followed her mother's gaze to the giant statue of the risen Christ intersecting the blue windswept sky. The face looked to the heavens, and the outstretched palms opened to the earth, raising the dead, as though Christ both mediated and melded Heaven and Earth.

Jessica spoke quietly, lost in her usual quandary over what to say. "I know, I miss him too." How she missed her father's robust strength: he had been larger than life. She missed his wide smile, his hefty grip, his sure hold as he twirled her at the father-daughter dance when she was nine, his hoisting her onto his shoulders in the Cal stadium so she could see better than her big sisters. Like turning the pages of a precious album, she returned to scenes in her memory, again and again, so that she would never forget. He had died too young at fifty-one, in his sleep, an aneurism they said. Was it from his college football years as a running back? Or maybe because of Samantha?

"Did you bring flowers?" her mother asked.

"I'm sorry. I forgot." She had meant to. She always brought flowers. Why didn't she remember? *The Fire Trail.*

"You can put these on your sister's grave." Carrie handed her daughter one of two bunches of red carnations. "I'll put these on your father's."

Jessica took the flowers and approached the headstone. With tender ceremony, she knelt and placed the carnations on the grass at the foot of the plaque.

Samantha Serena Thierry
1990-2009
Beloved daughter and sister
Rest in Peace

Carrie set her flowers in front of the neighboring grave.

Craig Stephen Thierry
1960-2011
A man of love,
Beloved by his family

"Let's walk, Mom," Jessica said, touching her mother's shoulder tentatively.

Carrie stood, smoothing her jacket and reaching for her tote. She wore a black jogging suit, red tee, and silver hoop earrings. Even in the confusion and heartache of grief, her mother dressed in her own confident style. They began to circle the garden, as they always did.

"Have you heard from Ashley?" Jessica asked, not unhappy that her older sister, Samantha's twin, rarely contacted them. Ashley was so different from Jessica, a terrifying example of lack of control. But her sister had turned twenty-four last week and perhaps, just perhaps, she had thought to call their mother. After all, Samantha would have turned twenty-four too, had she lived.

Carrie nodded. "I called her."

"Are things okay?" Jessica intuited they weren't.

Her mother shook her head. "In rehab again."

"Oh dear." Jessica adjusted her blouse over her jeans and checked that her cuffs were in place. She began to chant her own litany of self-help: discipline, self-control, delayed gratification; respect for the body, sex, mind, time; love as commitment and

9

mutual sacrifice. They were shortcuts for her rule of life, a rule that kept her safe and sane. She would not follow the path of her sisters. She would be different. She would do more than survive. She would succeed.

They walked in silence and soon left the twelve-by-twelve area of their family's graves where Jessica's father, along with her sister, rested with his French Catholic family. The living members were not so Catholic, time and inattention having eroded their beliefs. Even so, the Thierrys often chose to be buried together, some cremated, their boxes laid on top one another, some laid in full-body caskets, side-by-side. So be it, Jessica thought, not having a strong opinion one way or the other, except that she liked the orderliness of it, the planning ahead.

She turned toward her mother. "Mom, I need to tell you something." Her voice sounded deeper, more ominous.

Her mother waited, expectant, as though preparing for more bad news. "What is it? What's wrong?" she whispered.

"I . . . I . . . had a frightening experience yesterday."

"Go on." Her mother said, waiting.

Jessica spoke slowly, each word counting. "I'm okay, Mom, just a little shaken. But yesterday, a girl was assaulted—raped and murdered—on the Fire Trail." She hesitated, but the sudden silence was threatening. "I found her body."

Carrie reached for Jessica's hand. "Tell me about it, all about it." Her eyes widened. She had lost one daughter, a second was in rehab, and her own sweet Craig, the love of her life, was gone too.

Jessica described coming across the girl, but left out the encounter with the crazed man. There was no reason to worry her mother about that. The body was enough, maybe too much. Why had she said anything at all? She bit her lip.

"How terrible . . . are you okay?" Her mother sounded worried, less distant.

"Didn't sleep much last night." And she'd had nightmares, she recalled, darkness and blood and chaos.

"When does your roommate come home? You shouldn't be alone. Stay with me."

"Shelley gets back next week. But I have my research. I have my advisor meetings. I have a class in my doctoral program, a seminar. I'll be busy. I'll be fine."

"You need a job, maybe part-time. You need to be around people." Her mother thought socializing the best therapy. She had been at the top of her real estate sales when she left the Oakland agency to sell condos in Lafayette, hoping the change would help with her grief. It didn't.

"I *could* use the money," Jessica admitted.

"You need friends, Jessica. More friends. It's not healthy the way you live."

"I have friends." Did her mother want her to live like Ashley? Or as Samantha once did? They had friends, parties, drugs. They had pregnancies terminated.

"Shelley is your only friend, and she's a workaholic like you."

"I have my Fidelity meetings." The campus group had helped immensely, given her a powerful list of controls.

"You only attend their lectures, as I recall." Her mother raised a brow, tilting her head skeptically.

"Okay, I'll see about a job," Jessica said, appeasing her. She didn't need friends. She needed to focus on her degree. Her mother couldn't pay for everything. Her father had done well in construction and real estate, and had left her enough to cover her rent for a few years. Her mother paid her tuition. Two more years of school and she could teach undergrad History. Then she would pay her mother back. *Discipline and self-control, delayed gratification.* Simple really. Friends and socializing could come later.

Arriving at the risen Christ and the family plots, her mother paused. "I'm staying a bit longer. You go ahead. You have Shelley's car?"

"Such as it is." The windshield wipers didn't work and the idle was off. It had stalled a number of times. But it still ran, sort of.

Jessica embraced her mother, bending over the thin frame. She followed the path through the graves. When she reached the drive, she glanced back. Her mother was gazing at the surrounding hills, golden against the blue sky, her lips moving silently.

Three
Comerford House

That afternoon Jessica worked with the police artist, a criminology student, to create a version that somewhat reflected her description. But how could a sketch capture the curling lips, the vacant eyes?

Detective Gan stood nearby. As Jessica shouldered her pack to leave, he said, "You've gone through an ordeal. We have counselors if you need them."

"Thanks, but not now." What good would a counselor do, except take up more of her time? The image of the girl and the blood flashed before her. "Who was she? The girl?"

The detective hesitated as though weighing what to reveal. "We haven't reached her family yet. But I can tell you she was a Cal student, from Missouri. Her roommate identified her this morning."

"I feel so terrible for her."

"We all do. These things shouldn't happen."

"Did she know him . . . the murderer?"

"We don't think so. It appears random. Your description sounded like one of the People's Park regulars."

"He might still be wandering around the Fire Trail."

"We can't close the trail. Use caution, walk with a friend, don't go alone."

"Okay." Jessica's lip quivered as she turned toward the door.

"Let us know if you need anything, any help," Detective Gan offered.

She glanced back. "I will . . . Detective Gan . . ."

"Yes?"

"Will I have to testify?"

"Let's cross that bridge when we get there. If we find him, we want to convict him, don't we?"

"I'll testify." With these words she felt more assertive, in control.

She returned home, the crazed man's image more vividly alive in her mind than ever.

* * *

That evening Jessica worked on her outline, referring to her notes on the history of Berkeley, the subject of her dissertation. Her working title was "Irish Nuns and the Early Years of Berkeley, California." It was difficult to focus after recent events, but her advisor meeting was the next morning. What did she have at this point that she could show him? She disciplined her thoughts, channeling them into her subject.

She made a salad for her dinner break, washing green leaf lettuce, slicing tomatoes and avocadoes, adding a can of tuna. She skimmed the local news on her laptop. *Eminent Berkeley scientist dies by chemical suicide. Telegraph Avenue power-washed to revitalize historic shopping district. Two teens shot on Harmon Street. Student raped and murdered on Fire Trail, identity being withheld pending notifying next-of-kin. No leads as to suspects. Police looking for a white male, dark hair, medium build, facial scars, for questioning.*

The description was close enough, but she wasn't mentioned, and for that she was glad. She tried to shove the crisis to the back of her mind, controlling her fear. She worked until ten, reading and making more notes, then took two aspirin for a raging headache. But she slept better that night, the nightmares devoured by time, exhaustion, and her increasing interest in Berkeley's history. Early settlers, farmers, and an order of nuns populated her dreams, but they walked through pine forests and sudden clearings with flowery meadows, statues, and bloody headstones.

* * *

Friday morning, shortly after eight, Jessica watched Dr. Joshua Barnes, sitting behind a heavy oak desk, as he scanned her paper. Fearing her advisor's judgment, she studied his face for clues, his reading glasses slipping slowly down his nose. He was as dapper and formal as he had appeared in her European History class with his yellow bow tie and white collared shirt. A navy blazer draped the back of his chair. She thought he must be close to retirement, his crow's feet testifying to his experience.

He whipped the first page over, and it dangled on the corner staple, the snap of the page slicing the silence. He glanced up, eyed her intently, then returned to the page. As he skimmed and flipped the pages, he rolled a pen in his free hand. Occasionally he scrutinized the text and jotted in the margins with precise printing. Finally, he dropped the outline onto the piles of other papers and books domiciled in neat stacks on his desk. He waved his pen, as though giving it air, and leaned back in his swivel rocker. He touched his neatly trimmed mustache, then pulled lightly on his short beard.

"Substantive and significant, two qualities necessary in a good dissertation and can be developed from this outline," he began, staring at her and removing his glasses. "But I must say it is also remarkably brave."

Jessica sat up straight, scrutinizing him, squinting and tilting her head. "Brave? Is that good-brave or bad-brave?"

His smile held both irony and bitterness. "Both, I should say. Ms. Thierry, you have been admitted to one of the most prestigious doctoral programs in the world—History at UC Berkeley. Only ten percent are admitted annually. You come with an excellent academic record, and I can see why you were chosen. This early outline, to be sure, with your perceptive notes, reflects those abilities."

"But?" She could hear a qualifying tone.

"You must realize that the subject may be controversial—since it is not viewed through the lens of class warfare, indigenous peoples, race or gender issues, or America's imperialism. But I congratulate you that you are not bowing down to the academic powers that be. I'd like to see more of this kind of work, real history. To be sure, I'd like to see more students tackle what actually happened, not polemicize facts to fit a social narrative, *any* preconceived narrative for that matter."

"Thank you." Jessica knew there were codes of thought prevalent on campus, in class, among students, direct and indirect in texts and lectures. "I would like to do real history, as you say."

"If I might ask, Ms. Thierry, how you decided on a History major and then doctorate? What appealed to you? What interests you, what commands you? What drives you to fight the establishment?"

Jessica responded openly. "I actually began as a Psychology major. We had family issues growing up—and I wanted to be a therapist to help others as I had been helped." She grew silent, not sure how much information to divulge in this setting, at this time.

"Please continue," he said, clearly interested.

"I came to realize—through some lectures I attended here at Cal—that there are basic truths that surface from time to time in a society's culture. I learned and came to believe that if history isn't passed on to the next generation, the culture will starve."

Dr. Barnes steepled his fingers thoughtfully. "Indeed."

"One lecturer said that history is a cousin to philosophy, that history helps us create a philosophic structure with which to understand our world. Without history or a philosophic construct based on history, we choose to understand our world through pop culture—raunchy and violent movies, primitive music, coarse language."

"Ah," Dr. Barnes said, standing. "You remind me of my own college years, my own excitement with the study of history. I was told the same, but had nearly forgotten the words, the phrasing. Without history, we always said, we cease to ask T.S. Eliot's permanent questions, who am I, what am I, where am I going, or better yet, who are we, what are we, where are we going as a nation, as a world, as a planet." He sat down, again listening eagerly.

"That's it. So I changed my major in the first year from Psychology to History."

"And I appreciate the change. I agree to remain as your advisor, but you need to do a lot of work before I can fully approve this outline. You need to flesh it out. And you need primary sources. Have you been up to Comerford House?"

Jessica had heard of it. "The museum?"

"The Comerford family had a connection with early Berkeley and with your Irish nuns, the Sisters of the Presentation. You might visit."

Jessica made a mental note. "Okay, I will."

"It's not far from the Fire Trail base."

She blanched. "The Fire Trail?"

"You know where it is, of course?"

"I do," she replied, her throat dry.

"Good." He seemed to wonder at her hesitation. He handed her the paper. "Ms. Thierry, flesh it out, do the research, and good luck. We can meet again in a few weeks when you're further along."

As she left her meeting, she felt triumphant with Dr. Barnes' words, his tentative approval. But she decided to put off going to Comerford House and Museum, so near the Fire Trail. That could wait until her memory no longer stabbed her with the face, eyes, and swagger of the crazed man. She needed to forget, not remember. She needed a good night's sleep.

She needed, she decided, to cosset herself with familiar routines, and as she arrived home, she concentrated on lunch. She broiled an open-face sandwich (cheddar, tomatoes, nine-grain sliced bread) and poured a glass of milk. She reviewed her notes.

How would she spend her afternoon? The library? Internet research?

But Comerford House called her, and in her keen desire to understand the past, her curiosity trumped her fear. She checked online for more information about the house-museum. Photos showed it to be a charming early twentieth-century mansion in the hills, but best of all she could walk there without actually setting foot on the Fire Trail that ran behind it. The house would take her mind off recent events. The opening time was two p.m. She could do more research while her phone charged.

* * *

The day was warming up, the afternoon sun winning its skirmish with the morning fog. As she left her apartment Jessica reached for her Cal Bears cap to protect her face, pulling her ponytail through the back opening. She checked her phone. The time was 1:45, the battery charged. She added a bottle of water to her pack and decided to walk the mile to the house. It was good exercise and she had the time. She could take the hidden stairs that cut through the switchback lanes. She headed up Hearst, toward the hills, toward the Fire Trail.

The stairs led to a lane winding up and into a wooded hillside, and Jessica found the gated entrance, overshadowed by huge plane trees. The gates were open and she peered up the drive but couldn't see the house. A white sign with black script on a wrought iron post read:

Comerford House and Museum
Open Tuesday-Sunday, 2-5, Closed Mondays

Jessica shifted her pack and slipped a loose strand of hair behind her ear. She adjusted her glasses and stepped up the rutted drive parting the trees. A breeze rustled broad leaves high above and a pattern of sun and shadow danced on the craggy pavement. Not surprising, she thought, that a chain barred cars from the entrance, and you could only approach by foot.

The woods intrigued her. She glimpsed red roses beyond pines and eucalyptus. Were the roses wild? Was there a garden? The hum of town traffic that she took for granted faded into silence, leaving only the whisper of leaves and the crunch of her foot on the drive that soon became gravelly shards. The giant trees dwarfed her, and she felt as if she were walking through time, a single lone soul. What would she find in this Tudor-Revival mansion, close to one hundred years old?

She followed the drive around a corner and, continuing uphill, heard the distant notes of a piano tripping down the scale, like a waterfall skipping over rocks. The single notes were touched tenderly and lightly as though asking a question, then pulling her into the answer. What was the piece? Something classical, something romantic, something . . . perhaps Beethoven, she thought, recalling the movie *Immortal Beloved.* She drew near, and the notes trilled in groups, rising higher as she ascended the drive, and again downward as if searching for something lost. Then the melody returned, flush with chords, no longer lone notes.

Around another bend a magnificent white three-story house came into view, a queen on her grassy throne. Jessica paused where the forest met the lawn, listening to the music that seemed to come through an open window and studying the half-timbered façade. The shingled roof with chimneys on the sides and back was steeply pitched and gabled, rising above neat dormers with overhanging eaves and mini-paned windows. A broad porch aproned the front, and brick stairs descended to the lawn. The stairway, broken by three landings, parted unkempt grass dotted with daisies. An American flag flew high, rippling in the breeze and catching the afternoon light. As the windows reflected the western sun, Jessica took out her phone, tapped the camera icon, and captured the image.

Jessica knew that many of these hillside homes built around this time—after the 1906 San Francisco earthquake—had been destroyed by the firestorms of 1923 and 1991. Comerford House was one of the few that remained. She was glad it had survived and, welcomed by the music, she crossed the lawn and climbed the stairs. She guessed the pianist was practicing, for he or she repeated phrases and chords and then was silent as though waiting for other instruments to sound their parts. Marveling at the moment, touched with expectancy, she reached the verandah where a bay window curved alongside a heavy oak door with an etched wooden sign reading, "Welcome to Comerford House and Museum."

The music stopped. A bench scraped. Jessica tried the door, but it didn't give. As she searched for a doorbell, she read a notice in the lower corner of the window: "Help Wanted, Please Inquire Within."

Was the house closed? The sign at the entrance had read 2—5. She must have missed something. She turned around to survey the front yard. From this vantage, the faded brick stairs seemed smaller, tumbling into the grass. The towering trees guarded the yard and shaded the hidden drive. Beyond and above the trees, from this higher elevation, she could see the San Francisco skyline, the Golden Gate, and the Marin headland, a view similar to her Fire Trail lookout. The fog had disappeared; the day was fair. A cat meowed and a bird cawed in the distance. She turned back to the oak door. A brass lion's head knocker grinned. She raised the heavy ring and tapped lightly, then once again with more assurance.

Four
Zachary

As Jessica headed to her advisor meeting on Friday, Zachary Aguilar prepared breakfast in his studio apartment. He looked forward to running the Fire Trail. He had heard about the murder, but had grown numb to Bay Area crime reports. At twenty-six, he trusted his own strength and instincts. Though he was of average height, he considered himself fitter than most.

He often ran the trail, but he also pumped iron for upper body strength at the Cal gym, when he wasn't teaching Mondays through Thursdays. Fridays were unscheduled, usually devoted to working odd hours at Laurie's Fine Books on College Avenue or his exercise regimen. Some Friday mornings he met Matt, Jed, and Aaron, high school friends, for a few rounds of tennis so that he could keep his 4.0 level strong. Later, in the afternoon, he would often help his mother with her docent tours at Comerford House or with whatever else she needed. This Friday he hoped to practice Beethoven's Emperor Concerto on the grand piano in the music room. He dreamed of one day playing with the CCMS—the Comerford Chamber Music Society—but he wasn't good enough yet.

There was no piano in Zachary's room in the stucco bungalow on Short Street. There wasn't enough room even for his mother's upright, his practice piano from his childhood. Nonetheless he could listen to the concerto on his phone, the music streaming through earbuds as he made his breakfast in his kitchenette. He liked to create his own meals, controlling his intake of calories and nutrition, and keeping his expenses as low as possible. He scooped ground coffee into the filter basket of his coffee maker, added water to the well, and tapped the button. He poured nonfat milk over granola in a bowl, and as he stirred the mixture, the seeds and nuts and dried fruit swirled and surrendered. He carried his breakfast to his only window and slid onto a stool.

The window faced east and Zachary enjoyed the morning sun on his skin, his free Vitamin D, as he listened to the Beethoven concerto. Over the music he could hear Mrs. Zimmerman bustling downstairs and shouting to Mr. Zimmerman who often forgot to wear his hearing aids. Her admonitions were muted by Beethoven, and Zachary watched Short Street wake up to the sounds of the piano concerto. Even so, doors slammed and scooters gunned, as the bungalows sent their inhabitants into the day, one which, Zachary observed, promised to be fair. He rose and set his empty bowl in the sink, poured the coffee into a plastic cup, capped it, grabbed his keys, and headed for the door.

He paused before his books, lined on shelves covering the walls. Books flanked the narrow bed, surrounded the rickety chest of drawers, and rested under the window sill. He guessed he must have crammed hundreds of books into the room, and he was proud he had arranged them alphabetically by author. The collection was mostly English literature, with a smattering of American, and now he searched for the slim volume of Elizabeth Barrett Browning he had acquired while working at Laurie's. His long index finger found it—no dust jacket, yellowing pages, fair-to-good condition— and he tenderly pulled the book from its home between William Blake and EBB's poet-husband, Robert Browning. Clasping it, he bounded down the stairs, waving to the Zimmermans. He closed the front door behind him, flipped to the red leather bookmark, and glanced at the poem he had chosen to memorize, "How Do I Love Thee?," as he lowered himself into the driver's seat of his old Volkswagen bug.

He had the first three lines pretty much down, he thought, as he inserted a key into the ignition. If Elizabeth Barrett Browning was to be the subject of his doctoral thesis he wanted to understand her thoroughly, wanted to feel the words in his heart and soul. As he motored up Hearst Avenue, his car windows open to the fresh air, he recited, "How do I love thee? Let me count the ways./I love thee to the depth and breadth and height/My soul can reach, when feeling out of sight/For the ends of being and ideal grace."

He turned south on Shattuck and east on Dwight Way, heading toward the hills. As he passed People's Park he slowed, eyeing the makeshift tents and blankets sprawled haphazardly on the scruffy grass under the trees. How had this rebel community, formed in the 'sixties, survived so long? Crime lurked within the shadows, usually one squatter against another, and Zachary knew from the daily news reports that rapes were not uncommon, that drugs hardened consciences and empowered lust. Some of the park's denizens ventured into the surrounding neighborhoods, to Telegraph Avenue and beyond, where they shattered windows, battered parked cars, stole from careless pedestrians, and robbed shops. Laurie had long ago put iron bars on her ground floor windows on College Avenue, having relocated from Telegraph many years earlier. That such lawlessness was considered self-expression or free speech crossed the boundaries of logic, Zachary thought.

He drove into the hills, reciting his Browning, and by the time he reached the trailhead, he thought he had the lines down well enough to begin the next ones. He parked and checked the page: "I love thee to the level of every day's/Most quiet need, by sun and candle-light." He loved that part, *by sun and candle-light*. Zachary knew EBB lived from 1806 to 1861. Her home must have been lit by candles or possibly oil lamps. Gaslight was appearing in public spaces, but electric light would not appear until after her death.

He locked the car and turned to the trail, slipping on earbuds and touching the app on his phone for his playlist. Soon Borodin's String Quartet No. 2 in D Major, filled his ears. Zachary smiled, recalling that the Russian composer Alexander Borodin wrote the piece for his wife Ekaterina in 1881, setting to music their falling in love in Heidelberg twenty years earlier. For Zachary, the most beautiful of the four movements was the third, "Notturno."

As the cello and violin sang to one another, Zachary repeated his Browning. He soon fell into an easy stride, his soul overflowing with words, music, and beauty. But behind the words and beneath the music, counterpoint to Browning and Borodin, somewhere on the edges of his mind and memory, Zachary watched for the student from last year's Romantic Novel class.

She had been reserved, with large-framed glasses. She had sandy hair, kind of wavy and wispy, that she tied back with a band at the nape of her neck, no bangs, just a few strands that often escaped and fell into her face. She had large green eyes with flecks of gold and fair skin with a ridge of freckles on her nose. She had a habit of squinting when she talked and tilting her head when she was thinking. Sometimes she fiddled with her hair, slipping a strand behind her ear or adjusting the tie on the ponytail. She kept to herself, as though holding herself together, like a watertight ship in a stormy sea. She seemed complete, but fragile and mysterious at the same time. She wore loose, long-sleeved blouses and jeans, a bit boyish. The students gave oral reports, and hers was on Austen's *Pride and Prejudice.* When she spoke of Mr. Darcy she sounded ethereal. Sweet and ethereal. She "got" Mr. Darcy.

Now, her image returned to Zachary as he ran. He had seen her on the trail once before. Would he see her today? And if he did, what would he do? What would he say, if he had the courage to say anything at all?

Five
Father Nate

Friday morning, before Jessica Thierry met with her advisor and Zachary Aguilar ran the Fire Trail, Father Nathaniel Casparian, known as old Father Nate, laid out five bowls of dry cat food on the back porch of his cottage behind Comerford House. The floorboards creaked and a light wind blew through the eucalyptus trees.

"Come here, little ones, come here," he whispered, not wanting to wake his brother upstairs. "Breakfast time."

The cats soon bounded up the steps. He had named them after the cats in T.S. Eliot's *Old Possum's Book of Practical Cats.* Munkastrap, a white longhair, kept her nose high and her fur clean. Quaxo, sleek and black, with a bobbed tail and hypnotic green eyes, slid into view when not expected, silent and clever. Coricocat, a tortoiseshell, was shy and usually let the others go first. Father Nate thought she might have been abused, for if anyone appeared on the porch with him—except his brother Nicholas—she wouldn't show up for her feeding. Bombalurina, a dark gray shorthair who reminded the priest of approaching rain, had the sweetest temperament. She came to him first, before the food, and offered her head to be rubbed. "Good morning, Princess Bombalurina," he said, scratching behind her ears. Usually last, as though herding his sheep, came Jellylorum, a huge red tabby whose strong hindquarters testified to a wild life before finding Comerford House and the good Father Nate. Jellylorum appreciated affection as well and rubbed against Father Nate's legs, purring loudly and leaving swathes of light hair on his dark slacks.

Father Nate loved the cats for they loved him back, in spite of his damaged face. The explosion ten years ago, the gas igniting in the bungalow in old Berkeley, had been an accident waiting to happen, the news team reported. Father Nate and Nicholas were lucky to be alive.

The fire had left frightening red welts covering the priest's cheek, running from above his eye to his neck, a scary sight to most folks. Their reaction was understandable: averted eyes, glancing toward the angry scar one more time, then embarrassment that they had glanced. After the fire, he realized he could no longer be effective in a parish church and was grateful that Comerford House had taken him on as caretaker and gardener, giving him use of the cottage and the old chapel in return. His bishop had agreed, and while he couldn't celebrate the Eucharist in a deconsecrated chapel, he was given permission to hold prayer services. Not a bad bargain, he thought. Father Nate was thankful for what he had been given, but he was especially thankful for the cats. They never averted their eyes; they never showed embarrassment. They simply loved him. As did his brother, Nicholas.

And Father Nate loved Nicholas, his fraternal twin, diagnosed five years earlier with Amyotrophic Lateral Sclerosis, Lou Gehrig's Disease. The ALS was progressing steadily. Nicholas was wheelchair-bound, his arms partially paralyzed. He could form words, but speech was an effort; he slurred like a drunkard. Yet his eyes were the same as ever, alert and eager to connect. Father Nate could see and feel his frustration as though it were his own. One day Nicholas would need a tracheotomy, but not yet. He could still swallow.

The priest heard stirrings upstairs, and Nicholas peered through the open window, his head angled oddly. His brother was the handsome one, Father thought, as he waved back. Fortune was like that. Everyone had blessings and everyone had curses. It was the way of the world, at least this fallen world.

"I'll be right up, Nicholas my boy . . . oh, and, happy 77th birthday!" He shuffled into the kitchen to prepare a breakfast of scrambled eggs and bacon. He had bought Nicholas' favorite raisin muffins for the occasion. He lit the fire under the kettle and set out the chamomile tea bags.

Brenda, their home-care aide, pounded down the stairs with her ample frame. "He's all set for another glorious day," she said as she checked her watch and opened the front door.

"Have a muffin? Tea?" Father Nate asked.

"Gotta run. I'm late already."

"Many thanks, my dear, and blessings on your day!" He raised his hand and signed a cross in the air with a mottled finger.

Brenda's face lit up with the blessing. "See you tomorrow, Father Nate." She touched the medallion she wore around her neck, waved, and closed the door behind her.

Father Nate rubbed his hand over his thick white hair, smoothing down the stray ends, and shook his head. Brenda had a loving heart, a faithful devotion to God and her nurse's vocation. She never saw, or let on she saw, his ravaged skin. She never averted her eyes. And how did she manage so many cases, so many heartaches, so many crippled and dying? She was a treasure and didn't know it.

Father Nate said a prayer of thanksgiving on this the day of his and Nicholas' birth, for the cats, for Nicholas, and for the miraculous and beatific Brenda. He turned to the whistling kettle that sang like a chorus of angels.

Six
Anna

Around the time that Jessica met with her faculty advisor, Zachary ran the Fire Trail, and old Father Nate fed his cats, Anna Novak Aguilar, fifty-seven and trim, but not as trim as she wanted to be, settled herself in the driver's seat of her old Volvo and headed for her three-times-a-week CircleFit workout on Claremont Avenue. She had kept to her usual slimming breakfast: low-fat yogurt with protein powder, a whole-wheat English muffin (oh-so-lightly buttered), half a grapefruit, and Earl Grey tea with a dollop of milk and a drop of honey.

Anna could hear her pageant-protest signs rattling in the back of the car and made a mental note to secure them better next time. Made of short poles and white tag board, they were boldly printed, black on white: "Respect Children" and "Protect Childhood" and "Outlaw Children's Beauty Pageants." It was satisfying to have made them herself, but they were showing wear and wrinkling at the edges. She would make new ones when she had a chance, but these would have to do for today's gathering outside the studio by the bay. She hoped that her friend Laurie Warner would be there. Laurie might have suggestions as to making them sturdier, since she made signs for her bookstore.

For now Anna put the protest out of her mind and focused on her drive through her sweet Elmwood neighborhood of Berkeley. She considered, as she often did, how charming the houses were, as though each home had its unique personality. Many were shingled like her own two-story, inherited from her grandmother, but there were stucco cottages and colonials as well. The houses seemed grander as Elmwood merged into Claremont Canyon, where the neighborhood fanned down the hill from the century-old white hotel, which Anna called the palace.

But of all the houses in Berkeley, Anna loved Comerford House the best. Comerford was a historic house, on the official list of landmarks. Anna was a docent at Comerford and proud of it, passing on the history of Berkeley to visitors. But she worried that the house might close due to funding shortages. That would be sad. Father Nate and the others at Comerford House had become like family, a real blessing. Anna wouldn't have said she was religious, or even spiritual, but as she turned down Claremont Avenue she counted her blessings, just as her devout mother Marta had trained her. Comerford, for sure, was one of her blessings.

Another blessing was her roses. She glanced at the cut roses on the seat next to her. They looked okay, the stems banded in a wet paper towel in a plastic bag. Her three crops had been excellent this year, but she expected this would be the last before winter, when she would need to prune the stalks back.

Anna often mused that life was like a rose garden, that people were all roses growing in the garden of the world, different colors, varied markings and qualities, each one special. Some people were thorny, some smooth. Some were beautiful, some plain. Her own roses needed the discipline of pruning just like people did. If they weren't pruned, they didn't flower, which, Anna concluded, was true of both roses and people.

Anna knew she needed pruning a few years ago, when she was a tad too heavy. Now she needn't worry about being overweight, not with her new exercise program. The roses taught her about pruning, and Sue, her neighbor, told her about Cindy's CircleFit, where she soon learned how to prune herself and have fun at the same time, even make friends. Once size 16, now size 10! And she loved chatting with the ladies as they moved around the circuit, for her life was somewhat solitary since her ex, Luke, had left. With the music—fifties, sixties, seventies songs with an easy upbeat—the circuit was like a dance, both a dance of the body and a dance of friendship. She loved her CircleFit sisters. She would do anything for them . . . in a heartbeat, in a New York minute. They were another blessing.

As she parked and fed the meter, cradling the roses for Cindy, she wished Luke could see her now, admire her new slimness, in her black stretch-pants and purple jacket. When the fat melted from her face, her classic bones emerged. Her brown hair, slightly highlighted to cover early gray and cut in short feathery layers, set off her startling dark eyes, which now appeared larger. Her father had called them Slavic eyes, Croatian for sure, he had said with an appreciative nod. Anna wished her Luke could see her now, but it was too late for that. He wasn't her Luke anymore. He belonged to that Rosalind, half his age, and probably a size 2 or maybe even a size 0. Probably a minus 6, definitely unhealthy.

. At one time Luke had needed fat-pruning too. Still, he saw to it long before she did. He lost the weight, jogging and playing tennis with their son Zachary who lost his weight too. Not for the first time, regret rushed over and through her and gave her that awful sinking feeling in her stomach. *Such a loss.* How she had loved Luke, and still did, she would admit when she was honest with herself. How she wished she had seen it all back then, had pruned herself in time, but she hadn't, just hadn't seen it. And, as her mother often said, no use crying over spilled milk. It was water under the bridge, she would say. No point in beating a dead horse. After all, it was over two years ago that he moved out.

Today, Anna concluded as she entered the workout room, Luke needed sexual pruning, having run off to Lake Tahoe like that. Had Zachary seen the signs, the cracks in their marriage? He had been out of the house for years. Probably not.

Anna handed the roses to Cindy, who manned the reception desk. "Congratulations on your new granddaughter! How're mother and baby doing?"

Cindy smiled, her eyes alight with pride. "They're both fine and coming home today. Thank you, Anna. These are lovely. I'll get a vase."

Anna held her bar-code tag under the mini-scanner corded to the computer. A red line flashed on the tag and she heard the familiar beep as her name popped onto the screen. She placed her handbag in a woven basket along the wall and turned to the circle. She could see that half the circuit was humming with movement and chatter. She grinned her greetings to her lady friends and they grinned back as "We Are Family" played through the room.

* * *

There were twenty-four stations. Twelve were circuit machines, each one strengthening a different muscle set, with two-foot-square recovery pads in between, where the ladies stepped in time to the music, keeping their heart rate elevated, but resting their muscles. Every thirty seconds, a recording reminded Anna to "Change stations now." It was a line dance, a workout, and a coffee klatch all rolled into that half hour. She would make two circuits in that time, gently increase her circulation and heart rate, and she would leave, a little lighter, a little fitter, and a whole lot happier.

Nancy, Carol, and Jeannie were discussing movies they had seen recently, as Anna warmed up on a recovery pad nearby, stepping to the beat. She had assigned association labels to her friends to remember their names.

"It seemed like soft porn to me," Carol said, glancing at the others as she powered her legs forward on the leg press. A former teacher, she spoke with a certain authority. "I wish there could be better role models for the children."

Anna admired her, and not just because Anna had also once been a teacher. Carol was the Carer. She cared about everyone—animals, the sick, the lonely, the homeless. She volunteered at the local hospital and sometimes came to workouts in her smock. Anna had never worked in a hospital. It took a special kind of caring, she thought, to nurse the sick and the dying. There was old Father Nate at Comerford, but he helped her more than she helped him. She rarely thought about his face and the fire. And then there was his brother, Nicholas, whom she simply admired for his cheery temperament in spite of his paralysis. She had learned so much from both of them.

The ladies murmured their agreement to Carol.

"There's always sex and violence," Nancy said, as she pushed the Pec Dec with her forearms. "It seems nothing sells unless there's sex and violence." Nancy was the Novelist, and she was religious too. She went to church. But she didn't talk about her faith, and Anna sometimes wondered if that was a good idea. It was as if she were afraid, as if there were an unspoken ban on politics and religion in social settings, and CircleFit was no exception. Perhaps it was for the best.

"But you got published, didn't you?" Jeannie asked. "And you don't have that stuff in your books." Jeannie was the Jogger. Instead of resting on the pads, stepping lightly, she jogged in place, rotating outstretched arms. Jeannie was one of their younger members, probably late thirties, so she could increase her pace. She was a stay-at-home mom with a working husband. She, Anna could see, was one of the lucky ones, who took care of herself before it was too late.

Nancy laughed, loving to admit her small victory. "I did, but I was lucky. My publisher was the only one that would take a chance on me."

Anna considered herself a librarian, now that she worked at Comerford House and had filled two upstairs bedrooms with children's books. She slipped onto the seat of the Biceps/Triceps machine, placed her arms between the cushioned rollers, and began a vertical movement. "Young adult literature today is full of sex and violence and worse. Really dark stuff. I have to reject lots of books donated to Comerford. Even prizewinners."

"Any recommendations?" Jeannie asked, now on the Shoulder Press/Lat Pull, raising and lowering the handles vigorously. "My kids will be that age pretty soon."

Pleased to be asked and keen on sharing her knowledge, Anna replied, "Well, anything in *my* library. If I don't read them first, I read reviewers I trust. Come and visit. Honor system, no fees, no cards!"

"I should visit." Jeannie meant it, Anna could tell, as she nodded thoughtfully.

"I'm a pretty tough gatekeeper in terms of titles, some say," Anna added, stepping in time now to the Beatles' "Paperback Writer." "I like to think of Comerford children's library as a last refuge of civilization."

Carol glanced at her. "How did that tussle with the free speech people work out? I was rooting for you, Anna. I read about it in the paper. I thought it was awful the way they made you into some kind of censor."

Anna frowned, choosing her words carefully. "Free speech is important, so I have to say the accusations of book-banning really hurt. But porn is porn. And children are children. Adults are adults and should guide children, protect them, show them standards of behavior, not empathize with vampires and the living dead. You can't let darkness take over children's minds." Had she said too much? In the sudden quiet, Anna threw more fuel into her fire. This was her mission, and she couldn't stop. "Kidnapping and pederasty and incest and beatings. Real brutality!"

"I know," Carol said. "Even when I was teaching junior high— middle school—stories celebrated the criminal, the brutal, the heartbreaking. We were told it was good to experience the real world. I remember *Go Ask Alice*. I refused to recommend it . . . rape, drug addiction, prostitution, overdose. But I didn't have to deal with banning it, just avoiding it."

"It's worse today," Anna said. "Trust me. Mutilation and blood, vampires and sex, ghouls—the *undead*. Some say these characters reflect real life, but I say *please, give me a break*. Children are children. So today we have generations of adults that have been raised on this misery, with no heroes, no role models." Anna told herself to settle down. She was getting carried away. And then there were the child beauty pageants . . .

Nancy was jubilant. "Well said, Anna. Good for you." She fingered the gold cross around her neck. "I must have missed that news coverage. If I ever write a Young Adult novel, I'll be sure and let you know, but at this point I'm more interested in the grownups, such as they are."

"What are you working on now?" Carol asked.

"It's a mystery and a quest, set in Rome . . ."

As Nancy chatted about her novel-in-progress, Anna recalled the free speech issue of last year, how upset she had been when she had seen her name in the newspapers, but how, in the end, the board of the Comerford Foundation had supported her book choices. But for how long? It was a scary world, sometimes, when right was denied and wrong lauded. Where was it all leading?

Robin (the Reporter) had joined the group and was warming up on a recovery pad, stepping slowly.

"Any developments on the People's Park case, Robin?" Anna asked.

"Just that it wasn't 'stranger rape'." Robin shook her head.

"Stranger rape?"

"Meaning that in this case the man and woman knew each other. 'Stranger rape' is used to describe rape when the persons do not know one another, are strangers, as opposed to when they know one another but aren't on a date. When does no mean yes? If it happens at a party, not a date, is it date rape? As the law stands now, if the woman is intoxicated, the act is judged rape no matter what she said at the time, that is, if she's pressing a case. Of course, many women don't press charges at all."

Carol shook her head. "Crime is up everywhere, it seems. At least, it doesn't feel as safe as it was when I was growing up." She was working the Dip Shrug, standing straight, grasping the horizontal bar, pulling it up and pushing it down, like a railroad engineer.

They waited for Robin's analysis, their inside peek at the news media. Robin was too thin, Anna thought. She had worked out so often and dieted so strictly that, now in her late sixties, she reminded Anna of a prison camp refugee. Nevertheless, she was agile, and most likely strong, and she wore her blue spandex with style, her silver hair braided on top of her head, her aquiline features alert and confident. Anna figured that Robin didn't need pruning. She needed a vacation somewhere tropical with no exercise machines in sight and lots of tempting food, tortellini maybe, like Anna's mother used to make.

Robin turned to Carol. "Did you see how one of our photographers was robbed at gunpoint yesterday morning in West Oakland? Two men ran up to him and grabbed his gear."

"Were they caught?" someone asked.

"Not yet. Had a getaway car."

The ladies shook their heads and mumbled. It was not an unusual story, Anna knew, but the reaction was always the same. Disbelief. Denial.

"And," Robin added, moving onto the Squat Tip machine, "you've heard about the Fire Trail murder on Wednesday? Broad daylight!" She positioned her shoulders under padded bars and bent her knees, squatting, working her back leg muscles, pulling with her arms, pushing up with her legs.

"A murder?" Anna asked, concerned. "I work near the Fire Trail. It runs behind Comerford House. I didn't hear about it." But she had heard sirens Wednesday afternoon, she recalled.

"A girl was raped and murdered. The victim was a Cal student, but the police aren't releasing her name yet. They say the suspect is average height, thin, dark hair, scar running from ear to mouth. Caucasian. Will you let me know if you hear anything?"

"Sure," Anna said. She shuddered. A murder so close by. Was Comerford House safe? Was Father Nate safe? Was the trail safe? Her Zachary ran that trail. Did he know about the murder?

"Gads," Jeannie said. She stepped off her recovery pad and began her cool-down stretches. "I worry about my kids. I thought they would go to Cal, but it might be better to send them away, some small town."

Anna nodded. "Maybe so, but Cal's a great university, and you live here. They shouldn't have to go away to be safe."

Coach Cindy, her thick red hair swinging around her shoulders, stepped into the center of the circle. "My grandson would have been glad to get into Cal. But he never could discipline himself. His parents coddled him, wanted to be friends instead of parents." Her tone was edged with disappointment.

"You mean he didn't study enough in school?" Anna asked sympathetically.

"Exactly. Wanted to party all the time. He's a bright boy too, such a shame. Now he's on meds for depression. Can't find a job or his place in life. George and I feel so helpless." She showed Anna how to better position her hands on her machine.

"That's just it," Carol said. "Kids should be held accountable, held responsible for their actions. What happened to standards? Adults are afraid, it seems to me. Afraid of the kids. So the kids expect to slide through life with all this feel-good stuff, demanding positive self-esteem."

Cindy's tone was hopeful. "I think our new grandbaby will be raised differently ... my daughter has lots of common sense. Parents are getting wise."

"I hope so," Anna said, thinking of Zachary. At twenty-six, was he drifting? Going for his doctorate in English Literature? But he taught part-time and worked at Laurie's on weekends, loading, unloading, shipping, even making deliveries, writing book descriptions for the website. Before that he had been a steamfitter, repairing pipes, and he even had helped Father Nate with plumbing repairs. He was self-supporting. He paid his own way — rent, food, tuition. Maybe she and Luke had done something right after all. And Luke, in spite of his philandering, had worked hard as a grocery cashier, brought home a paycheck. He supported them. He made it possible for Anna to stay home and be a mom. For that she would always be grateful. Of course, Anna had inherited her grandmother's house, which helped with the budget.

Carol waved as she left the circuit, heading for her wicker basket. "Bye, ladies! See you next time!"

Terri (the Tiny) entered, fiddling with her bar-code tag. She reminded Anna of a water sprite, always surprised, always happy.

Anna moved to the Ab machine, tightening her stomach muscles, raising the weights and lowering them to the tune of "Mama Mia."

"Seen any good movies?" Terri asked the group. "I saw a fabulous one last weekend . . . the best love story . . . the cast was *so* good . . . It was called *Hana-lani* and it was set on Maui . . ."

Ten minutes later Anna left CircleFit. She checked her watch. The pageant protest would be starting soon, and she didn't want to be late. They were depending on her for those signs she had crammed into the back of her Volvo.

Seven
Sisters

Jessica's sharp clap with the lion knocker on Comerford's oak door was answered sooner than she anticipated, and she jumped slightly as the door swung open. A young man, broad-shouldered and slightly taller than she, peered at her, his brows raised. He wore jeans and a navy tee. Short dark hair framed a clean-shaven face.

"Welcome to Comerford House." He adjusted rimless glasses over brown eyes. "Sorry, the door must have been locked. We need to fix this." He wedged a rubber doorstop with a sandaled foot. "The tour has begun, but you can catch up with them." He pointed to a group at the base of the stairwell in the large paneled entry. "Mom . . . er . . . Anna," he said with a trace of embarrassment, "the docent, that is . . . er . . . she's right over there . . ." Nervously, he pointed again.

Jessica stepped over the threshold, nodding, and shifted her pack. "Thank you." His stare was discomfiting. Did she know him from somewhere? She crossed the foyer with its gleaming wood floors and joined other visitors gathered around the woman speaking. As Jessica found a place on the edge of the group, she continued to feel the man's gaze. He seemed familiar, but she couldn't place him. She turned her attention to their guide, who welcomed her with a slight wave.

"Please join us," the docent said. "We've only just started." Her resonate voice was low-pitched, a singer's voice. Jessica judged she was mid-fifties. She was petite with layered brown hair with streaks of amber that framed a heart-shaped face. She had an air of satisfied delight, Jessica thought, as though she had run into an old friend and couldn't believe her good fortune. She wore a green twinset over a floral, tiered skirt, and dangling earrings. A canvas tote with a lantern logo hung from her shoulder, and she clasped five-by-seven pastel index cards in one hand. As she leaned toward the group, making individual eye contact, Jessica was drawn to her warmth.

"Please allow me to repeat for our new arrival," she said cheerfully, as she handed Jessica a shiny brochure from the tote. "I'm Anna Aguilar—please call me Anna—and I'm the docent of Comerford House and Museum. Comerford House was built by Beatrice and Patrick McKinnon in 1914, so we're celebrating our centenary! The house has an intriguing history. There are many photographs of old Berkeley on the walls, a unique collection of antique chalices, and a children's library upstairs that is free, operating on the honor system. The house is also home to the Comerford Chamber Music Society. There is a historic chapel, and we even have a gift shop."

Jessica glanced back toward the front door, still ajar. The young man was gone. Was he the one who'd been playing the piano?

Anna caught Jessica's glance and beamed proudly. "You may have heard my son practicing the piano earlier. He's not supposed to play during opening hours, but this time I let him finish up his Beethoven. His dream is to be part of the chamber group one day."

Some of the visitors nodded, fingering their brochures. There were men and women of varied ages, and Jessica thought some might have been parents since they clearly shared Anna's pride. What would it be like to be a mother, to have children you were proud of? She wished her mother was proud of her, but couldn't tell, and mostly sensed that Carrie was far away and didn't want to return to mothering any time soon. Jessica could understand that, given the twins' troubles.

"Now for a wee bit of history." Anna folded her hands over the cards and leaned toward the group thoughtfully. "First the name, Comerford. Why *Comerford* when the family that built this house was named *McKinnon*?" She raised open palms. "The McKinnons were cousins of the Comerfords and greatly admired them. The family emigrated from Ireland, farmed, and made their fortune in early land development in Berkeley and Oakland. Beatrice's and

Patrick's portraits," she said, pointing to black-and-white photos on the wall, "date to about 1910, and you can see other family photographs throughout the house."

Jessica considered Patrick's image. He wore a jacket and tie, and while not smiling, he gave an impression of immense kindness. Beatrice, too, with her high frilly blouse and curly hair, had a composed quality, yet also a sense of goodness and deep satisfaction. Jessica thought they had probably been in love; in their twenties, they appeared to own some kind of happiness.

Anna continued. "The McKinnon family was part of the Irish emigration in the mid-nineteenth century. Why did the Irish emigrate, and who were the Comerfords? You may recall that gold was discovered at Sutter's Mill in 1848 and the historic Gold Rush began. First came the miners, then came those who wanted to profit from the miners. Then came the farmers who settled the land. Many farmers were Irish Catholics escaping the terrible potato famine in their homeland."

Anna moved toward two other photos on the wall. "One of those settlers was James McGee." She gestured to a black-and-white formal portrait of a serious man, bearded and balding, with a high forehead, in a dark jacket, white shirt and bow tie. "Next to him is Catherine, his wife."

Catherine's image was severe, her hair evenly parted and tamed close to her head. A brooch clasped a high collar. Jessica had seen the photos online, but these were larger, sharper and, located in this historic house, they seemed more real.

Anna moved toward another photograph, this one of a Neo-Gothic church with tall vertical windows, pitched roof, gabled entry, and bell towers. "James sailed from Ireland to Boston," Anna explained, "then took the ship *Areatus* to San Francisco in 1849. Five years later he settled in what is today central Berkeley, where he farmed grain. He must have done fairly well, for in 1878 he donated a parcel of property to Irish Catholic nuns in San Francisco. The land was bordered by Grove Street—today Martin Luther King

Way—Addison, Sacramento, and Dwight. A convent and school, as well as St. Joseph's Church, were soon built." Anna motioned to other drawings of the church complex.

Jessica opened her brochure, glad to see some of the photos, as well as a floor plan of the house and property.

"The nuns were called the Sisters of the Presentation of the Blessed Virgin Mary." Anna moved across the hall to a painting of a young woman, her hair hidden in a white cap. The young woman's eyes were loving and knowing, her face determined. "Here we have Venerable Nano Nagle of Ireland, founder of the order. Nano wanted to help the sick and needy, especially women and children. She founded Catholic schools in Cork when they were illegal and is credited with saving Catholicism in Ireland. She is called the Lady of the Lantern because she traveled the winding lanes of Cork in the dark of night with her lantern, visiting the poor and ill, bringing food and medicine, giving hope to those without hope. As she approached the last years of her life, she opened her first convent in a cottage on Cove Lane where she and four other women lived until Nano's death in 1784."

Anna paused, honoring this woman of good works, then moved to the next group of photos. "Now we come to Sister Mary Teresa Comerford of Kilkenny who, along with four Presentation Sisters from Midleton, County Cork, came to San Francisco in 1854. They established convents, and opened free schools for the city's children." She pointed to a photo of a nun with a tent-like veil. "As I mentioned, they were cousins of the McKinnons in Ireland."

Sister Mary Teresa leaned toward the photographer with questioning eyes, as though asking, "How will *you* help us feed, clothe, and teach the children of the world?" Jessica tried to imagine those times of such certain belief, such faith. She touched her own high collar, unbuttoned at the top and, for a brief moment, wished she had been born back then, when the world seemed more civilized and safe. Had humanity progressed or regressed? She knew from the study of history it was a question asked by many. She guessed there was no simple answer.

Anna turned to an etching of several buildings. "So a church, convent, and school were built on the property: St. Joseph's Church, St. Joseph Academy for Girls, which later became Presentation High, and St. Peter's School for Boys."

A gentleman in a tweed jacket, holding an unlit pipe, smiled and nodded. "My mother went to Presentation High. Didn't the Comerfords found the schools?"

Jessica observed the interchange, appreciating the living history in their group.

Anna grinned. "Lovely to have you here, sir. There are Presentation High alumni scattered throughout Berkeley and the Bay Area. And indeed, there were three famous Comerfords involved in these foundings. Mother Mary *Teresa* Comerford established the Presentation Sisters in San Francisco and Berkeley and built the schools. Her younger sister, Mary *Bernard* Comerford came to San Francisco and later Berkeley where she would be called *Mother* Mary Bernard. Their brother, Father Pierce Michael Comerford, came to Berkeley in 1878 to serve as parish priest of St. Joseph's Church." She eyed the gentleman with appreciation. "You are right indeed."

One of the women in the group asked, "Did the McKinnons know any of the Comerfords personally?"

Anna nodded. "A good question. Of course the families were related and from Ireland, but also, Beatrice McKinnon mentions Mother Mary Bernard, one of her teachers, in her letters. She may have known Father Comerford as her parish priest, but the older sister, Mary Theresa, who came first to San Francisco, died in 1881, before Beatrice's birth."

The gentleman with the pipe added, "Is that lantern on the bag referring to the Lady of the Lantern, then?" His eyes registered genuine curiosity, and Jessica guessed he had a keen interest in family history.

"It is." Anna held up the bag with the lantern emblem. "Beatrice and Patrick McKinnon named their house Comerford House. They adopted the emblem of the Presentation Sisters to honor their contribution to Berkeley's early days."

The group moved from photo to photo, and Jessica stepped back in time. Buildings were built, gardens planted, a Lourdes grotto created. After the 1906 earthquake, she could see that many survivors fled San Francisco to the East Bay. Little did they guess, she thought, that there would be earthquakes and fires here as well.

Anna opened her arms wide as though to embrace the house. "So you see, in 1914 Beatrice and Patrick McKinnon built this lovely Tudor Revival home in these hills, designed by Wexford Reynolds. Throughout the house you can see more photos and letters and mementos."

"World War One began in 1914, I believe," the gentleman said thoughtfully.

Anna nodded. "Although America did not enter the war until 1917."

"Of course," he agreed, stroking his mustache. "Interesting, though, to imagine the times. The McKinnons would have heard about the events of the summer of 1914. Do we know when exactly they moved in?"

"Not until the following year. Beatrice's brother would be killed in the war. The reports from Europe must have been troubling to say the least."

"And changed the twentieth century for all of us."

Jessica watched the gentleman with interest. His words entered her mind and were immediately filed on a shelf with other vital historical moments. In her studies, she had learned that there were, as one author had memorably stated, "hinges of history."

July 28, 1914, the day that Archduke Ferdinand of Austria was assassinated by a Serbian rebel, was one of those hinges, Jessica realized. That event aligned the major powers in the First World

War, a war that in many ways caused the Second World War, which produced many of the movements and trends of the last sixty years. It was a watershed moment, a pivotal time. The old world of class, formality, and manners began to crumble and a new world of equality, informality, and casual, even coarse, manners replaced it. Jessica recalled reading that it was as if barbarism had crossed the borders of civilization. It seemed to Jessica that when the Vandals invaded Italy in the fifth century, the Church civilized them. But in the twentieth century, with the ebbing of faith, the barbarians had the upper hand. Islands of civilization remained, continually threatened by the jungle culture washing their shores.

The story of the nuns and their work, as well as the life of the McKinnons, touched Jessica, and she looked forward to exploring the house and grounds and gift shop. She was intrigued with the timeline of the nuns and their presence in San Francisco and Berkeley.

"Now," Anna continued, "let's consider the decor, beginning with the entry. The floors are oak. The beams and trim are redwood, woods repeated throughout the house. The grand staircase with the oriental runner," she said, turning with a graceful gesture, "meets a landing with leaded windows. Let's now visit the library, which we call the music room so as not to be confused with the children's library upstairs."

They entered one of the front rooms to the side of the foyer. A grand piano anchored a corner, opposite windows that opened to the lawns. Books lined two walls, some behind glass, some on open shelves. Folded chairs and music stands grouped to the side. A moist breeze drifted in, carrying salty air from the Pacific Ocean.

"The house had several owners after the McKinnons," Anna explained, "and their stories are detailed in our book, *Comerford Tales Through the Years*, available in the shop. In the sixties, during anti-war demonstrations and Berkeley's drug culture, the house was ransacked and windows broken. It was locked and shuttered, and sold to a psychiatric clinic. Around this time these front rooms were expanded to allow for group therapy meetings. When the clinic closed in the 'eighties, a foundation formed to create a museum, a venue for the arts, historic exhibits, concerts, that sort of thing. There are classes for all ages, offered to the Berkeley community by the Comerford Foundation throughout the year."

Anna stood alongside an antique rolltop near the piano. "The house faces west, and the view may have been even more panoramic from here when the trees were young. Beatrice did most of her writing at this desk." Anna laid her hand tenderly on the old maple. "She was a novelist in the style of Jane Austen, but today her works are no longer in print. You can see her first editions and other nineteenth-century first editions in the glass cases. After the devastation of the First World War—as you recall, Beatrice lost her brother in the fighting—both Beatrice and her mother were interested in preserving Victorian culture, 'civilized culture,' they called it."

And little did they know, Jessica thought, that a young woman would be raped and murdered on the Fire Trail so nearby, their fears realized. The girl, the blood, and the woods flashed into her mind. Jessica shivered and tried to steady her shaking fingers by gripping the brochure tightly.

"Is this where the Chamber Music Society performs?" someone asked.

Anna smiled. "Indeed. They practice here as well, and sometimes hold concerts in the gardens."

They left the music room, crossed the foyer, and entered the room opposite. Jessica recognized the bay window she had seen from the porch. The space, in spite of the dark woods, was bright and airy and appeared to extend far to the back of the house, as though two rooms had become one. Greenery rustled beyond paned windows. Sofas and chairs were grouped congenially. It was a friendly room.

"This is the drawing room," Anna said. "Originally there were two *withdrawing* rooms, where women withdrew after dinner, leaving the men to their port and cigars. But over the years the wall separating them was removed to make a larger meeting space. Note the two redwood-paneled fireplaces. Here in this front parlor the family gathered to read to one another, to play musical instruments, and even perform short plays. The McKinnons had eight children, three boys and five girls, born in the 1920s and 1930s."

Jessica and the others followed Anna through a wide doorway. "And here we have the dining room. Note the tiled fireplace. Stained glass windows face the back gardens. The McKinnons held school fundraising dinners here from time to time. Now we go through these double doors into the kitchen."

The spacious kitchen looked out on a terraced hillside. Jessica could see a stone chapel hidden in the pines beyond.

"This room," Anna continued, "has been modernized many times. Even so, the basic proportions remain, a large area for cooking and washing. It once incorporated an ice room and a smoke room for curing meats. The old hearth, where game roasted on a spit," Anna said, pointing to the south wall, "has been replaced by commercial ovens and refrigerators."

They stepped outside onto a brick patio, where a manicured lawn ascended to garden beds, and pine and eucalyptus trees.

"Through the trees," Anna said, "you can see the stone chapel where a priest once said daily Mass. Today the chapel hosts a local choir who sing *Evensong*, Anglican chant dating to the sixteenth century and earlier, on Sundays at five during the school year. If there are any Roman Catholics in the group, you might ask why Anglican Evensong is allowed in a Roman Catholic chapel. The chapel was deconsecrated in the sixties when the house was closed. It was reopened as an interdenominational chapel, used by the university and other groups."

An elderly woman with white hair nodded appreciatively. Her black cardigan hung low over her slacks, and she wore a cross in the vee of her white blouse.

Anna glanced at her with reassurance. "The cottage next door to the chapel was once the greenhouse but now is the caretaker's residence and garden shed. Our gift shop is next door."

Someone asked, "Is there another access to the house, besides the parking area below and walking up? It seems a long way for events."

Anna nodded. "Upper drives are open for events, deliveries, and handicap access. There is a parking lot there as well." She waved to someone in a window of the caretaker's house.

"I heard there was a rose garden," a woman said.

"The rose garden is beyond the chapel—just follow the path. It's open to the public. It replaced the old kitchen garden. And so . . . we now conclude our tour." As Anna handed out small magnets with the image of the Comerford lantern, she added, "Please feel free to walk the grounds, visit the shop, and ask any questions. Upstairs you can see period furniture in the bedrooms and browse the children's library."

"You mentioned a chalice collection?" a young man asked.

Anna smiled with appreciation. "The McKinnons collected chalices once used in historic churches. They are displayed in the chalice room with other antiques, second floor at the end of the hall. Please respect our roped-off areas. And, since we don't charge for tours or restoration projects, donations are always welcome in the shop."

"Do you have a concert schedule?" an elderly woman asked. "I'm afraid I don't do the Internet."

"We do," Anna said, smiling with understanding and pulling a flyer from her bag.

More questions were raised, hesitantly at first, then with greater assurance. Some visitors thanked her and wandered toward the gift shop.

Jessica wanted to ask about the job posting, but Anna was busy, chattering and answering and laughing, so Jessica decided to explore the rest of the house. She climbed the stairs and peeked into the children's library, then the chalice room. Rows of glass cases contained writing implements, jewelry, domestic heirlooms such as Beatrice's comb and brush, and a number of brass and silver chalices, some rustic and discoloring, some engraved with Latin phrases and symbols.

She climbed more stairs, narrowing now, to the third floor, where attic bedrooms were furnished with period antiques. She crossed to a dormer window and peered out, over the front lawn to the forest and the bay. The fog had settled into a narrow strip bordering the horizon.

She wondered if Anna might be free now and headed downstairs, thinking to visit the shop before leaving, and maybe even the chapel and the rose garden.

All the while the girl in the woods, the open eyes, the blood seeping into the forest floor, haunted her.

Eight
Family

The house had grown quiet as Jessica stood before a large beveled mirror centered over a bench in the entry. The girl returning her gaze was boyish, with her jeans, shirt, and high-top shoes. Jessica took off her cap and unloosed her hair, combing it with her fingers.

She found Anna alone in the music room, sitting at the rolltop desk. Tapping lightly on the open door, Jessica asked tentatively, "Could I speak with you for a minute, Anna?"

Anna glanced up and smiled. "Of course. Did you enjoy the tour? Please have a seat." She pointed to a chair facing her own. "How can I help you?"

Jessica introduced herself, sat down, and set her pack on the floor. She smoothed her cuffs, wishing she had worn something more attractive, more professional, maybe a tailored jacket. "I wanted to ask about the job posted in the window."

"Are you interested? It hasn't been filled yet. I only posted it this week."

"Could you tell me about it? I'm a History doctoral student. And Berkeley is the subject of my dissertation."

Anna leaned toward her with interest. "Really? That's remarkable. I need an assistant to help with the tours so that I can spend more time in the children's library. Part-time, maybe fifteen hours a week, Fridays, Saturdays, and Sundays." She angled her head and watched Jessica respond, as though summing up her suitability in a glance.

Jessica tossed her hair to one side and folded her hands. She too leaned forward, endeavoring to make friendly eye contact. "That would be perfect. My schedule is pretty flexible on weekends."

Anna swiveled to the desk and pulled an envelope from a cubbyhole. "Take this job application packet. I'm afraid all we can give you is minimum wage."

"That's fine." Jessica opened the envelope and read the description of the hours: 1-6, Friday, Saturday and Sunday.

Anna appeared relieved. "Good. Then if you are free tomorrow, you can start right away—bring in the completed application. We can make it a trial basis until the Foundation approves the application and you approve the job. They will have to do a security check on you, given the antiques and historic documents on the premises. And here's a set of the history cards used for the tours."

A bell rang five, a thin clanging through the trees. Anna grinned. "The chapel. Father Nate will be saying Evening Prayer with his brother Nicholas and anyone who shows up. I usually go. Want to come?"

Jessica was studying the job description. Was Anna Catholic like the McKinnons? "Sorry, not today, I have a commitment." Why did she say that? Her only commitment was to her studies. But she hadn't planned on it, and she didn't like sudden changes in her plans.

Anna rose. "I understand. But know that you are welcome to join us anytime. It's peaceful in the chapel. I find it calms me. Sometimes we have tea beforehand, but I was too busy with the visitors' questions today. Let me walk you to the door."

"Maybe I *will* join you another time," Jessica said, as a peace offering.

"I'm not religious, but it calms me—they read the psalms, and Father Nate is a dear. He's become a good friend. He's the Comerford caretaker and lives in the back cottage with his brother."

"About tomorrow—should I come at one?"

"Please do. That gives us an hour to review the history of the house. Then you can assist me with the tour—we usually have a good-sized group on Saturdays—and you can stay for tea. We'll discuss any questions and concerns you might have."

Jessica nodded. She wanted to ask about the Fire Trail and safety, and did Anna know about the murdered girl? Did she know the murderer was still at large, probably wandering the trail? But what to ask? And why should she ask at all? In the end, Jessica didn't want to hinder her job chances with these worries. She stood, shouldered her pack, and said, perhaps too abruptly, "Sounds good. See you then. Thank you."

They parted on the front porch, and Jessica descended the brick stairs. As she crossed the lawn to the gravel drive leading into the forest, she turned to look back. Was that Anna's son watching from a window? Anna's reassuring form stood in the doorway, her face bright, her hand raised in farewell.

Jessica waved and stepped onto the drive that disappeared into the trees. She followed the rutty pavement down the hill into the deepening shadow, then emerged into the sudden rush and bright noise of Berkeley, her heart lightening.

* * *

Jessica sensed someone following her as she took the Bancroft Steps linking Prospect and Warring. When she quickened her pace, he did too. She slowed, he slowed. She glanced back, and thought she recognized the man on the Fire Trail with his rangy lope. Was it him?

She decided to take the route home that crossed campus, hoping other students provided safety in numbers. She felt for her phone and pepper spray. Was she being paranoid? She couldn't let fear affect her life like this. She walked on, determined to be in control, and soon found herself on busy Hearst, nearing Arch Street. She glanced back, from time to time, and decided she had lost him. Perhaps it was all in her imagination. Was it safe to go home? She stopped before a street vendor and pretended to look at jewelry displayed on velvet cloths. The man following her had disappeared.

She entered her basement studio with extra care, scanning the room, then bolting the door quickly behind her. She pulled out her phone and tapped Detective Gan's number. Her words tumbled out.

The officer sounded stern. "You should have come to the station, not gone home."

"I was afraid of that."

"But I'm glad you let me know. He might be lingering around the trailhead. Call with anything else. You should be okay for now. And, Ms. Thierry, we released the victim's name: Verona Bradley, a junior, majoring in communications."

"And her family?"

"Her parents are coming in tomorrow from Missouri."

"Should I see them?"

"Only if you want to and they agree."

She ended the call and turned on her laptop to scan the headlines. *Earthquake damage in Napa. Outrage over beheadings by ISIS. Rape in People's Park. Fire Trail murderer at large, victim identified as Cal student Verona Bradley.* Jessica scrutinized the article. Verona Bradley seemed so innocent, and yet, could this girl have prevented, in any way, what happened? Could she have been more cautious? Did she have any intuitive warnings? Her image would, she feared, be forever burned into Jessica's memory. She shook her head, not knowing the answer, the question a familiar one, one she had asked about her sisters, about Samantha's drowning and Ashley's drugs. And did she want to see Verona's parents? What grief they must be feeling. Would there be a funeral?

As the questions gathered and huddled, clouding a corner of her mind, she checked her messages. Her roommate Shelley had texted: "Can't come back yet, Jess. Grandma's in bad shape, and I need to stay with her another week at least. Good thing I haven't any classes this semester. Call when you can."

Jessica sympathized. Shelley was her grandmother's only living relative who cared enough to call and visit. Disappointed, Jessica stared about the small, dark studio—the bunk beds, the dressers, the kitchenette with its single-burner stove, the yellowing sink, the open shelves, the torn couch.

The owners had fixed up the basement, but it was still a basement. A narrow window ran horizontally at ground level, close to the ceiling. A vertical window bordered one side of the front door, and through the glass Jessica could glimpse steppingstones climbing up through a bed of ivy to the street. She had thought the setting quaint at first, but now it seemed dark and dingy. Nevertheless, she didn't spend much time there, except to study, and her desk lamp was light enough for that. The rent was good, especially since she shared with Shelley, who was also working toward a graduate degree, hers in Philosophy. When the place got her down, she reminded herself it was only temporary, necessary and temporary.

She missed Shelley, a high school friend, but Jessica didn't feel the same about Shelley's boyfriend, who flirted with her when Shelley wasn't looking. Thankfully, he hadn't called or shown up. He must have read Jessica's signals loud and clear. She would invite Shelley again to a Fidelity meeting. The Fidelity Society, dedicated to sexual integrity, marriage, and family, hosted lectures that helped navigate the confusing map of relationships today. Her roommate needed to learn the safety controls and warning signs. Shelley was far too naive. Not all guys were nice. Not everyone was trustworthy.

Maybe this attack on Shelley's grandmother had been a wake-up call, Jessica considered, as she rummaged on a shelf for a can of chicken noodle soup. The elderly woman had been a victim of home invasion, had opened her door to a couple who claimed to admire her garden, asking friendly questions. As they chatted, the couple worked their way into the house. They beat her, stole her jewelry and silver, and emptied the medicine cabinet of prescription drugs. A neighbor was suspicious, found her bleeding on the floor, and took her to the hospital.

Jessica tried to concentrate. She sipped her soup, spooned the noodles, and worked to memorize the Comerford history cards. The material should dovetail with her dissertation. She would study the cards tonight and be ready for tomorrow. She wanted Anna's approval.

She turned to a family photo on the fridge, tilted, attached by a Cal magnet, and placed the Comerford magnet on another corner of the picture, righting it. The photo had been taken when her sister and father were still living. Her parents, their arms around each other in a comfortable embrace, appeared happy. Jessica stood on the other side of her father. Her twin sisters framed the three of them. Her siblings were attractive, she thought, with long auburn hair and heavily made-up eyes and lips, but their low-cut tops and mini-skirts were too revealing. Jessica, younger by two years, wore similar clothing, but had little yet to reveal. The picture had been taken after a family therapy session, date-stamped 2005. She was thirteen, the twins fifteen.

Jessica examined her own image in the photo. She had a knowing look, a calm, purposeful look, but her brow was pulled together, her eyes pinched. She recalled she had learned that day about Dr. Stein's theory of sex, the two systems of growth, one of emotion/motivation versus one of control/delayed gratification.

Dr. Stein's theory claimed that these two systems of growth had become separated in today's society. They used to run parallel, complementing one another, but not so anymore. Adolescents had great energy, he explained, which comprised the emotion/motivation system. They were motivated by energy and emotions. But over the last few generations they had less of the control/delayed gratification system. They had less ability to control and thus direct this emotional energy to a goal.

Dr. Stein claimed that these control systems develop from learning real-life skills, skills that earlier generations had been forced to learn. Agrarian cultures trained their young in practical tasks, and the training itself informed the control centers of the brain. In other words, today's children were isolated from this system by being in school, away from these practical life moments. So the urges were there—lots of energy—but the urges were not

controlled. Sexual energy—and other forms of adolescent behavior
—would go berserk. That's why adolescents took risks. Their brains
were only half developed. They couldn't say no to the energy. In
addition, marriage was delayed far beyond the time of sexual
maturity, allowing for few approved outlets for that energy.

The knowledge was a life preserver for Jessica. It explained so
much. She wasn't a nerd yet when the photo was taken, but the
seriousness was starting to take hold.

Jessica examined Ashley's face. Her features reflected boredom
and even embarrassment. The therapy session was part of Ashley's
drug rehab program; the photo was family-strengthening medicine
prescribed by Dr. Stein. They were supposed to take the picture
after every group session. Little did Jessica know then that Ashley
would leave home the next year at the age of sixteen, she would
continue to fight addiction, and she would move in with a boy with
a similar problem, probably an enabler, a boy she met in their
therapy group.

Jessica now turned to Samantha's image. Her features mirrored
Ashley's, since they were identical twins, but she was smarter and
more practical about what she wanted and how to get it. She could
pretend she was fine when she wasn't. She knew how to hide her
pregnancies. She knew how to get an abortion once their mother
had walked her through the first one. Sure, she did drugs, but she
didn't appear to. She was clever about details and appearances, and
their mom and dad had high expectations for their bright, beautiful
Samantha, who posed for the camera with calculated innocence.
Ashley would run away, but Samantha would stay and graduate
and go on to college.

Jessica saved the study of her parents for last, for she loved
them so. She saw her mother as a tragic figure, a simple woman
who trusted the authorities in her life, a deer caught in the
headlights. She had complete faith in her children's teachers and
what they taught, believed journalists and what they wrote,

worshiped Hollywood stars and what they expressed in their movies.

Jessica studied her father's image, his open, loving features. He gazed at her mother, not the camera. His thick wavy hair was cut short, brushed back. He had a hefty build, with a square jaw and broad shoulders, a man's man. His arm gripped her mother's waist as though protecting her from the therapy session and her disappointment in Ashley. He, like her mother, was trusting, but he worked long days and didn't pay attention to what was going on at home. He trusted her mother to solve school and family issues and considered the twins' mood swings and parties to be normal adolescence. In this photo, Jessica could see he was worried about her mother more than the rest of them.

Jessica loved her parents' love. Even in this family portrait from nine years ago (what had happened to the others?) her mom and dad were lost in one another's presence. They didn't notice Jessica, gripping her father's other arm.

Jessica checked the time on her phone. Nearly eight. She reread her Comerford cards and studied the shiny brochure with its floor plan. She filled out the job application. Soon she was able to return to her dissertation.

What was she proving with the paper? What was her thesis, her premise, her argument? It had to be *substantive* and *significant*. Perhaps it was the influence of the Church upon the State in the quality/cost ratio of secondary education, especially considering the taxpayer and government deficits. Catholic schools appeared to be closing because of government's growing intolerance, and American education, Jessica posited, was suffering for it.

What would happen when the only schools on offer were public schools with unionized teachers who couldn't be fired for incompetence or rewarded for excellence, or high priced private schools? It seemed the divide between rich and poor would widen. Perhaps she was arguing that the state had an interest in encouraging schools founded and funded by churches. As her advisor said, her premise (and argument) might be risky and unpopular, but that could be a good thing here in the Free Speech capital of the world. It might be an attention grabber, even *substantive* and *significant*.

UC Berkeley was celebrating the fiftieth anniversary of the Free Speech Movement this fall, not necessarily encouraging to Jessica, who guessed that Berkeley's idea of free speech was liberal speech, politically correct speech, not free speech at all.

Nine
Goodness

Jessica was nervous when she arrived on Saturday for her first day as assistant docent, but she tried not to show it and concentrated on learning as much as she could. Anna reviewed the tour with her, and when the visitors arrived Jessica handed out brochures. Eventually she grew more comfortable as Anna's assistant. She gave the short talk in the dining room so that she could "break the ice." She thought she dressed more suitably this time, wearing charcoal slacks and a tailored jacket and plaiting her hair in a French braid. She found that wearing a more formal outfit encouraged her to act the part. She thought she might shop for a vintage skirt one day.

After the last visitor had left, Jessica helped Anna prepare tea in the kitchen. She arranged pink roses in a vase and set out cups, saucers, small plates, paper napkins, knives and spoons, for three persons on a linen-covered table. Anna removed the oval lid from the pewter butter dish, engraved with the Comerford lantern, and Jessica placed a pewter pitcher of milk alongside a bowl of sugar, a jam pot (tiny red flowers on white ceramic) beside the butter, and another pot of clotted cream next to the jam. Lastly, Anna set brown flaky scones, the raisins peering out like tiny eyes, in the center of the table next to the roses. Jessica wondered who the third setting was for. Perhaps Father Nate or even the young man.

"Zachary will look after any visitors who might come by," Anna said. "It's after four and most folks from the tour have left by now or are in the gift shop. We lock up the main house at five."

"What about Evening Prayer in the chapel?"

"That's part of the reason for locking the front door. More people are coming for Evening Prayer, so we keep the grounds and the gift shop open until six, but the house has to be locked to maximize security. We don't have the staff we once had. It's a miracle we were able to arrange funding for your job. I was told that someone on the board stepped up to cover the cost."

"I'm grateful," Jessica said. Her mother would be happy too. She eyed the third table setting.

"Father Nate should be along soon," Anna said.

"The priest you mentioned?"

"Indeed. Afternoon tea is one of his rituals before Evening Prayer. And he wants to meet you. Sometimes we have tea on the back porch of his cottage, sometimes here."

Through the window Jessica could see an elderly man stepping confidently across the lawn from the chapel. A straw hat shaded his face, and he wore his black clericals and white banded collar. As he entered through the French doors, Anna rose to meet him. Jessica smoothed her slacks and straightened her cuffs.

"No need to get up, my dear," he said to Anna, bending and kissing her lightly on the cheek. He turned to Jessica. "This must be our promising history student, our new guide?" He removed his hat and held it genteelly with both hands like a suitor come calling.

Seeing the elderly man's scarred face, Jessica gasped. Clearly he had been in a fire. The red skin, amoeba-shaped, formed shiny smooth hills and gullies along one side of his face and over the bridge of his nose. Jessica hoped he hadn't noticed her slight outcry. She concentrated on his blue eyes twinkling with reassurance.

Seemingly unconcerned with her reaction, he held out a thick hand. "I'm Father Nathaniel Casparian, but you can call me Father Nate or Nate or Father or whatever you like. I'm most pleased to meet you, Miss Jessica. Welcome to Comerford House."

Jessica half stood and placed her hand in his, nodding. "My pleasure, er . . . sir . . . er, Father Nate." She hated her confusion and glanced away. She mumbled, "And please call me Jessica."

Father Nate took a seat between them, settling himself comfortably and unfolding his napkin. "It's okay. I understand my appearance is a bit of a shock at first."

Anna patted his hand. "We get used to it and never think about it again. It's your badge of honor, perhaps your halo. Angelic, at the very least, to my way of thinking. Have one of my whole-wheat scones, Father, and tell me what you think."

"You've been baking, my dear?" He rubbed his hands in anticipation. "Now that you have an assistant you can go to your exercise classes more often and therefore bake more often? These smell divine. And warm!"

"That's my plan, Father, to clock in more CircleFit time and library time too." She pointed upstairs. "Anyway, these scones *are* nutritious. They have wheat germ and protein powder." Anna nodded sagely. "Grace, Father?"

Father Nate raised his hand over the scones. He drew a cross in the air and intoned, "For what we are about to receive, make us truly thankful, in the name of the Father, the Son, and the Holy Ghost, Amen."

"Amen," Anna said. "But you might not be so thankful after you taste them. There is butter involved, I *will* warn you. How can you make scones without butter? But I think the recipe is a little salty, and the oven time might not be quite right, for they seem a bit dry, and—"

"Not to worry, Anna, not to worry." Father Nate helped himself to a scone. He reached for the strawberry jam ("made from your garden strawberries, aha!") and the clotted cream, spooning dollops of each onto his plate and passing them to Jessica. He sliced the scone in half with his knife, spread the thick cream, topped the cream with the jam, then eyed it with pleasure. He took a bite carefully and closed his eyes, savoring.

Anna waited for his reaction. Jessica observed them both, entranced.

Father Nate opened his eyes. He beamed. "Marvelous! Absolutely marvelous! You are a wonder!"

Anna sighed with relief and arranged her own napkin on her lap.

Jessica laughed. She copied Father Nate's movements, as though performing an ancient ritual. As the scone and cream and sweet strawberry preserves melted in her mouth, the whole wheat adding a unique and not unpleasant texture, she recalled spring and high grasses and fresh air and her mother calling her in from outside when she was little. Why was that? It was comfort food, she guessed. "Delicious, Anna. Thank you . . . melts in my mouth."

Anna poured the tea through a tiny strainer that captured the saturated leaves. She filled the cups three-quarters full, leaving room for milk, and placed the strainer on its own caddy. Jessica stirred sugar into the steaming amber liquid and added milk. She noticed the Comerford lantern also on the teaspoons.

"We sell them in the shop," Anna said, proudly. "Also the pewter items . . . very popular, especially around Christmas."

Jessica imagined Comerford House decorated with lights and greenery. "Christmas! Do you decorate and have special events like they do at Dunsmuir House in Oakland?" She recalled her family visiting once.

Anna daintily tapped the corners of her mouth with her napkin. "We do. It's splendid. Maybe you can help us. And the chamber group works with a local chorus to perform Handel's *Messiah*. But we're not sure about this Christmas." She eyed Father Nate.

The priest reached for a second scone. "No, we don't know about this year. But something will turn up. It usually does." He studied the sky and winked. "I have friends in high places, very high places."

Anna turned to Jessica. "The Foundation is cutting back on our budget. Donations have dropped since the recession. There's talk of closing completely."

"I'm so sorry. That would be sad," Jessica said.

"And we've been accused of building code violations as well," Father Nate added, eyeing Anna with concern. "In fact I've noticed a cracking in the back of the chapel, probably earthquake damage."

Anna frowned. "Last Sunday's quake in Napa? Oh dear. I haven't seen obvious damage in the main house here."

"It's probably nothing, but the city seems to be looking for revenue and they've cast their eye in our direction for fees and fines." Father Nate, having finished his second scone, sat back in his chair, cradling his cup with his hands. "Now, Miss Jessica, let's hear about how your first day went."

"It went well, at least I think it did . . . I enjoyed it." Jessica nodded with enthusiasm.

"She was perfect," Anna said, tapping the table for emphasis and grinning at Jessica.

"Good. And tell us about your studies. I understand you are working on your doctorate in History. The study of history is important, vitally important to our culture. Each generation must pass to the next generation all they've learned."

Jessica described her program and her possible thesis, the importance of parochial schools to public budgets and private taxpayers.

"Excellent. This is a premise, or thesis if you will, that needs to be argued loudly. Our culture *should* seek the support of religious institutions, for the common good, especially those institutions that formed our founding principles of freedom and individual liberty, not to mention social welfare and free speech."

Anna nodded. "We're both concerned about the culture, Jessica—how America can survive without belief, without the faith of the Founding Fathers."

"How so?" Jessica asked, confused. Were they talking about a theocracy? She sipped her tea carefully, watching the steam rise.

Father Nate ran his hand through his white hair. "Cult, that is, religion, creates culture. Nicholas taught me that. Our laws are based on Judeo-Christian beliefs. When our people lose their faith, they lose respect for those laws."

Anna added, "But many folks who aren't believers—like myself—see the need for the Judeo-Christian tradition. We see how important it is to our way of life, to keeping the peace and protecting the freedoms we take for granted. Even if I don't believe, I'm glad others do."

"And so," Jessica ventured, "you remind people of our country's history here in this house? The Comerfords and the Presentation Sisters?" She nibbled on the last bit of scone.

Father Nate tapped his nose. "She's very smart, Anna, very smart."

Anna laughed, and Jessica felt her cheeks burn with the compliment.

"Father, you knew some of the Presentation Sisters, didn't you?" Anna asked.

"Indeed. They still do excellent work, although they aren't located in Berkeley anymore. They have a school in San Jose, Presentation High, and their motherhouse is near the University of San Francisco. They serve in elementary schools and various social ministries. I knew them from my parish life when Presentation High in Berkeley was going strong. Anna, aren't there some journals or letters or such in the attic archives that might be of interest to Miss Jessica? Anything about the sisters?"

Anna tapped her head. "Of course, I should have thought of that." She turned to Jessica. "Beatrice corresponded with several of the nuns. I believe she even went back to Ireland with them on a recruiting trip. You're welcome to look at the letters or anything else in the archives."

At that moment Jessica felt that her life was taking a turn for the better. Her advisor had mentioned primary sources, and she had few at this point. "That would be useful, thank you both. I really appreciate it."

"Good," Anna said. "Now Father, I'm keeping an eye on the time for you. Is Nicholas coming to Evening Prayer? Shall I send Zachary to fetch him?"

"He's coming. I'll bring him to the chapel tonight, not to worry. We have that lift on the stairs now, remember, and the ramp." He turned to Jessica. "My brother taught history at Cal. If he could speak he would enjoy talking to you about your project. But he's dying slowly, suffering from increasing paralysis, can barely communicate. But he's safe with me as long as I'm around." A deep sadness passed over his features.

"And me too," Anna said, patting Father Nate's arm, then whisking crumbs off his sleeve.

"Is your brother Dr. Casparian?" She had heard of him, even read one of his books.

Father Nate beamed. "The very same. He had quite a career. We are all so proud of him."

"Will you be joining us for Evening Prayer in the chapel, Jessica?"

Jessica evaluated the approaching dusk, thinking of safety and her walk back, recalling the man who had followed her the evening before. "I'd better go before it gets dark." She would drive next time, she thought, although she liked the exercise. She had Shelley's car, after all.

"Stay for Evening Prayer," Father Nate said. "Are you worried about walking home? Walking alone? Since . . . the terrible incident on the Fire Trail?"

Anna began to clear the dishes. "The Fire Trail! I'd nearly forgotten. Have they found the man yet?"

Jessica felt cold, icy cold, and Father Nate touched her shoulder. "Are you okay, Miss Jessica? You're whiter than a sheet."

Jessica stood to help Anna clear the table. "I saw him," she whispered.

Anna and Father Nate repeated her words, "You saw him?"

"On the trail. I found . . . the girl . . . her body." She dropped back into her chair.

"That's terrible. You don't have to tell us, if you don't want to," Anna said, clearly concerned.

"It *was* terrible," Jessica said quietly. She explained in bursts of words that trailed after one another like falling stars.

"You witnessed evil among us," Father Nate said. "Come to Evening Prayer, my dear. It will do you good."

"It will," Anna agreed. "And Zachary can walk you home. You shouldn't be going anywhere alone, especially at night."

Jessica shook her head. "No, I'll be fine, but I should leave soon. I think someone might have been following me yesterday." She needed to go home, to safety.

Zachary appeared in the doorway. "I heard my name. Anything I can do?" He glanced at Jessica and nodded to Father Nate. "Good evening, Father."

Father Nate smiled. "Good to see you, Zachary."

"Zachary," Anna said, "you've met Jessica, haven't you?"

"Well . . . sort of . . ."

Jessica sensed his nervousness, wishing she could put him at ease. She noticed he wore the same jeans, blue shirt, and Birkenstocks that he'd worn on Friday. He studied her through his rimless glasses, as though she could make him more comfortable by saying something.

Jessica stood and shook his hand. "Nice to meet you, Zachary." She flashed him a smile, then turned to Anna. "Zachary opened the door for me yesterday and kindly showed me where the tour was starting."

Anna's face registered curiosity, then recollection. "Of course. How silly of me not to have introduced you sooner."

"I didn't arrive at the house today until three and you were upstairs," Zachary said. "I was at Laurie's."

Father Nate was heading out. "Blessings, Zachary, don't forget I can use another acolyte at Evening Prayer. And it was a pleasure meeting you, Miss Jessica," he said, turning in the doorway and waving. "But I've an appointment with God." He lumbered toward the cottage.

"I'll be along soon, Father," Anna called after him. "Jessica, now that you two have officially met, please allow Zachary to walk you home."

"I'd be happy to," Zachary said seriously.

"Thanks," Jessica said, heading toward the foyer, "but—"

"You might have things in common," Anna continued. "You're both working on your doctorates, after all." She half-smiled as she carried the tea tray to the sink and glanced back. "Don't forget to lock up the front, Zachary. And Jessica, you did a fine job on the tour. See you tomorrow at one. You can give the whole tour." She turned on the faucet and began washing and rinsing with great energy.

Ten
Poetry

Jessica waited on the Comerford front porch for Zachary to securely lock the massive oak door behind them. She checked her backpack for the history cards, her phone, her wallet, and her studio keys, then turned to the lawn sloping to the forest. The fog had rolled in, blanketing the city and the bridges beyond. A cold damp breeze blew her hair across her face, and she slipped a strand behind an ear.

"You don't have to walk me back, Zachary," she said as they stepped down the stairs. Yet she didn't want to discourage him, so she added, "But thank you. I appreciate it."

"It's my pleasure." He bowed from the waist. "I'm at your service, Miss Jessica."

They laughed at the name Father Nate had given her. Crossing the grass, they followed the drive through the trees, slightly awkward in one another's company.

As they reached the road, Zachary said softly, "You don't remember me, do you?"

"Should I?" Jessica studied his face. He had seemed familiar. But she couldn't, even now, place him. High school? Undergrad classes? Friend of Shelley's? Could he be connected to her sisters? That would not be good. "I'm sorry," she said honestly, shaking her head.

"I had a beard. That's probably it. I was the teaching assistant in one of your classes last year."

Jessica imagined him with a beard. She recalled a young man, a Mr. Aguilar. Aguilar! That was Anna's last name. "I remember now. I'm sorry. The Romantic Novel, right?"

They continued down the hill, toward the first set of stairs.

"Right. I recognized you yesterday, but I could see you didn't remember me. It's okay. You're working toward a doctorate?

Mine's in English, naturally, and it's going slowly, I have to say. What's your field?"

"History. But narrowing the dissertation thesis is the hardest part," she said, glad to have something objective to talk about with this young man whom, she had to admit, she did find attractive. There was a gentle strength about him. "I'm only beginning the program. I graduated last May in History. I'm entering the combined Masters/Doctorate program."

"I was admitted to mine two years ago, and I'm still figuring out my thesis. I'm working two jobs, at a bookstore and as a teaching assistant, not counting helping my mother at Comerford, but that's fine since I'm allowed to practice on their piano." He pulled into himself. "I'm talking too much."

It was true his words had poured out like the falling notes of the concerto that afternoon. Jessica was amused. "Not at all. And I loved hearing the piano. I heard you playing as I walked up the drive on Friday. It was lovely. What was it?"

"Thanks. It was Beethoven's 'Emperor Concerto, Piano Concerto No. 5'. It's astonishingly beautiful. It always surprises me in a new way, like another facet of a jewel catching light from a different angle. Beauty is something I crave, but then, I suppose everyone does. I collect beauty—moments, notes, words, images." He glanced at her. "When I find it, I try and hold on to it. It's so rare and so wonderful and it takes so many different forms."

"How do you hold on to it? Write the words down? Like journaling?"

"Even better, I memorize or try to memorize bits . . . mostly poetry."

Jessica wondered if he was a poet-philosopher. He seemed to be meditating on the meaning of life. As they crossed campus, she said, "I live on Arch Street, Northside, off Hearst. Lots of routes from here, but I like the campus walk." Another reason for not driving, she thought.

"Me too. Cal is picturesque, the way it's landscaped with old trees and winding pathways, and the two forks of Strawberry Creek. It's good exercise, and I like being outside. I bike sometimes. I run the Fire Trail . . . did you hear about the murder?"

Jessica blanched. "More than hear about it . . . I . . . came across . . . the man . . . coming out of the bushes. I found the girl."

With an abrupt halt, Zachary faced her. "How terrible," he whispered. "I'm sorry I mentioned it."

"It's okay. I'm trying to put it behind me."

They passed Bancroft Library and Moffitt Library, and turned up the north fork of Strawberry Creek.

"I haven't been back," Jessica said. "I'll face the trail when my roommate comes home, and we can go together. I miss it. I love the Fire Trail. I love the views from the hills." A chance to rise above this bone-chilling fog and feel the sun, she thought. She turned up her collar against the cold.

"They haven't found him?"

"No, and . . . I think someone might have been following me yesterday when I walked home from Comerford. I'm glad you came with me. I should have driven. Thank you."

"It might be wise to drive rather than walk, all things considered. Some fears are worth listening to."

They continued in silence for a few minutes, turning on Hearst and heading down to Arch.

"Do you have a working thesis?" he asked suddenly, as though words were needed to create a comfort zone. "I'm told the statement often changes as you do the research."

"I want to do something about Berkeley history, probably dealing with the Presentation Sisters, maybe examining church-state issues."

"The Irish nuns who immigrated in the early days? The ones in the story of Comerford House?"

"Exactly. They were established in Berkeley in 1878. So after the 1906 earthquake the nuns in San Francisco joined the sisters here, then returned to San Francisco to rebuild, doing relief work and opening schools. I'd never heard of them, and they did so much for Berkeley and San Francisco. Anyway, one thing led to another, and the history of Berkeley sort of beckoned me." Was she rambling? Last night she had a thesis drafted, but she couldn't seem to pull it together again. What words had she used with Father Nate and Anna?

"Sounds interesting. The McKinnons certainly admired the Presentation Sisters."

As they walked up Arch, Jessica said, "I'm not Catholic, but the early settlers had such a rough time. I admired how the religious institutions contributed to the early communities in so many ways, lifesaving ways, especially here in the East Bay after the earthquake. I thought the story should be retold to our generation. Churches and their foundations and charities might be useful and worth supporting from the state's point of view. It seems they are too often threatened by government mandates."

"You mean like the new healthcare law not allowing religious exemptions—that kind of thing?"

Jessica nodded. "That's a good example. The state is forcing religious institutions to operate against their beliefs. Government should be encouraging groups that benefit society, those that found schools, hospitals, and shelters contributing to the common welfare."

"The healthcare law is controversial, that's for sure. I do think that churches should be encouraged, not discouraged. They are a stabilizing force for good. They give people meaning. They inspire and answer the big questions about life. Church life and belief inspired the Victorians, and I admire their world as well as their faith."

"The Victorians? You said you were writing about poetry? Victorian poetry?"

"Elizabeth Barrett Browning, her poetry, the pull of beauty and the human desire for transcendence, even the vision of God, the beatific vision. I like Gerald Manley Hopkins as well, so I'm not sure. Maybe both."

"Yes, beauty." They had arrived at her house. "Here we are, home sweet home. I share the basement studio with my roomie, Shelley. She's working on her doctorate, too."

They followed the steppingstones down through the ivy to the door, and Jessica gasped, her heart pounding. A dead bird lay on the mat, bleeding onto a scrap of paper.

"Zachary, it's a tiny sparrow." The innocence, the loss of something so precious, pierced her.

"Let me help." Zachary pulled a tissue from his pocket, cradled the bird in his palm and moved it into the ivy. He picked up the note.

Jessica read the scrawl that ran through the sparrow's blood:

You next

She shivered. "I thought someone was following me last night. He was here today."

"Better call the police."

Jessica breathed deeply and fumbled with her key. She opened the door. "Come in. I'll get a plastic bag for the note."

They entered and glanced around the room.

"Things seem okay?" Zachary asked.

"I think so. Doesn't appear that he broke in."

She found a bag and Zachary slipped the note inside.

"Are you going to be okay?" he asked.

Jessica breathed deeply, wanting to reassure him. "I'll be okay. I'll call Detective Gan right away. Thanks for walking me back," she said as firmly as she could, but her throat was dry, her voice hoarse.

"Better take your car tomorrow," he said, as he turned toward the door.

She followed him to the entryway. "I will."

"Are you sure you're okay?"

"I'll be fine. I'll lock the double bolt after you leave. I'll be fine." Her lower lip trembled. "Maybe see you tomorrow at Comerford House."

"Until then, Miss Jessica." He smiled, nodded, and headed up the steppingstones.

Jessica watched him leave and bolted the door. She sat down and considered the bloody note in the plastic bag, trying not to panic. There was a Fidelity meeting the next day. It would strengthen her.

She pulled out Detective Gan's card and dialed.

* * *

"Please, have a seat, Detective." Jessica motioned to the torn couch.

"No need, but thanks. I'll just take a minute of your time, Ms. Thierry. You have evidence, you said?"

She handed him the plastic bag with the bloody note. "I found this on my front porch. Along with a dead bird."

"Where's the bird?" He read the note through the plastic and placed the bag in his pouch.

"In the ivy. You want the bird too?"

"We want anything connected to the case. Who knows what we might find?" He raised thin brows. "That poor girl," he added.

"Did her parents arrive?"

"Yes, but they don't want to see anyone. When the time comes, they're taking their daughter's ashes home for burial."

Jessica was relieved. Meeting the parents would have been heartbreaking, but the mention of ashes brought the murder home with double force. A life lost, a girl loved, a daughter gone.

"I'll show you the bird," she whispered. She led the detective outside and pointed to a tiny bundle resting in the ivy. "There."

He frowned, reaching for the sparrow, and held its body with tender reverence. "This is a tough job sometimes, Ms. Thierry. I see a life like this and think of so many others, so many innocents on our streets hurt each day. You never get used to it. I want to cry."

"I do too."

They stood together, hushed by the moment as though honoring both the innocent lost and the loss of innocence.

He eyed her with concern. "I'll have a patrol drive by from time to time."

"Thank you," she said, with some relief.

"Good night then, Ms. Thierry." He saluted her, then stepped slowly, reverently through the ivy.

"Good night, Detective." She entered her studio, bolted the door, and left the porch light on.

Jessica felt safer that night. She was glad she had called Detective Gan.

Eleven
Love

On Sunday morning, September 7th, Jessica found a seat in St. Joseph's hall for her bi-weekly Fidelity meeting. With half her attention held hostage by the events of the last few days, she set down her bag and concentrated on the banner hanging over the speaker's platform, words similar but not the same as her own list:

Fidelity over infidelity, selflessness over selfishness,
honor over dishonor, truth over lies, restraint over indulgence

She scanned the room, recalling that this block, bordered by Addison and McGee, once home to the Presentation Convent, was today home to University Terrace, St. Joseph's Catholic Church, and a charter school. On an earlier visit she had walked around the block, snapping photos of the pink stucco condos built after Presentation High closed in 1989.

Jessica pulled out a pen and a lined pad to take notes, and now, as she waited for the speaker, recalled her walk home with Zachary. She felt both anticipation and dread at the thought of seeing him again, emotions she wanted checked. Today the speaker would steer her back toward a course of sanity. She had nearly forgotten her list of controls, her goals. Her firm focus was not as firm as it once was or should be.

She didn't recognize anyone from earlier meetings. She knew some had come from the church nearby, perhaps even the organizers themselves. But you didn't have to be religious or of any political persuasion to attend.

The event flyer read, "Falling in Love: Realities and Myths." The subject sounded interesting, sounded useful, just as the other talks had proved to be. The lecture was to be delivered by a professor, Dr. Susan Jacobs, PhD Philosophy, who now stepped to the lectern. She appeared to be in her early thirties, with dark curly hair that fell to her shoulders. She wore a black skirt, tweed jacket, and crisp white collared shirt. Her oversized horn rims seemed designed to lessen the impact of her feminine features, so that she would be taken seriously. Dr. Jacobs held the microphone with practiced poise.

"Welcome, victims of the sexual revolution," she began, provoking a ripple of laughter, perhaps one of recognition as well as curiosity.

As the room quieted, she continued. "We are all affected by the sexual revolution, those who caused it and those who were taught by those who caused it: parents, educators, media. The rest of us have been influenced by the status quo, the resulting culture surrounding us today. Let's face it, we women have been abused by this creed of self-gratification and so-called freedom, and it's time to say so and stand up for ourselves. We thought we had it all, with the pill and free sex, anytime sex, anywhere sex, but the revolution backfired. We women have been victimized far more than men, although men have been hurt as well. When we treat others as objects, as both men and women have been encouraged to do, our hearts harden and the ability to love is damaged if not altogether lost."

Jessica wondered whether the room had grown silent because of shock or agreement. She leaned forward, forgetting her note-taking, just watching Dr. Jacobs' animated face and absorbing her words, following her line of thought.

"Now, after decades of casual sex and campus hook-ups, it is remarkable that some of us crave romantic love at all, a need to find 'the One.' There are those who argue that with the loss of faith in God, in transcendence personified, we have shifted our human need for worship of a deity, and union with him, to the worship of a person. There is a long history that supports this interesting theory, but that is for another lecture.

"Today I'd like to address what is particularly true in the modern world, especially on campus, even this campus, so that we women, and men as well, can make sense of sex and love and create a better recipe for happiness on this planet."

Jessica admitted she longed for romantic love, the kind of love her parents had, but how did one find it, if it even existed at all? Was it as simple as embracing chastity before marriage? An earlier speaker had stressed that aspect.

Dr. Jacobs spoke without notes, holding the microphone with one hand and gesturing with the other. "First of all, know that the college years are the best time of your life to find your soulmate, so don't wait until career goals are met and you deem yourself financially stable. Here and now is the place and time to find a likeminded person, one who shares your drive, your interests, your degree of intellect, and even your future plans. Here and now is the place and time to find a friendship that might lead to long-lasting love with the commitment of marriage."

The speaker surveyed the room, weighing her audience, making eye contact where possible. Jessica could see she was eager to communicate.

"We are designed, created, to love and be loved, to be lovers, and to be friends. And friendship is the precursor to love, in fact, it is the precondition, the requirement for true love to develop. Dating—that old-fashioned exploration of friendship-with-possibilities—is immeasurably more productive than hooking up, which is simply a shortcut to despair. I ask you today, I implore you, if you desire true love, begin with the basics: set limits and acknowledge definitions. We here at the Fidelity Society can help you do that."

Jessica considered her lack of male friends. She had truly run away from men. Once she had dreamed of boyfriends, but her experience with boys had only caused the running away. There had been innuendoes and groping in her teens, promises not kept, assumptions not warranted, demands she refused. All had been breeches of trust.

Should she now be open to dating? Was she any wiser? Even when she had so much going on in her life, working toward her degree? Where would such dating lead? Could she control the relationship, once begun? She could not, would not, forget her sisters and their lack of control.

"We must encourage an atmosphere where sex is dignified, respectful, and beautiful, built upon a commitment to the future. Our relationships with one another should be affirming and supportive, ones in which we are not transient objects of desire, where we are not abused or used for another's gratification. We at the Fidelity Society believe that the best way to achieve these goals is to live a chaste life outside of marriage, developing friendships leading to love, to sexual integrity within the relationship, love that honors the commitment of traditional marriage."

It was definitely a step beyond her chastity creed, Jessica admitted to herself, a step on the path toward love and marriage.

"Even our definitions of love have become twisted beyond recognition. To love, in our society, means taking care of number one, embracing sexual license, slipping into the addiction of self-gratification. Love today means never judging, never having to say you're sorry. It denies suffering and sacrifice. These definitions of love are the very opposite of the historical idea of love, a definition that humanity has valued and upheld for thousands of years. These modern tortured twists have turned love upside down and inside out. Whatever happened to love that brings genuine goodness, wholeness, happiness, generosity? What happened to love that sacrifices for the other, truly caring for one another? For those of us who believe in God, love turns us into who God wants us to be. True love, transcendent love, reflects God's eternal and perfect love for us."

Jessica listened, barely breathing. Zachary would like that last part. Transcendence. To Jessica, the words were like water in a desert. Here, in this room, she was no longer alone. She had meaning and purpose. Once again, she had a way forward.

Dr. Jacobs spoke of friendship, the first step, as being necessary to weed out the lightweights, the chaff, from your life. But she also spoke of having too-high expectations placed on suitors, too-unrealistic demands, of worshiping your potential spouse, seeing him or her as the answer to everything. She spoke of recognizing one's own imperfections and the need to forgive one another. For Jessica, Dr. Jacobs completely redefined love.

The meeting adjourned, and Jessica ate her sandwich and sipped a coffee in the back of the room. She picked up a flyer cataloging the lecture series for the semester:

1. Falling in Love: Realities and Myths
2. What Is Marriage?
3. Contraception and Designer Babies
4. Man and Woman: The Same or Different?

Jessica wanted to attend them all, but she would have to see how her schedule developed. She checked the time on her phone as the audience broke into small group sessions. It was nearly one and she needed to head to Comerford House. This time she was prepared. She had brought Shelley's car.

Twelve
Laurie

That Sunday morning as Jessica drove to her Fidelity meeting, Zachary left Short Street and walked up Hearst. He would retrace their route through campus as he made his way to Laurie's Fine Books on College. He wanted to clock in a few hours of work before heading up the hill to Comerford House. He might see Jessica along the way, for one never knew what might happen. Serendipity was everywhere, the stars were out, and the sun was shining. He knew that Jessica was giving the two o'clock tour, so he would see her then for sure.

Zachary's emotions jumbled together like words on a page, unedited, thrown together in the rush of inspiration. His concern over Jessica's safety in the aftermath of her ordeal vied with his relief that she had re-entered his life at all. The relief won for the most part but the concern was growing.

After all those months, all those days, all those yearning, sleepless nights, wondering if it would ever happen, wondering if he should track down her number and call her, trying to summon courage but finding only shameless cowardice. Robert Browning would not have acted this way, to be sure. Or Mr. Darcy. Or Alexander Borodin. Period. And now Jessica was the reason he couldn't keep his mind on his thesis, and a most excellent and welcome reason it was.

As Zachary walked east along Ohlone Greenway, he didn't pay much attention, as he usually did, to the sun sparkling through the mist, or the dogs walking their owners, or the stillness that settled over a Sunday morning in Berkeley neighborhoods. Instead, his thoughts returned to Friday and his encounter with Jessica.

On that miraculous afternoon at Comerford House, when Zachary had heard the knock on the front door, he wasn't sure he had truly heard it. He had stopped playing the Beethoven concerto and listened for the second clap. He had stepped from the music room into the foyer, wondering why the front door was closed, annoyed at the intrusion into his precious practice time. He had opened the door, even more irked that it was locked like that. And there she was, on the porch. He was stunned. For a moment he was tongue-tied. He must have stared at her like a complete moron.

He had relived that moment many times in the last couple of days, clasping it and memorizing it in case she should disappear again from his life, but hating his own idiocy in doing so. He recalled that her sandy hair, while hidden inside the Bears cap, was trying to escape, and a golden strand that fell onto the side of her freckled cheek had caught the afternoon sun. She wore a pale pink long-sleeved shirt with a Ralph Lauren logo stitched in blue near the collar, and jeans and faded high-tops, clothing that made her look younger than he guessed she must be. After all, she had been in his upper division class last year, so she must have been around twenty at least, but she looked sixteen that Friday afternoon on the Comerford porch. She carried a small knapsack over her shoulder, worn and faded like the shoes.

As Zachary continued up Hearst, crossing Martin Luther King Way and then Shattuck, he recalled how Jessica hadn't recognized him when he opened the door. What to do? He was approaching panic. Should he pretend? Should he explain who he was?

She had had an expectant air laced with impatience. A frown was forming on the edges of her mouth. He worried that she had been waiting a long time. Had she been listening to him play? Was that a good thing? He wasn't sure as he thought back again and again how he had played, how many mistakes, how many perplexing pauses there had been. Would she realize that the pauses were for the flutes, French horns, bassoons, and strings?

He was now moving into the busier section of Hearst, along the campus border, where eateries and shops and Starbucks competed for the student market. As he approached Arch Street, he recalled how flustered he had been and what a jerk he must have seemed as he stammered apologies for the locked door and pointed to his mother and the tour like the simpleton he truly was. His happiness, in the end, vanquished his misery as he reflected on the scene, for after all, she *had* reappeared in his life without his having to phone her. His main concern afterward had been whether or not she would return. He had acted the fool before with girls, girls in high school, girls in college, and they usually drifted away.

But Jessica had returned, and he had been surprised again when he discovered her with his mom and Father Nate having tea on Saturday. And his mom asked him to walk her home. It was all too good to be true. Granted, he wanted to ask her out but didn't think it appropriate considering the note and the bird. But all great love stories had difficulties. They all had beginnings, middles, and happily-ever-after endings. This was their beginning; she simply didn't know it yet.

He turned up Arch and stood opposite her house, dreaming. This was her home and it was this Northside street that held his future. He would step carefully, for he sensed she had been hurt, and not just by the experience on the Fire Trail. There was something fragile about Jessica, and yet something strong as well. She had the power to devastate him, to turn his nerves on fire, to make life so real all around him that it was piercingly beautiful. How could he ever be worthy of her? How could he show her his respect and devotion and not trespass into her private world? For Zachary could see she had fenced herself in, built a high wall circled by a deep moat. She must have done this for good reason. In some ways, he supposed, he had done the same thing. After his overweight years and the bullying, he had found safety in sports and books. In college he had occasionally braved the confusing world of women, but only occasionally and not for long. Why enter the fray?

Zachary returned to Hearst and followed the pedestrian path he had walked with Jessica across campus. The sun had finally banished the fog and was slanting through the old oaks shading the lawns. He followed the north fork of Strawberry Creek, past the libraries to busy Bancroft Avenue, then turned south to College. As he pulled out his Browning, he repeated his latest line: "I love thee to the level of every day's/Most quiet need, by sun and candle-light."

He turned to the bookmarked page as he walked, and read the next two lines: "I love thee freely, as men strive for right./I love thee purely, as they turn from praise."

When he thought he had the stanza memorized, he slipped on his earbuds and found Mozart's Clarinet Concerto in A Major, Second Movement, which reminded him of the theme from *Out of Africa*. Soon, weaving between colorful street vendors, Zachary found himself at Laurie's Fine Books.

* * *

The hanging bells on the door jangled as he entered the antiquarian bookstore, and Laurie Warner rose from behind an antique cash register.

Laurie was one of the blackest blacks that Zachary had ever known. He loved the way her teeth shone so white against her skin, and her eyes seemed bigger and brighter because of the rich dark hue around them. Her hair, cut short in a silvery Afro, spun a medieval halo around her face. Zachary was sure she must have been a great beauty when she was young, for even now she radiated a self-confidence that only the beautiful possess.

He knew little of her history, except that she had been born in Kenya and had lived in Berkeley since the sixties when she graduated from Cal. She had seen a great deal of action on Telegraph Avenue, too much, she often said, especially relating to the folks living in People's Park. She spoke with a slight British accent, a lilt that lifted her words through their phrases as though they danced.

She was indeed musical, for she played the violin and conducted the Comerford Chamber Music Society. Zachary knew he had been fortunate with this job, since his mother was friends with Laurie and had mentioned him to her, so he didn't take it for granted. It would be too much to expect favoritism regarding the Chamber Music Society as well, but somewhere in the back of Zachary's mind, he hoped one day she would let him audition again. He hadn't made the cut the last time, but he thought that if he kept practicing he would one day.

The bookstore was empty this Sunday morning, but to Zachary it was alive with all the stories peopling the pages. Laurie kept the store tidy, with neat aisles and shelves packed with faded spines. Old posters decorated the wall space remaining. From time to time, a string quartet played in a corner, and there were wing chairs for reading with good light to read by. Authors discussed books in a back room; etched over the door were the words *Virtue exists for truth, but truth does not exist for virtue, St. Maximus the Confessor, seventh century*. The Warners had converted an old cottage, turning the downstairs into the shop, an enterprise that expanded into the backyard and garage and out to the alley. Laurie's reputation had grown as well; folks stopped by from all over the Bay Area, the Napa Valley, and Marin County.

"My, oh my," she said, flashing that dazzling grin. "You are one happy fella."

Zachary knew he was blushing when he said, "Laurie, I'm in love." With Laurie, he could hold nothing back. She could usually read his mind anyway.

"Tsk, tsk." She lifted a box of books onto the counter. "Take your lovesick face to the back office and make condition cards for these, please."

"Be happy to, Laurie."

"Do you believe in love, Zachary Aguilar?"

"Of course," he said, hugging the box. "Love is everything."

Laurie looked into the distance. "I was in love with Mr. Warner, you know."

"You told me."

"He was a violinist like me—that's how we met. Say, how's the piano coming along?"

Zachary tried to communicate optimism. "Great. I'd like to audition again sometime."

Laurie studied him, pondering. "We'll see. It might be useful to have a substitute pianist. Maybe you can practice with us on Tuesday? Hector, our solo pianist, also plays the cello, so it might be a good idea. We couldn't pay you, you understand."

"I understand. I'd be honored to practice with you, Laurie."

The bells jangled. A customer entered and began browsing the children's literature aisle.

Laurie leaned toward him with her bright earnest eyes. "Zachary, listen to me. I'm glad you're in love. I was so much in love with my Mr. Warner, God rest his soul. It's good to be in love, and it's good to be reminded how good it is." She flashed her smile as she turned toward the customer.

"It's better than good," Zachary said to himself, as he settled into the closet storeroom where a computer, printer, and more books awaited his evaluation and recording.

In the next few hours, Zachary examined each title and judged its condition, deciding whether to keep it or give it to charity, sometimes to the Comerford library. If the book passed the test, he searched online to see how rare it might be, then created a short description from his research. Finally, he priced it and added it to their database, one shared with other dealers worldwide.

All the while he worked, Jessica lived in the borderlands of his thoughts, her safety nagging him. He didn't want to alarm her further by his own concern, so he had tried to play his fears down. He wanted to be strong. But what could he do about it? This madman knew where she lived.

Around noon, Zachary reported to Laurie on his progress. He signed the work log for the day. He lingered by the front door.

Laurie glanced up from the counter. "Thought you were gone, young man. What's the problem? I can see there's a problem and you may as well just tell me what it is."

Zachary returned to the counter and the refuge of Laurie's kindness. "It's Jessica."

"Your new love?"

"She may be in trouble, and I don't know how to help."

"That's the worst kind of trouble, the kind where there doesn't seem to be an answer. When those crazies vandalized our Telegraph store in the sixties, friends said the same thing. They wanted to help, but didn't know how."

"The People's Park protests?"

"It was ugly. Listen, I love trees and grass and free speech just as much as anyone, probably more, but private property is private property. We sacrifice and work hard for our property. And we have laws that protect us, or should protect us. That's what makes civilization civil, as my dear Mr. Warner would say."

"Jessica found the body of the girl murdered Wednesday."

"The girl on the Fire Trail?" Her eyes widened in shock, then narrowed in concern.

Zachary ran his hand through his hair and adjusted his glasses. "She saw the murderer as he was leaving."

"Did *he* see *her*?" Laurie asked, as she led him to a corner where they could sit and talk.

"He did, and it appears he followed her home last night."

Laurie held up her hand. "Wait one minute. Derek!" she shouted to the back. "Come here please, we need you."

A tall young man with a lighter complexion, but the same winning smile as Laurie, approached them. He wore overalls, and Zachary could see he had been painting. "Excuse my mess," Derek said. "I've been touching up our St. Max room—the moldings and such."

"You remember Derek, my grandson?" Laurie asked.

"Sure, I remember Derek," Zachary said. "We were on the tennis team together."

They shook hands firmly, and Derek grinned. "Still on the team. Parks and Recreation—but I'm coaching this time around."

"And helping me in exchange for his room," Laurie said. "Zachary, tell Derek what you told me."

Derek pulled up a chair and listened to Zachary repeat his concerns about Jessica. "Could she identify him?" he asked.

Zachary rubbed his hands and eyed Derek seriously. "The police hope so, she thinks she might be able to, and the murderer must think she can or else why follow her home and threaten her?"

"Derek," Laurie said, "do you have any connections with People's Park? Could you find out anything about this guy?"

"You know I don't."

"You did once." Laurie's eyes grew large and commanding.

"Gran, not anymore!"

"Well, if you hear anything, you'll tell me, okay?"

Derek nodded. "Of course."

Zachary knew the park was an eyesore and there was crime. "Why don't the police clean up People's Park?" he asked them.

Laurie turned to Zachary. "It's private property. It all began in 1969. The Vietnam War was on. The military draft had begun. The country, for the most part, was against the war, so students absorbed the culture of the time and staged free speech—antiwar—protests. This property bordered by Dwight, Bowditch, and Haste was owned by the university. They had the right to use it as they wished, but students who were part of the Free Speech Movement wanted it to be a park. They took it over and planted trees and a garden. It lasted three weeks. In May of '69, Berkeley police and the National Guard confronted thousands of protesters and many were hurt. It's had a troubled history ever since, and it's still a haven for drugs and crime."

"Taking private property doesn't sound like free speech to me," Derek said.

"Freedom demands responsibility," Laurie said.

Zachary listened to them debate the park, the people, the university and the City of Berkeley. "What about Jessica? What about this madman?"

Laurie tapped his knee. "She can stay here, if she wants to."

"Really?" Zachary stood, glancing at his watch. "That's a generous offer, Laurie." He kissed her on the cheek. "You're amazing."

"Talk to her and see."

"I will, and now I need to get up to Comerford House."

Derek walked him to the door. "Let me know if I can help in any way, man."

They shook hands and Zachary nodded. "Thanks, and let's play tennis sometime."

"Sounds good."

Armed with Laurie's offer of a safe house for Jessica, Zachary left the shop and headed toward Comerford. He walked back up College Avenue, turned east on Dwight, up and into the hills. Reaching the Comerford drive, he followed the rutted road through the forest to the house, his heart full, his hopes high, the image of Jessica ever present.

* * *

At two o'clock Zachary stood in the doorway of the music room looking onto the foyer. From here he could watch Jessica begin her tour. Anna was in the group, and she motioned to Zachary to join them. Jessica smiled and nodded. So he joined them, keeping an eye on the front door, now held ajar by a thick volume from the library. He scanned the mixed-age gathering. There were about ten others who, Zachary hoped, would be friendly and respectful and pay attention. He turned to Jessica as she began to speak.

"Welcome to Comerford House," she said, smiling.

Jessica had a lovely smile, Zachary thought, as though she were smiling behind the smile and behind that one too. It was a controlled smile, as if holding something in reserve, nearly teasing. She wore no makeup, and her eyes sparkled as she spoke. Her clothes were the same as Saturday and she was endearingly professional with the dove gray jacket and white shirt with its fine pleats. Her hair was pulled into a French braid with two soft strands falling to the sides of her face. She wore pearl earrings. But most of all she embodied sweetness and innocence. Every fiber in Zachary's being desired to protect her from all pain and provide her with all joy.

Jessica glanced at her history cards, using much the same phrasing as his mother had used, and adding a few details when coming to the wall photos of the Presentation Sisters. Zachary could see that his mom was happy with the extra information, and he felt a sudden surge of pride. He studied Jessica and, as he watched her speak and gesture, he absorbed her open palms and long fingers and the curve of her neck and movement of her arms as she pointed. He liked how she stood so straight and tall. She didn't fidget, but leaned forward, in imitation, he thought, of his mother, and made eye contact with her audience, but only briefly with him, moving away too soon, as though afraid to linger. As the group followed Jessica into the music room, he watched, and as they moved again across the entry with its gleaming floors, he watched. Then he returned to his piano, not sure what to do next, knowing he wasn't supposed to play during opening hours.

He closed the door and played anyway, emboldened by love, but he played as softly as possible, and he played solo arrangements for piano, Mozart's Piano Concerto No. 21 and Beethoven's "Moonlight Sonata", and the music stole under the door and through the entry and barely permeated the rooms. It wove up the stairs past the leaded glass to the library and the bedrooms. It spilled out the windows onto the gardens.

When he guessed the last visitor had left, he reverently lowered the fallboard over the keys, listening for the tap of contact. Then he stood, released the lid prop, and allowed the huge curved lid to drop slowly, the weight both heavy and light in his hands, so that it covered and protected the strings. He ran his long fingers over the lid's black lacquered hardwood, and as often happened, he experienced a curious joy as though this remarkable instrument truly knew him, was part of him.

He heard footsteps and turned toward the door. His mother peeked in, Jessica behind her. "Zachary, could you bring Nicholas down for Sunday Evensong? It's four-thirty already, and too late for tea since the singers have arrived and are practicing in the chapel already, and Father Nate needs to be there."

"With pleasure." He smiled and half-waved at Jessica, as they allowed him to pass through. "Good job! Nice tour . . . you sounded so professional! Coming to Evensong? It's beautiful." He didn't want to sound pressuring or betray his desire with his voice.

Jessica nodded coolly, smiling her enigmatic smile. "Your mother talked me into it."

Zachary grinned and opened his palms. "Great, that's great." He couldn't recall ever feeling so nervous, so out of his depth.

"Afterward, could you see Jessica home in her car?" his mother asked.

Zachary waited for Jessica to nod assent. "I would be honored," he said.

"Good," his mother replied in her efficient voice. "We don't want her driving home alone in the dark, all things considered."

"No, we certainly don't," Zachary said. "I'll meet you in the chapel." He headed for the cottage to escort Dr. Casparian, all the while pondering recent events, one happening after another in miraculous patterns, like motifs in a Bach fugue layering and weaving upon one another.

Thirteen
The Chapel

St. Augustine's Chapel, popularly called Comerford Chapel, nestled in the forest behind the house. It boasted an age of nearly one hundred years. This particular Sunday evening the chapel was filling up, much to Zachary's surprise. He hadn't been to Evensong in some time, he realized. Evening Prayer, entirely spoken, was said weekdays and he had attended with his mother from time to time, then had dinner with her at their Elmwood house where he had grown up.

But an article in the local paper announced that the event was free and the Comerford Singers would be chanting an ancient psalmody, prompting the curious and the thrifty to attend. Such a thing as Anglican Evensong had become avant-garde; it was so old, it was new. Father Nate's prayer processions through campus had also advertised the chapel as something out of the ordinary and had drawn in more visitors.

As Zachary pushed Dr. Casparian in his chair up the side ramp to the chapel door he could hear the organ playing in the loft. He guessed it was a Bach prelude and he marveled, as he often did, how welcoming music could be. The gentle notes, rich in timbre and tone, floated lightly toward them, circling and weaving, then returned to the organ loft like homing pigeons. As he and Dr. Casparian entered the chapel, Zachary was glad the chanting hadn't started, for he looked forward to the singers' procession up the aisle.

His mother and Jessica sat in the back, and Zachary placed Dr. Casparian, in his chair, in the side aisle. Zachary took the seat next to him, at the end of the pew. The elderly man rested his hand on Zachary's shoulder, then let it fall into his lap, limp. He mumbled something from the side of his mouth, his eyes beseeching Zachary to understand his gratitude. Zachary took the hand towel draped on the arm of his chair and wiped the corner of the professor's mouth where a bit of drool lingered from his attempt to speak.

"My pleasure, sir," Zachary replied, and it was, to be sure, his deep pleasure and great honor, since he knew who Nicholas Theodore Casparian had been before stricken with this horrible humiliating disease. His distinguished career had begun with a stellar education at Columbia where he studied under Dr. Jacques Barzun, the highly esteemed cultural historian. Dr. Casparian had followed in his mentor's footsteps, teaching History at Columbia. He had been an advisor to two presidents and written over thirty books. When he came to UC Berkeley it was to chair a new Department of Western Civilization and develop faculty and curricula that would teach students the roots of democratic culture, roots traced to Athens and earlier to the Judaic tradition of Israel. He was known worldwide and shortly before his diagnosis had received a Pulitzer in History. To Zachary, Dr. Casparian would always be that distinguished scholar, no matter the damage ravaged by ALS. Zachary was honored to escort him to Comerford Chapel.

The chapel had been built as a replica of an English country church made from fieldstones. A pitched roof rose over an arched door and shallow porch. A bell tower stood to the side of the door. One central aisle, uncarpeted, and two side aisles led to a marble altar abutting the back wall. Antique ecru linen draped the altar, falling to the floor. The rough stone of the undecorated interior added to the chapel's simplicity and, Zachary considered, encouraged an attitude of anticipation, like a vessel waiting to be filled.

Zachary had been told that there had once been a tabernacle and a crucifix on the altar, but they had been stolen in the sixties. Two pewter candlesticks were all that remained. Rabbi Rosen, an old friend of Father Nate, used the chapel from time to time for blessings and weddings. Couples, often of no particular faith or no faith at all, had been married there. The house itself had become popular for receptions. The wedding industry had provided a steady income that the Board of Comerford Foundation appreciated and encouraged.

Above the front entrance a choir loft was home to various musical instruments as well as the organ, owned and installed by the university, and housed in the chapel by mutual consent. The arrangement had worked out well over the years.

A young man in a black cassock entered from a side door, and Zachary briefly considered helping Father Nate as an acolyte. He watched as the young man lit the altar candles and carefully set a wooden cross between them. The candlelight would be the only light in the dim space, except for two stained glass windows, depicting the Comerford lantern, one above the entrance, the other high over the altar. The windows were modern, for they had been commissioned by the Foundation to replace those broken by vandals.

The steeple bell clanged five mournful notes, muted by stone and fog, and soon Father Nate entered from a side door, his black robe cinched by a rope, the signature of his order of friars, his head covered by a cowl shading his face. He bowed his head as he walked, his hands folded inside wide sleeves. Zachary recalled that Father Nate would not face them, but would sit in the front and ring a hand-bell placed on the floor or, facing the altar, would stand to read the lessons from the sixteenth-century *Book of Common Prayer*, a treasured gift from Father Paul, an Anglican friend. Father Nate took his seat in the front pew. After a moment, he rang the hand-bell to signal the singers' entrance.

They processed in, intoning *Our Father who art in heaven . . .* and the five men and five women, robed in black, took seats alongside Father Nate.

The chanting began, responsorial, one side, then the other. *Fret not thyself because of the ungodly; neither be thou envious against the evil doers* was heard from the left; *For they shall soon be cut down like the grass, and be withered even as the green herb* came from the right. With the third verse, Zachary joined the congregation, following in a tattered coverless prayer book. *Put thou thy trust in the Lord, and be doing good; dwell in the land, and verily thou shalt be fed* was answered with *Delight thou in the Lord, and he shall give thee thy heart's desire.*

Thy heart's desire . . . Zachary glanced at Jessica on the other side of his mother who scrutinized the print in the dim light with great care, following with her fingertip, her head bowed low to see better. Jessica, however, was not singing. She grasped her book between her palms and, as though in a trance, posture straight, stared around the chapel, at the people chanting, at the choir, at the altar, and up to the window high above. Finally, she rested her eyes on the flaming candles. As though she felt Zachary's gaze, she turned toward him. Their eyes met and she smiled, this time unguarded and open. But she quickly looked away.

The voices soared, gathering strength, then receding, like the easy, rhythmic ebb and flow of the sea washing the shore. The choir sang an anthem in three parts, Father Nate read from a large Bible, and they all sang another psalm. Then The Comerford Singers recessed out, a mere thirty minutes after they had processed in, this time chanting, *My soul doth magnify the Lord.* Zachary turned to Dr. Casparian whose eyes were fixed upon the altar cross. Tears rolled down his cheeks, and Zachary gently dabbed them. Somehow, he sensed they were tears of joy.

* * *

After seeing Dr. Casparian to his room, Zachary met Jessica in the upper parking area. She was waiting in the driver's seat with a dreamy expression on her face.

"Thanks for the ride," Zachary said, lowering himself into the seat alongside.

Jessica turned to him as she inserted the key in the ignition. "I appreciate the company, after last night. I'm not sure what might be on my doorstep."

"I'm glad to do it. And I can walk to my place from there."

"Maybe you'd like a bowl of soup? A thank-you for your time?"

"That would be most kind, if it's not too much trouble. It would save me time later . . . er . . . and I'd also love to share supper with you." Couldn't he say anything right?

"Good." Jessica laughed, keeping her eye on the road as they descended into Berkeley.

Zachary observed her profile. "How did you like Evensong?"

"It was beautiful. I've never been to anything quite like it."

"My mom finds it peaceful. I do too."

"Are you religious?" She glanced at him.

Zachary wasn't prepared for such a direct question. "No, I guess I would have to say I'm not. I don't go to church. But I *wish* I believed in God." He surprised himself. Did he wish that? That would be the ultimate transcendence. "I'd like to believe in a loving God. Who wouldn't? The order, the design, the meaning and purpose of life all spelled out."

Jessica nodded. "My father's family were French Catholics. But he didn't go to church. I guess you would call him a lapsed Catholic."

"My mom doesn't go to church either. But my grandma Marta did. She was Catholic. Croatian."

Jessica turned onto Piedmont Avenue. They passed fraternities and sororities and International House, then followed Gayley Road along the east side of campus, turning left on Hearst, and right on Arch. She parked, pausing before getting out of the car.

"You okay?" Zachary asked, sensing her nervousness.

"I'm fine." She opened the car door and moved slowly toward the top of the steppingstone path.

Zachary ran ahead of her, descending quickly through the ivy to her door. There was no bird, no note. "All clear."

"Thanks, Zachary." She stepped carefully. "I appreciate your sensitivity. I was afraid —"

"I know."

Jessica unlocked the door and Zachary scanned the room for signs of intrusion. It was larger than his place on Short Street, but then she shared with a roommate.

"You like it here?" he asked, as she set her pack down and turned on her laptop.

She glanced up, her news site appearing. "It's okay for now. I'm on a tight budget. Please . . . have a seat."

He sat on a couch of an indeterminate color, avoiding the tear. "I'm on a tight budget too. I understand."

She opened a can of tomato soup, poured it into a small pot, and set it on a burner. She sliced a brick of sharp cheddar. "No loans for me. I want to graduate free and clear."

Zachary nodded. "That's what I want. But it's easier said than done." He grimaced and rubbed his forehead. "With two jobs it's difficult to find time to study. I may not make the deadline my advisor set, rather *reset*."

Jessica placed a bowl of salsa and crackers on the counter and glanced at the laptop screen. "Just checking local news. Looks like they haven't found him yet. Here's today's police report." She angled the screen toward him as he approached the counter: *Boy attacked by mountain lion; Killer sentenced in brutal knife attack of Berkeley woman; Burglary on Magnolia Street; Felony assault on College Avenue.* "By the way, I saw Detective Gan last night."

"Good. You gave him the evidence?"

"I did. He was optimistic they would find him. He said the suspect might be from People's Park."

"The university should clean that place up. It's a breeding ground for crime."

"Aren't they just homeless folks, down and out on their luck?"

"Dangerous homeless folks. Listen, you might not be safe here—"

"I'm okay." Jessica turned to the soup and stirred it silently, then asked, "You said you hold two jobs?"

Zachary thought the time was wrong to offer Laurie's room. He sat on a stool, his arms resting on the counter. "I teach most mornings, Monday through Thursday, three classes. On the weekend I work odd hours at Laurie's Fine Books on Telegraph. You should meet her. You'd like her."

"The antiquarian bookstore? That must be interesting."

"It's a great job and I'm lucky to have it. My mom knows Laurie and arranged it for me. Can I help you with anything?"

"Just talk to me. I enjoy listening."

"The store is fun. I write descriptions of books Laurie brings in. I make deliveries. Laurie's a bit quirky—I like to think colorful. Anyway, it's a lot better than the industrial job I had as an undergrad."

"What was that?" Jessica eyed him with interest. "I can't see you working in a factory."

"Steamfitter. It paid well, which was the idea. When I decided to go to college and pay my own way, I went to community college, lived at home to save money, and took the counselor's advice as to the most in-demand and highest paying certificate. I worked for a group in Emeryville all through my undergrad years. It paid the bills. When I graduated, I was able to make enough with the bookstore job combined with my teaching hours. All told, I make less than I did as a steamfitter. But it's okay."

"What's a steamfitter?"

"We repaired pipes, sometimes installed them, usually plumbing systems in commercial buildings."

"Sounds difficult." Jessica set a small tub of sour cream on the counter. "Supper's ready."

They sat at the counter and ladled their soup. They nibbled on crackers and cheese. Zachary wanted to pinch himself. It was probably his best meal ever, and not just because he hadn't eaten since breakfast. It was his first meal with Jessica. He would memorize this meal so he could share it with their children.

"Drink?" she asked.

"Water is fine."

"Me too." She held mismatched glasses under the tap. "You're the guest. You get the one without the crack."

They laughed at their shared poverty, and Zachary knew this was a moment to cherish, this was a moment of great beauty, a beginning, a budding, the moment when they felt at ease in one another's presence for the first time.

"Cheers," he said, raising his glass.

"Santé," she replied, clinking his and slipping a stray strand of hair behind her ear, studying him.

They chatted as they ate, weaving words together, dancing with their thoughts and phrases, testing out here, retreating there, ever careful.

Reluctantly, he checked his watch. "It's seven-thirty, and I'd better go, got papers to grade." He walked to the door, halted, and turned. "Next time, Miss Jessica, I'd like to be the host, but I'm afraid my counter has only one stool and my room is way too tiny. But let's go for a walk sometime. Are you ready to revisit the Fire Trail, this time with a friend?"

Jessica nodded. "The views are great and I do miss it. I'm not sure when Shelley is getting back and can hike it with me."

"But . . . are you ready?"

"I'm putting it behind me." She breathed in deeply. "So let's be brave and walk the trail."

"Then it's a date," he said, his heart pounding. "This week?"

Jessica frowned. "We'll see. Maybe next week. This week seems too soon. And it's not a date-date. Maybe a walk with a friend." She kissed him on the cheek.

"Good, we'll be in touch." Zachary grinned and mumbled good night to the doorstep.

As he stepped through the ivy, he touched the place on his cheek that held the kiss. He walked straight down Hearst, past the trendy eateries and watering holes. He continued west toward the bay, through the Ohlone Greenway to busy Sacramento Street. Soon he turned onto Short Street and climbed the stairs to his room in the stucco bungalow. Later, when he thought of that momentous evening, he didn't recall walking home at all. His heart—and his mind it seemed—were in a basement studio on Arch Street, locked up tight. And, as trite as it sounded, Jessica Thierry had the key.

Fourteen
Nine-Eleven: Zachary

On Thursday, September 11, close to four p.m., Zachary parked his car at the trailhead where the East Bay hills bordered Berkeley. It was the anniversary of a horrific day of national tragedy and he needed to see the silvery bay, the San Francisco skyline, and the Golden Gate. He wanted to think. His mind and heart were a jumble. He needed to sort things out.

He began with a few stretches, but could feel the chill of the fog moving up from the water, so turned up the uneven path toward the Fire Trail at a slow jog, watching his step and soon hitting his regular rhythm. He could feel the pull of his leg muscles, a sweet ache he loved, as his cross-trainers arced through the air. Soon he was flying low, his bent arms relaxed, a trickle of perspiration caught in his headband, and another running down his spine.

Zachary ran, pounding softly the packed earth, parting California bay laurel, passing under gnarly oaks, their aged branches turning and twisting into the air. He ran through stands of cypress pines, their trunks straight and strong, punctuating broad meadows of green grass. He ran through patches of lingering fog and splashes of sudden sun. When he reached the hilltop he stopped, breathed deeply, and stretched his fingers to his toes.

He had not seen Jessica since Sunday, but he had called and left messages. She had not returned the calls, and he tried not to dwell on this. He would see her tomorrow, Friday, at Comerford, and he held on to this idea, slim but definite.

In the meantime, his life had grown terribly complicated. He had settled into his teaching program, Introduction to Poetry, Introduction to the Novel, and the upper division class, The Romantic Novel. Things seemed okay, books ordered and delivered as needed, assignments assigned, expectations explained. Attendance was not bad, considering some lectures were online, and the numbers enrolled were sufficient to continue the class. Things seemed okay, except for the poetry class.

The girl's name was Ellie Sarton. She had taken Introduction to the Novel last year. He had been relieved when the semester was over and he could forget her. She was provocative, no question about it, proudly and carelessly, wearing low-cut tees and miniskirts, exposing breasts and legs, leaving little to the imagination. She often lingered afterward for help, leaning toward him or crossing and uncrossing her legs. Zachary read her message loud and clear. She was the modern student from hell: teasing, tempting, manipulating, controlling.

He had tried to ignore the signals, but she kept on. He refused to give her a gratuitous grade and recommended a C. She was not pleased with his honest assessment and threatened him with sexual harassment. Things settled down over the summer, and he chose to believe that she had moved on to another, easier mark.

How had he managed to survive the year? And now she had shown up in his class once again, with the same routine, only this time with a vengeance. Yesterday, she followed him home, a new low. He ignored her shadowy presence, and finally she went away.

He pulled his T-shirt loose from his shorts for air and resumed his run. Life was full of contradictions. If he had not lost all that weight as a teen, if he had not stayed on his diet and exercised out of sheer fear of obesity, if he had remained as he had been that September of 2001, heavy and unattractive, he wouldn't have the problem of Ms. Sarton today. He supposed that was one of life's ironies, that no matter how green the grass was over the hill, it was never as green as you thought it would be when you got there. It was as though it had turned brown with your stepping on it.

His metaphors reflected his running as he loped along the narrowing trail through low grass in a wet and foggy hollow. He plowed through more bay and laurel and on through live oaks to another crest. Soon he would emerge onto a vista point. Hopefully, he could see the San Francisco Bay, if it was not yet engulfed by fog. He could stare at the city and figure out his life, what to do next, as he had done many times over the years.

The long bench was welcome and he sprawled on it, pulling out his water bottle. The San Francisco skyline and the Golden Gate glistened in the encroaching mist. Berkeley dipped low and shadowy toward the shoreline.

Thirteen years ago today, 2001, the year of the New York City attacks, he was only thirteen. Zachary could not imagine what it was like to have been in New York on that Tuesday morning, September 11th. He didn't recall much about the day in his own life. He remembered being afraid, as usual, of going to school. He could never forget those bullies. They tormented him because he was fat and because he went home instead of roaming the streets with them. When did his mother finally sense his fear? When did she learn about the gang? How relieved he was when he changed schools. He took up tennis with his dad. He lost weight. And he stayed fit.

Zachary drank long and deep and watched the sky change over the bay, the city, and the bridges. He rummaged in his pack and found a baggie of almonds, grabbing them with his fingertips and tossing them into his mouth. Salt free, fat free, healthy almonds.

His mom had been overweight too. His dad had lost the extra pounds when he started walking to his job at Foodmart and back home each day. His mom was still heavy then, probably because she loved cooking and feeding them. She loved being a mom, a homemaker. Zachary could understand it would be difficult to stop nurturing in that special way.

His dad should have understood as well. He should have been more patient with his mom. Instead, his eyes wandered at work and soon his body—his new body—wandered as well. Then, only two years ago, his dad moved out and, although Zachary had been living on his own by then, it felt as though Luke had left them both. It hurt.

Zachary missed his father but didn't want him back in his life, not after what he had done. His mother looked great now, with her exercise program and her diet. But she must miss his father. Zachary knew they were once in love, once close. He knew she must have suffered when he left her for a younger woman, way younger.

He, Zachary, would be better than that. He would be true. He would love, protect, be always faithful to the woman he married, and he would make vows for life, in sickness and in health, till death parted them, all those vows you read in novels and see in old movies. To Zachary this was true love and without true love, committed love, sacrificial love, what was the point?

With the Trade Center attack, the recent wars, and now the beheadings, trust and truth and commitment were more important than ever. Life became serious when it was threatened.

Nine-eleven. Zachary stood and stared at the skyline, imagining the planes attacking San Francisco as they had attacked New York. He had seen the images on television year after year, and each time was astonished that others would hate America like that, hate their freedom. Such hate and such tyranny were so opposed to the innate human desire for love and transcendence. Those terrorists chose the bestial way, the way of the jungle, the way of illiteracy and babble, the way of chaos and death.

And yet America had its own communities of chaos and death. There were moments, Zachary admitted, that he desired greater control over criminals, greater safety on their streets. Was that a desire for tyranny? He hoped not. But he recognized his passion to defend Jessica from rapists and murderers. He could see where that passion might lead, without laws duly respected and rightly feared. He could see the boundary between liberty and law was not always easily seen.

Zachary suddenly felt a great love for this skyline, this bay, this American city with its bridges. The nation had been at peace for many years before 2001, so that events like Nine-Eleven were shocking. They burned the mind and memory, seared images onto the soul. In this way, Zachary judged, the attack pulled Americans out of their lethargy and into paying attention, to watching, to being alert. Just so, the recent beheadings of American journalists James Foley on August 19 and Steven Sotloff on September 2 by the

Islamic State woke up Americans. Even home-grown horrors like the Boston Marathon bombings of 2013 and the Fort Hood massacre of 2009 nudged the nation to evaluate who and what America was and is, and how best to re-form this perfect union of cultures, races, and beliefs.

But America, Zachary believed, still held close to her heart the values of freedom, even in the face of the hate flying into New York City on that clear, September morning. America still valued free speech, democracy, and peaceful assembly. America still had the will and the resources to protect the world from tyranny. The nation wasn't perfect, the balance precarious, but that was the price of freedom.

Today was Thursday, nine-eleven-fourteen. Tomorrow was Friday, nine-twelve-fourteen. He would see Jessica tomorrow. His world had survived another year, and Jessica was in his life. He wanted to use tomorrow well and not stumble over his words. He should do something about the madman that followed her home. But what could he do?

Zachary stood, stiff from sitting, lost in reverie. He hadn't solved the Ellie Sarton problem. He felt for his earbuds and phone, but he had forgotten them. He decided silence was best on a day like today, as though he joined the nation in mourning. He fell into a slow jog, along the trail that would take him through the grove of trees where Jessica had seen the murderer.

Zachary ran, touching the earth tenderly with his soles and watching for the stand of pines, watching for the man with the scar and the wild eyes.

* * *

It was dark when Zachary's phone buzzed and he entered his upstairs room on Short Street. He pulled the phone out of his pocket and swiped the screen. As he listened to Laurie's tense voice, he gazed out his window into the shadowy cul-de-sac through the trees. A street light sputtered, and the BART station glared beyond.

Laurie sounded as if she were trying to hide what she felt, smothering the urge to be blunt. "Derek connected with an old friend. He says this fellow, this suspect—this *murderer rapist*—is known in People's Park, but hasn't shown up for at least a week."

"What else?" Zachary was sure there was more. "Please, Laurie, I need to know."

"Okay, but I hate talking about these things, you know I do. It's all so horrible. You wonder what's going to happen next. I'll have nightmares tonight, but I promised to call you. Derek said that the People's Park homeless are afraid of this fellow, this suspect. They're relieved he seems to have moved on."

"And?" Zachary wanted it all. This wasn't all.

"Okay. Okay. This is it. He likes killing birds and squirrels. Cuts off their heads."

Zachary breathed in deeply, pulling himself together. "Are you okay, Laurie?"

"No, I'm not. But yes, I guess I'm okay. I'll be okay. It's just today's Nine-Eleven. The terror's still with us. The beasts in the jungle, you know what I mean? They come from everywhere now, out of their caves and holes in the ground. Be careful, Zachary, just take care of your Jessica."

"I'll try, Laurie."

"That's your main job, Zachary."

"I know, Laurie."

As he ended the call, Zachary gazed into the dim street, into the eerie film of light, the pale glare angling through the leaves onto the broken pavement, enshrining late workers tumbling from the trains, drifting like ghosts, silently into the night. He shivered and switched on a light. He needed to make supper. He needed to work a few hours before bed.

Fifteen
Nine-Eleven: Anna

As Zachary ran the Fire Trail on Nine-Eleven, Anna busied herself in the Comerford kitchen, making tea. A grandfather clock tolled four. The notes, Anna thought, sounded mournful, appropriately so, on this day of such remembrance, such national tragedy. The day had cast a spell of sadness over her. She had skipped CircleFit and instead worked steadily in the library upstairs. No one showed for the two o'clock tour, now that school was in session, and she turned on the small TV in the pantry, muting the sound, simply wanting reassurance that her country had not been attacked again.

Having set the table with a bowl of sliced apples and a plate of oatmeal cookies (steel cut oats, whole wheat), she added a vase of red roses from the garden. She waited for the water to boil, glancing from time to time at the TV screen, reading the running news panel along the bottom: *Trade center rises from ashes, opens 13 years after terror attacks; Berkeley Free Speech Movement rally planned; Militants behead British hostage in video; Suicide risk on the rise for elderly; Fire Trail suspect still at large ...*

Comerford House was quiet, as though a pall had fallen over the grounds. Anna vividly recalled September 11, 2001. She had been thirteen years younger then, only forty-four, and Luke had not yet left them for that young Rosalind, and they were a family. California time was three hours earlier than New York time, so Anna first learned about the attack shortly before six in the morning and Zachary was still sleeping. She had risen early to see Luke off for his shift at Foodmart and was making breakfast, the portable TV blinking and flashing its morning news.

Zachary had been in that awful class with the bullies, so he must have been in middle school. Anna winced. They should have transferred him sooner; she should have seen the signs sooner; she should have noticed her boy's withdrawal, his fear of leaving the house and going to school. Fear tells us something, Anna thought in hindsight, and we should pay attention to its signals.

The first TV bulletin had been nearly unbelievable. The voices of the reporters moved from pragmatic concern to astonishment to horror at what they were seeing, and then saying, as they described the planes diving into the towers. Today, thirteen years later, Anna could see it so clearly: the black smoke of the first plane and the fiery explosion of the second. It was, she recalled, when the second plane hit, that she, along with a stunned nation watching, concluded this was not an accident. The United States was under attack. But who would do such a thing? Later, she learned, four passenger airliners had been hijacked by nineteen terrorists who had turned the planes into suicide bombs.

That morning Anna had stared at the screen, dumbfounded, as American Flight 11 and United Flight 175 dove into the North and South Towers of the World Trade Center. She witnessed men and women jumping from upper windows to their deaths. She saw the towers implode and fall to the earth, and she could even now feel the terror of it, as though she were there. She could taste the dust billowing through the cavernous streets, the heart of America's financial markets, as terrified workers ran from flying debris. The third plane, American Flight 77, crashed into the Pentagon and the Department of Defense in Washington D.C. The last plane, United Flight 93, diverted by passengers rushing the hijackers, exploded in a Pennsylvania field. Over three thousand died, including hundreds of firefighters and police, the deadliest attack on American soil in the history of the United States.

The kettle whistled. Anna turned off the burner, the flame died, and she poured boiling water over tea leaves in the pewter teapot. Leaving the tea to steep, she moved from the kitchen into the foyer and crossed to the music room. From there she could see the San Francisco skyline, its misty shape still visible, still intact. Comerford's porch flag flew at half-mast, and she watched the heavy canvas ripple in the growing damp, its stars and stripes waving as though holding the past and the future in its weave.

Anna heard the French doors open and close in the kitchen. Father Nate had arrived for tea.

* * *

The priest seemed unusually somber as he rubbed his thick fingers through his hair. His mood suited Anna's.

"How's Miss Jessica working out?" he asked. "She seems eager."

"I like her. She's sweet and bright. She's different from others we've had."

"I felt that too. Dresses differently."

"What do you think of her? First impressions?"

Father Nate sipped his tea thoughtfully. "I think she's running away."

Anna scrutinized him, surprised. "From what?"

"I'm not sure. Some hurt, either done to her or those she loves."

Anna reflected on Jessica's cool calm, her control, her measured way of speaking, her old fashioned clothing—covering herself, arms, legs, never showing a hint of cleavage, which most girls flaunted. "I can see that. She's almost in hiding, at least by today's standards."

"Well said. And then to go through such an ordeal on the Fire Trail. To find that young woman's body." Father Nate rubbed his scarred cheek. "How's she holding up?"

"She seems to have a hidden strength."

"I sense that too, rather like your Zachary. Speaking of hidden, I found something curious today."

"What did you find?" Anna asked, offering him the oatmeal cookies, and glad he could see her son's hidden strength.

Father Nate reached for one, took a bite, and a dreamy look came over his face. "These remind me of cookies my grandma used to make. Delicious, Anna."

"Thanks. You were saying you found something?"

He pulled from his pocket a long key, dark and discolored. "It's probably quite old."

Anna held it in her palm, turning it over. "Where did you find it?" It was about the length of her hand, cool to the touch, heavy.

"You know how the wall behind the altar is rough stone? Some of the crevices are quite deep. I believe the Napa earthquake last month may have loosened some of the contact points. I found this in one of the gaps."

"What's it for?"

"I have no idea. It's too large to be a tabernacle key. That was my first thought. Must have been a key to a door or even a gate. It doesn't fit the chapel door. Curious, wouldn't you say?"

Anna set it on the table. "Should we display it?"

"Not yet. Perhaps we'll find its lock. I'll put it somewhere safe for now."

In the quiet of their thoughts Father Nate reached for a third cookie and Anna munched on the apples.

"I found something else, although I don't want to frighten you," he said.

Anna waited. "Please, go on."

He observed her carefully. "In the woods above the parking lot, before you reach the Fire Trail, I found a small clearing where a campfire might have been made."

"What does that mean?" Anna's heart seemed to stop. The silence in the room deepened.

"Fires are dangerous in these hills. And it's a wonder I didn't smell smoke during the night. He must have been careful and quick."

"Who would squat on Comerford property like that? You think the murder suspect?"

"Could have been anyone. I reported it to Eddie Gan." Father Nate rubbed his hands thoughtfully.

Anna recalled the detective, whom she considered trustworthy. "What did he say?"

"Eddie said there had been sightings of the suspect on the Fire Trail. He's coming by to take a look."

Anna rubbed her forehead, which was beginning to throb. "Are we safe here? Are you safe living here?"

"Not to worry about me, Anna. I'm sure the man's just looking for a night's rest. But be sure and lock up before leaving. I'll walk you to your car after Evening Prayer."

"Thanks." Anna's mind was whirling with possible dangers, but she didn't want Father Nate to worry about her worrying, so she said as calmly as she could, "I'm glad you like the cookies. They're Zachary's favorite."

"They're excellent." He looked relieved at the change of subject and Anna was relieved that he was relieved. "Thank you for preparing this. I do enjoy teatime. Zachary is blessed to have a mother like you. How's he doing? I haven't had a chance to chat with him lately."

"I'm so proud of him, Father. He works so hard to support himself and finish his doctorate so he can teach."

"He has a big heart. He'll be a good teacher."

"You've taught him a lot, Father. And me too."

The priest raised his brow and shook his head, as though in wonder. "He's in love with God but doesn't know it." He touched his nose. "I think you might be coming close to belief as well."

Anna chuckled. It was a familiar attempt to convert her. "How so, as far as Zachary is concerned?"

"He speaks from time to time about his desire for beauty, goodness, and transcendence. That shows a deep desire for God in his life."

Anna nodded. "I suppose so. He sees transcendence in the chapel service. And beauty too. And maybe even goodness."

"Yes, the chapel service, a daily joy. And tonight Evening Prayer will be in memoriam. I'm saying prayers for the dead, since it's Nine-Eleven."

"I've been thinking about Nine-Eleven."

Father Nate nodded. "A horrible attack on America. But we should not forget. We must remember. It was a holocaust. Did you watch the President's address last night?"

"I missed it. Are we at war?" she asked, thinking of the recent terrorist attacks.

"I'm not sure. Not officially. But he's indicating a change of course. He's talking about greater military action. No boots on the ground, but selective bombing."

"Is that good?"

"Probably too little too late. This could have all been avoided. We never should have left Iraq when we did, the way we did. And he's weakened our military with the sequestrations. He's undone so much of President Bush's work to protect us."

Anna found the Bush years confusing. The media vilified George Bush, but Father Nate described the times differently than she had read in the papers and heard on TV. And she had come to trust the priest.

Father Nate wrung his hands, then refolded them as though praying. "And now we have the beheadings—executions—of civilians. Videotaped! They've declared war on America."

"What should be done? What does Nicholas say?" Anna's fears soared when she thought of the beheadings, and Nicholas would have the last word, being their expert in residence.

He eyed the stone chapel in the trees. "Nicholas says the borders should be tightened immediately. He said there is a *clear and present danger* to the United States."

"But what about the immigrants?" She thought of the children; she thought of the political unrest and violence that forced them from their homes.

"They're welcome, if they come legally. It's only fair to this country, and especially now that terrorists are traveling with Western passports."

"I do think everyone should learn English."

Father Nate sat back and nodded in agreement, his features expressing *what can they be thinking*. "You would assume that would be a priority. That one issue, over the years, has been Nicholas' mantra. *If a people has no common language, it has no common culture. If it has no common culture, it will divide upon itself, and will have no future.*"

"Like Abraham Lincoln said, 'a house divided upon itself cannot stand'?"

"And Lincoln was quoting Christ." Father Nate locked his eyes on hers. " 'Every kingdom divided against itself is brought to desolation; and every city or house divided against itself shall not stand.' "

"But we welcome immigrants, we welcome diversity. That's who we are. The great melting pot." Anna loved the image of multiculturalism. It was colorful and rich, like a vegetable stew. Her own family had come from Croatia, then called Yugoslavia. And Father Nate's family, she knew, was from Armenia. Her ex-husband, Luke, had family in Brazil.

"Ah, the melting pot. Nicholas would say that first of all, we love those who respect the law, so come here legally. And second, our melting pot is our strength, but there must be some kind of melting, and the first common flavor *must be language.*"

Anna considered his words as she bit into an apple wedge and eyed a cookie. She saved the cookie for last, strengthening her delayed gratification. "Is that why we have these homegrown terrorists? Like the Boston marathon bombings last year?" She recalled the race and the crowds and the explosions. The maimed, those who had lost their legs, would be crippled for life. She thought of the children who witnessed their siblings and parents mutilated.

"At least they knew English. We are beyond the language issue, I suppose. Nicholas complains now about the lack of civic education in UC Berkeley, but even more so in high schools and grade schools."

"You mean like patriotism? Flying the flag? Honor and pride in country, that sort of thing?"

"Exactly. Without such educated patriotism, America has nurtured by default pockets of revolution, communities of fanaticism. And oddly enough, anti-Americanism has been encouraged, even taught, in our universities."

"Is that why there's so much crime today?" It wasn't like that when she was growing up, at least not that she could recall.

His tone was deeply sad. "Nicholas often claims that Americans don't know who they are. They don't know their history. There are reasons for traditions and structures and the way things are done. New is not always better. Changes should happen for good reason, not for the sake of *new* or to make news. So we need to understand the *why* of history as well as the *what*. I was once a liberal. Now I'm a conservative for this very reason."

"You were once a liberal?" Anna found that difficult to believe.

"Ah, my dear, Western liberalism stems from Christian roots. Originally, St. Paul and St. Augustine built upon classical ideals. The importance of social charity and the dignity of the individual are unique to Christianity. Some say the Western mind is closing down and we are entering a time of anti-enlightenment, of darkness."

"Liberalism came from Christianity?"

"The Enlightenment was Christian-based. Man's reason was encouraged by the Judeo-Christian tradition, in which a rational

Creator created rational beings. The scientific quest, freedom of speech, thought, and worship, are Judeo-Christian ideas."

"Just sometimes poorly practiced?"

Father Nate squinted at her, rubbing his chin. "Indeed. But they are still Judeo-Christian ideals. This is who we are. To deny these roots is national suicide. And then there are the lies of modernity."

"The lies of modernity." Anna thought she knew what he meant. "I see a lot of modern lies in the books donated to my library, I can tell you. I have to vet them carefully."

"I'll bet you do."

"So what are the lies you are talking about?"

"One was spread by Darwin who said man was merely animal."

Anna knew what he meant. "That would explain what I'm seeing, Father, in these violent and pornographic novels. Children are in hopeless situations."

The priest nodded. "Despair and hopelessness are modern hallmarks. Another lie was promoted by Marx who said that man has no free choice, an idea called social determinism. Freud called this psychological determinism, and Nietzsche said there is no truth, an idea called nihilism, encouraging the rise of a superman."

"Might makes right? Like Hitler."

"And Russia's Stalin and China's Mao. Anarchy invites a police state to produce order. These patterns repeat again and again in history. Students need to learn the patterns."

"More tea, Father?" Anna reached for the pot and refilled their cups. How could she help him to a better place, a softer tone. His face was redder than usual. It wasn't healthy.

Father Nate smiled. "Thank you, my dear. I'm afraid I'm on a tirade just like Nicholas. You *are* a good listener."

Anna laid her hand on his. "I'm listening because I'm interested, interested in the truth, in what really happened, how we got where we are today." She tried to look as sincere as she felt, but her words sounded thin. Sometimes she couldn't find the words she needed. Sometimes she didn't know whether to speak or be silent.

Father Nate poured milk into his fresh tea and reached for the sugar. He looked out the window again, toward the chapel.

Anna followed his gaze to the shady hillside, the eucalyptus and pine, as she absorbed his ideas and they tumbled about in her thoughts. She wanted to ask him about his memories of Nine-Eleven.

But as she sipped her tea, about ready to ask, she heard a loud clap from the lion knocker on Comerford's front door.

Sixteen

Nine-Eleven: Nate

Father Nate opened the door, pleased to see Eddie. Anna stood close by.

"Good afternoon, Father." The detective's face was both open and urgent. He wore his uniform, but took off his cap in deference to the priest.

"Good afternoon, Eddie. Thanks for coming by." The priest ushered him into the foyer. "Would you like some tea?"

"No thanks, Father. I'm here on serious business, I'm afraid. He glanced at Anna who smiled reassuringly.

"Of course," the priest said. "You've met Anna?"

The detective nodded and smiled. "I have, and am happy to see her again." He cleared his throat. "I think both of you should come up the hill with me."

"Let's go out the back." Anna led him through the kitchen and out the French doors.

Father Nate bolted the front door and followed.

They crossed the lawn, passed the chapel in the pines, and took a path parting beds of roses and sunflowers, azaleas and camellias, up to the parking lot. On the other side of the lot the path continued into the woods, overgrown but apparently used. Eddie led the way, Father Nate close behind, Anna last. The priest looked over his shoulder as he stopped for breath. "Not many know this trail is here, it's so hidden."

"I didn't know about it," Anna said.

Eddie turned toward them. "It goes back to earlier days and has been re-found, you might say. It connects with the Fire Trail."

Soon they arrived at a small clearing.

"Is this the place you mentioned, Father?" Eddie asked.

"Yes," the priest said, wheezing slightly. He breathed deeply. "I check the grounds from time to time. I knew about this upper path—more of a deer path—but had never come across anything like a campfire, or signs of human use."

"Father, maybe you should sit on this log," Anna said.

"I'm fine, Anna." He glanced at her gratefully, then turned to Eddie. "What do you think?"

"It's the remains of a campfire, that's for sure, and not that long ago. Hard to tell when exactly. Probably in the last week."

"Anything else?" Father Nate intuited that Eddie was hiding something.

"I . . . er . . ." he began, glancing at Anna.

The priest knew that Anna would be better off with the full story. She clearly desired to know. "Out with it, Eddie. Anna is a tough lady. It's okay, right, Anna?" He didn't want to keep secrets from Anna.

"I need to know. I work here." Her eyes demanded the truth.

Eddie Gan moved to the edge of the clearing. He pointed to the ground. Dead animals, birds and squirrels, lay scattered about, decapitated.

"Good Lord!" Father Nate called on the Almighty in the most literal sense, as a cry for help, and not in vain.

"Oh." Anna placed her hand over her mouth, and her eyes met the priest's. "It's like ISIS."

Father Nate shook his head and folded his hands prayerfully. What evil prompted a man to do this? What hate compelled him? He offered a prayer for the estranged stranger, the man who had crossed the borders of sanity, had stepped outside the human community and into the jungle. He prayed that the demons leave him and he be healed, made whole again.

"Awful, I know," Eddie said, trying to soften the sight. "This is hard to see, but I wanted to show you, since, as you say, ma'am, you work here. You just need to be careful."

"Thank you." Anna moved back to the path and sat on the log, her eyes on the detective as if he were a refuge.

Eddie stood nearby. "And we have sitings of the suspect on the Fire Trail. We'll get him, don't you fear, Mrs. Aguilar."

Father Nate joined them. "What should we do?"

"Would the Foundation consider a fence and alarm system?"

"As in gates and entry codes?" the priest asked.

"These are dangerous times, and it will probably get worse."

Father Nate shook his head. "It would add to the expenses, budget, future viability for Comerford House." And it would not be welcoming, he thought.

Anna stood, looking resolved. "We'll mention it to the Board."

"Good," Eddie said, turning to the path. "That's it. I wanted to give you a full report."

"And we're grateful," Father Nate said, following Anna.

"Are you sure you can't stay for some tea, Detective Gan?" Anna's voice was unusually tense. "We have some nice cookies."

They entered the parking lot and Eddie hesitated alongside his car. "Not today, Mrs. Aguilar, but thanks. A rain check maybe?" He lowered himself into the driver's seat.

"Absolutely," Anna said, raising her hand in a wave.

"He's a good man, Eddie Gan." Father Nate said, watching the detective drive off.

"He has a tough job these days. Father, it's late. I've got to clean up the tea things before Evening Prayer."

Father Nate recalled his change of schedule. "Not as late as usual. Evening Prayer is an hour later tonight because of Nine-

Eleven. Others might want to come after work, so I set it for six rather than five."

"I'd forgotten. Good. We can take our time getting back. It's nice up here."

Standing above the cottage and the house and the stone steeple with its cross intersecting the sky, they watched the sun slide into the fogbank. The earlier mist had thickened and now blanketed the bay, but the hazy sky still held the last rays as if too lazy to send them over the horizon.

"What a panorama," the priest said.

"It is, isn't it? The view up here is better than from my library window."

"And better than from Nicholas' room."

They laughed lightly, releasing tension, comforted by the warmth of friendship.

"San Francisco is still there," Anna said, "and it's Nine-Eleven."

"No attack so far," he said, rubbing his chin.

"Thank God."

"Thanks be to God."

Anna turned to him. "So, in Evening Prayer we're offering prayers for those who died and for their families?"

"Yes."

A sudden silence fell over them like a pall as they stepped slowly and carefully down the gravel path through the gardens, hearing only the sounds of their footfall and the caws of unseen birds high in the pines.

Pausing, they looked out to the pale sky spread over Comerford House. When Anna spoke, Father Nate could barely hear her. "I was making breakfast when I heard," she said. "Where were you on Nine-Eleven, Father?"

The question jabbed the priest's memory, but he didn't mind. Memory, he knew, could be healed by love. Anna wouldn't probe too deep. He trusted her to heal and not hurt. He could see, when she glanced at him that she simply desired to remember the day, to mourn for America then and now. He tried not to waver, but his face must have betrayed him, for she added, "You don't have to tell me."

"It's okay, Anna. Stories are good. Especially true stories that explain the present, like all true history, all good history, handed down to the next generation. But let's sit so I can rest my legs again." He motioned to her to join him on a bench in the garden. Taking a deep breath, he said a quick prayer, forcing himself to give voice to that time of sudden, shocking loss. "I was a parish priest and friar. Nicholas was teaching at Cal. I lived near the church, St. Joseph's. I remember hearing the news when I turned on the TV early in the morning."

"Me too."

"It was before the fire." He touched his crimson cheek. "And before the ALS."

"Two more tragedies."

"But the worst tragedy was . . . Louise."

"Louise?"

"Louise Casparian, Nicholas' wife."

Anna grew silent, and Father Nate could see an array of emotions pass over her face. She waited for him to speak.

"She died that morning," he said, focusing on a pale pink rose in the garden. "She was visiting a cousin at her office in New York at the Trade Center. They never had a chance."

"Oh, no."

He turned to Anna and met her soft dark eyes, caring eyes, eyes that understood loss. Encouraged, the words tumbled out, and he found himself gesturing with open palms, standing, pacing, and sitting again. "We didn't realize, at first, where she was at the time, but when we didn't hear from her ... well, we learned soon enough. Nicholas was devastated, as were the children. They were adults, of course, a son and a daughter with families of their own. But it was so violent, so unexpected."

"How did he manage such a loss?"

"He plunged into his work. But his academic colleagues claimed that America asked for it, citing our imperialism, capitalism, and wealth, and saying that the terrorists were the real victims. Nicholas was furious. It became his mission to correct their lies."

"What did he do?"

"He fought them with words and ideas. He set up courses to teach the next generation the truth: America's history, her institutions, what defines her, his six grand pillars."

"Six grand pillars?"

Father Nate ticked them off on his fingers. "There were the three L's: *Limited* government, individual *liberty*, rule of *law* . . . let's see, the other three were free markets, personal responsibility, and traditional values."

Anna repeated them as if committing them to memory.

Father Nate continued, venting the concern he shared with his brother and welcoming the healing tonic of Anna's friendship as though she could carry his burden by gathering it up, at least for a time. "Nicholas claimed that our country had grown weak and vulnerable to another attack. Clinton eviscerated the CIA, he said, so intelligence was ineffective. He used the word *eviscerated*, I remember. I had to look it up."

"And President Bush?"

"Nicholas admired Bush, said he would go down in history as one of our great presidents. He thought the liberal media had reached a barbaric low when they made fun of him. He often said that the guarantors of freedom and free speech were their close cousins, respect and responsibility."

"I remember how the papers and TV made fun of President Bush, even little things, personal things. I don't like sneering and bullying. It isn't right. It isn't civil."

Father Nate nodded. "It crosses the border between the civil and the uncivil. But the media bias soon was out in the open. When President Bush's term was up in 2008, the media orchestrated the next election. The new president, their man, *eviscerated*, my word this time, the military across the board, leading to our current crisis."

"And this encouraged the rise of Islamic terrorism?"

"Yes, to put it simply."

"Americans don't like war." Anna looked doubtful, and Father Nate knew she voiced the feelings of many, that if you don't like something then it must be wrong. Even national defense was now guided by feelings.

Father Nate breathed deeply and spoke firmly, as though explaining to the daughter he never had, telling the truth, emboldened by love. "Nobody likes war. But balance of power keeps the world safe, prevents war and protects peace. War is inevitable when you have tyrants in the world, regardless of their reason. Russia is another rising tyranny. So the balance of power has now been tipped in tyranny's favor."

They headed downhill, following the path.

"What happened to Nicholas' son and daughter? And their families?" Anna asked as they neared the chapel.

"They're fine, in Arizona and Maine. Each invited their father to come live with them, but he didn't want to be a burden. So he sold the house in the Berkeley Hills and moved in with me."

"He wanted to keep teaching."

Father Nate nodded. "He lived and breathed academia and the free exchange of ideas. Working was the therapy he needed. And now he was on a mission, to correct the media's lies, the lies taught on campus, politically correct lies."

"Was it really that bad?"

They crossed the lawn to the French doors. He wanted Anna to understand what it means to be a refugee, to emigrate to America. "Anna, our grandparents fled the Armenian genocide of 1915 in Turkey, where their own parents—our great-grandparents—were murdered. They worked hard when they came to this country. They farmed near Fresno, living in a refugee community. Nicholas and I grew up during World War Two. We were raised to deeply value liberty—the freedom to think, speak, and worship as we choose. We loved America. We loved the culture of the Western world. We didn't have much, but we had America. We were *Americans*."

"I understand, Father." She opened the door. "I'm so glad to hear your story. Thank you."

"Not an unusual one, even if ignored or forgotten. Thanks for listening to an old friar, Anna."

"But what happened to Nicholas' Western Civ program?"

"It struggles. Many faculty still think the West is the *cause* of the world's problems, not the solution." Father Nate shook his head. "I can't figure them out. Do they want to be like Russia? Or China? Or Iran? Do they want women to be enslaved, children raped? Do they want Jews, gays, and Christians slaughtered, beheaded, crucified? Blasphemers whipped and adulterers stoned? What are they thinking? I'll never understand the America-haters, and there are lots of them with powerful tenure in respected universities today. They're teaching our children and grandchildren to hate their own country."

They stood in front of the table, and Anna tasted her tea. "Cold."

"I'll help you clean up." He should help Anna more often, he thought.

"Thanks."

As he cleared the dishes, Father Nate added, "You're a good friend, Anna Aguilar. That means a lot to an old man like me, especially in these uncertain times. And I know I've been rambling. The older I get, the more I ramble."

"I like your stories and your ramblings, Father. They help me understand my own stories." She washed and rinsed the cups, setting them carefully on a rack. "You can dry these if you like."

Father Nate picked up a towel and reached for a cup. "This Fire Trail killer is a victim of our not enforcing the law. We've grown lax because many don't believe in the source of our laws. Nicholas sometimes quotes Jefferson: 'Can the liberties of a nation be secure when we have removed a conviction that these liberties are the gift of God?' The words are etched into the Jefferson memorial in Washington, D.C."

Anna glanced up at him. "He means that if we don't believe in the source of the gift we might not believe in the gift itself?"

"Exactly."

"Religion is important, I've come to see, even if I'm not very good at believing. Now go and fetch Nicholas. I'll meet you in the chapel. We have lots of prayers to say tonight."

Father Nate bowed from the waist with a gallant flourish. "I think one day I might convert you, my dear. One day you will have a vision of God." With those sudden words, he prayed that it would be so. Why didn't she believe? She was so close to glory but didn't see it all around her.

Anna laughed and raised her brow. "Maybe so."

As Father Nate stepped into the back garden and crossed the lawn to the cottage, he could feel Anna's eyes upon him, and he prayed his prayer again. Some things, he knew, he must leave to the mercy of God's great love for those who love.

* * *

As Anna watched the old priest cross the lawn, she thought, *I'd like to believe in God, if I could, so I'll pray to Father Nate's God. I'll remember those who died on this terrible tragic day. I'll remember Louise, for Nicholas' sake, for all our sakes.*

Anna put away the dishcloths and tidied up. She checked the front door locks. She turned out the lights, except for the one on the porch so the flag could be seen. After Evening Prayer, Father Nate would lower it, fold it, and put it away carefully. Sometimes, she thought, he prayed over the flag. Was he a saint? What was a saint, anyway?

Anna picked up the vase of roses and, holding it close with one hand, locked the back door behind her with the other. She stepped across the grass as a light mist gathered around the chapel. All seemed peaceful for now, except for a distant siren. She glanced up the hill toward the gardens.

Father Nate stood on the chapel steps, his head hooded. He reached for the heavy rope hanging by the door and pulled down, then released it. As the bell tolled, Anna entered the chapel, placed the roses on the altar, and sat beside Nicholas, his eyes on the flaming candles. He turned to her with beseeching eyes, immensely kind eyes. He opened his hand, and in his palm lay a creased photograph of a young woman.

"Louise," he mouthed, pulling his lips around the letters.

She took the photo and nodded to Nicholas. "I know," she whispered. "Nicholas, I know. We'll pray for her together."

Anna's eyes moistened, and tears streamed down Nicholas' handsome face. She pressed the photo into his hand. "She was beautiful, so beautiful."

His eyes on the flames, Nicholas nodded slowly.

Seventeen
Nine-Eleven: Jessica

On that same Thursday, about the time that Zachary Aguilar began his run and Anna Aguilar made tea, Jessica Thierry decided she would not return Zachary's calls from Monday, Tuesday, and Wednesday. She wanted to concentrate on her thesis, and she set to work. She spread out her papers and photos on the counter. She turned on her laptop and checked the national news.

Immediately images of Nine-Eleven filled the screen: the smoke, the imploding towers, the screams. Jessica drew in her breath. She had forgotten the date. Today had been a normal day on campus. She had attended her seminar on research methods and visited the Berkeley Historical Society downtown, all the while haunted by every scruffy straggler, every sinister footstep, every stranger's glance. The Fire Trail ordeal was recent, she told herself, and the horror would recede with time, but the police sketch that confronted her at the Post Office, the bank, the market, and the library kept the man alive in her thoughts. No wonder she had forgotten the date.

The headlines had been the usual ones; she did not recall a mention of Nine-Eleven in her local news report: *Live Oak Park celebrates 100th birthday. State may fine UC Berkeley for violations related to custodian death. Police seek help in solving four-year-old Berkeley murder. Business burglarized on Shattuck Avenue. Fire Trail suspect still at large . . .*

Jessica turned to her notes, trying to concentrate, but unable to focus on Berkeley history, as the New York attack flashed through her mind. Her own fears seemed silly. Where had she been on that terrible day? She was nine; Samantha and Ashley, eleven. September 2001 was before Facebook and sexting and selfies. It was before Ashley's drugs got out of hand and before Samantha's drowning. It was before she met Dr. Stein in family therapy and learned the two systems of growth, emotion and control, that so changed her. It was before she discovered that knowledge coupled with self-discipline was empowering.

Jessica recalled her mother had picked them up early from school and driven them silently home. Ashley and Samantha were giggling about a boy, and their mother shushed them angrily. And then, at home, the television on, her parents tense. Her father got off work early.

A persistent scraping noise returned Jessica to the present. She stood and peered through the vertical pane by the door, but could see nothing but the ivy. All was dark and still in the deep shade. A few leaves rustled. She unbolted the door and peered through a crack. She re-bolted the door quickly and turned to the counter where her phone lay ready, Detective Gan's number on speed dial. She wished her landlords were home, but they had left for a long weekend. She pulled herself together and turned to the papers on the counter.

Jessica read through her notes. She opened a new Word document, and typed:

Thesis

> _The presence of religious institutions in the late nineteenth century were key to the development of the city of Berkeley, and thus give good reason for government support today. I shall argue this through examination of the work of the Presentation Sisters in the nineteenth and twentieth centuries and its impact on the community of Berkeley. I shall consider the change in the community with the erosion of such religious institutions, changes seen in education, medical care, and public safety, areas of vital interest to city, state, and federal governments._

Background

> _Originally settled by the Ohlone tribes, the area that is now Berkeley became home to the first Europeans in 1776 with the arrival of the De Anza Expedition, largely financed by the Catholic Church. This group established the Spanish_

134

Presidio of San Francisco, the military defense at the mouth of the Golden Gate. For his services, the soldier Luis Peralta was granted 44,000 acres of land on the coast opposite to San Francisco, contra costa, where he raised cattle. Rancho San Antonio was divided among Peralta's four sons, and it was Vicente's and Domingo's parcels that eventually became the town of Berkeley. The brothers lost most of the land to Gold Rush squatters and died in poverty. Domingo lived from 1795 to 1865, and his house on Codornices Creek was the first non-Ohlone dwelling in Berkeley.

More settlers meant more children. In the early 1850s, Archbishop Joseph S. Alemany invited groups of women religious to come to California from Europe, including the Daughters of Charity, the Dominican Sisters, Notre Dame de Namur, and the Sisters of Mercy.[1] When the Sisters of the Presentation in Ireland were invited in 1854, they said yes. Five sisters arrived from convents in Midleton and Kilkenny; by the end of the first year three returned home due to illness. Their order was called the Sisters of the Presentation of the Blessed Virgin Mary.

The Presentation of Mary refers to an event recounted in the apocryphal Infancy Gospel of James. Mary's parents, Joachim and Anne, had been childless when they received a vision that they would have a child. When Mary was born, they presented her to the temple to be consecrated to God.

Jessica admired the dedication of Joachim and Anne. To be childless and to offer their only child to God took great faith. She glanced at her own family photo. In the nineteenth century families considered children a precious gift since so many died in infancy. They had larger families, for they hadn't learned how to avoid conception when inconvenient or undesired. She thought of her sisters' abortions, of the nieces and nephews who hadn't survived her sisters' choices. If there was a Heaven, would she meet them there? Reading about the many children of early San Francisco and the nuns sailing from Ireland to teach them was comforting and enriching. In contrast, her own world seemed barren in its celebration of childlessness.

The leaves rustled outside, and Jessica turned with renewed determination to her text. Who were these Presentation Sisters, after all?

The Foundress

Nano (Honora) Nagle (1718-1784) founded the Sisters of the Presentation. Cousin to the statesman Edmund Burke, she was born into a wealthy Norman-Irish family in County Cork, Ireland. When the young Nano visited the tenants on her family estate, she was troubled by their poverty and lack of education. She began a life of prayer and good works to help their children. She opened a school in 1754 in Cork City and six more schools over the next fifteen years. She cared for the poor and built homes for the elderly. She became known as the Lady of the Lantern, for she visited the sick, the elderly, the lonely, and the poor in the slums. She lived among them, spending her fortune on their education and care. In 1775 she founded a community of women religious, sisters who would continue her work. She died of tuberculosis in 1784.

The Sisters of the Presentation have continued Nano Nagle's work throughout the world in Ireland, England, the Americas, India, Pakistan, Australia, New Zealand, the Philippines, Papua, New Guinea, Eastern Europe, Africa, and Palestine.[2]

Such goodness, Jessica thought. Did such goodness exist today? It appeared so, in spite of today's creed of self. What was the source of their goodness? Jessica intuited the source was faith in God, as though God empowered them to be good. Is that what Father Nate meant by "cult creates culture"?

St. Joseph's Convent, Berkeley

Into the rough and lawless world of the California Gold Rush came the first five sisters in 1854. They had sailed from Kingstown (today Cobh) to Liverpool to New York, then to

Panama. They rode mules across the Isthmus, through mud and high rivers, following rocky trails along precipices, and forging their way through dense tropical forests. They sailed up the coast to San Francisco on the steam clipper Golden Gate of the Pacific Mail Steamship Company[3] and arrived in cold and damp San Francisco shortly before dawn on Monday, November 13, 1854. No one met them at the wharf, for the bishop, not notified, was visiting a mining camp. Some Irish Catholic gentlemen came to their rescue and took them in their horse-drawn carriages up Market Street, "the widest street in the world," to Third Street, to the small convent and orphanage of the Daughters of Charity of St. Vincent de Paul. Today the Palace Hotel stands on the site.

That year their first school and convent opened on Green Street behind St. Francis Church in North Beach. Two hundred girls enrolled. In 1861, more sisters, including the second Comerford sister, Mary Bernard, came from Ireland and opened a second school in San Francisco.

In 1877 Mother Maria Teresa Comerford searched for land on the "contra-costa" side of the Bay to build a convent in a sunnier climate for her nuns convalescing from tuberculosis. Several tracts were offered, and she chose McGee Meadows, the most central, to best serve the children of the scattered farms in the area. Offered by James McGee, these two acres along Strawberry Creek were close to the new Central and Southern Pacific Railroads running through Ocean View on Shattuck Avenue.

By 1878 the convent was constructed. The Oakland Evening Tribune wrote:

> The building is a large square, two-story structure, situated on a gentle slope which extends from the mountains to the bay and is about equidistant from East and West Berkeley. The site is excellent, and the view finer than any

other point in the vicinity of San Francisco. It is directly opposite Alcatraz Island and the Golden Gate, and on a clear day the Farallones [sic] are discernable. To the left is Oakland, a handsome expanse of houses, trees, and spires; in the left background is San Francisco; to the right the picturesque mountains of Marin, and in the rear the bald hills of the Contra Costa Range. The prospect was indescribably lovely, and the site could not have been better chosen. [4]

The building would soon house a school and chapel, in addition to a convent:

The size of the building is 60 x 70 feet and two stories high. The cost of erection was 13,000 dollars. There is one school-room which is divided by rolling-doors. There are also four music rooms, refectory, chapel, spacious corridors, and bath floors [sic] and dormitories. [5]

Sister Mary Rose Forest writes that the sisters, on the day of their moving in,

took the afternoon ferryboat which left San Francisco at two o'clock on Thursday, June 27. Mr. McGee met them with carriages at the pier in West Berkeley and drove them up University Avenue to their new home. From afar the sisters could see it across the fields, standing alone, the only two-story house in sight except for the one red brick building which then comprised the great University of California. [6]

St. Joseph Presentation Academy opened July 16 with nineteen girls and became known for its high academic standards. The convent bell, the first steeple bell in Berkeley, rang three times a day, calling people to services. Soon a neighborhood parish formed, and Mother Comerford's *brother, Father Pierce Michael Comerford, came from Ireland to serve as pastor.*

A parish boys school was built (1880-81) for elementary grades, funded by Father Comerford from the sale of his horse (comparable to a car today) and called St. Peter Boys' School. St. Joseph's Church was constructed, "a single story, gable roofed, Gothic Revival with narrow lancet windows and ornamental buttresses."[7] It seemed appropriate that the church was dedicated to St. Joseph, patron of a happy death, for eleven sisters had died of tuberculosis by 1880. Young and eager, their ages spanned seventeen to thirty-two.

By 1889 Presentation Academy had grown to seventy-five high school students. The parish added a girls elementary school to complement the boys school in 1892 and opened with 150 students.

Jessica was glad she had majored in History, had switched from Psychology early on. Every book, every class, every research project, enriched her understanding of the present. She could see that students needed to learn their own nation's history, as part of their core curriculum. And it was equally important that this history be passed on to the next generation.

With that thought, she turned to her notes on the founding of UC Berkeley and began to knit her bits and pieces together in logical patterns.

<u>The University of California</u>

In 1866 the private College of California in Oakland, led by Congregational minister Henry Durant, taught a classical core curriculum modeled on Yale and Harvard. The trustees decided on a new site alongside Strawberry Creek in the foothills of the Contra Costa Range. It is said that,

> *at Founders' Rock, a group of College of California men watched two ships standing out to sea through the Golden Gate. One of them, Frederick Billings, thought of the lines of the*

Anglo-Irish Anglican Bishop George Berkeley, *"westward the course of empire takes its way,"* and suggested that the town and college site be named for the eighteenth-century Anglo-Irish philosopher. [8]

Bishop Berkeley (1685-1753) had spent four years in New England and had written a poem, "The Prospect of Planting Arts and Learning in America," the last stanza being:

Westward the course of empire takes its way;
The first four acts already past,
A fifth shall close the drama with the day;
Time's noblest offspring is the last.

Bishop Berkeley had planned a town and college on Rhode Island, but funds had not arrived from England. Instead, he returned to London to build London's Foundling Hospital, an orphanage for abandoned children.

Although he never saw Berkeley, he was correct about the course of the British Empire taking its way westward to the New World and on to the coast of California. America was, after all, the child of England and thus the child of classical education in the English language, with studies in Latin, Greek, history, English, mathematics, natural history, and later, modern languages.

America's colonial colleges had been founded by religious institutions: Harvard, Yale, and Dartmouth by Puritans (Congregationalists), Princeton by Presbyterians, the College of William and Mary, Columbia, and the University of Pennsylvania by Anglicans, Brown by Baptists, Rutgers by the Dutch Reformed. The University of California at Berkeley, a century later, was no exception. The degree of religious influence varied and lessened over time, but the drive to achieve and to educate the young was a key aspect of Christianity. This "course of empire" was driven by Christian assumptions and worldviews and, of course, was *meant to reflect the positive aspects of empire: peace, law and order, public health, and a solid education in the liberal arts, all considered necessary for democracy to thrive.*

While much has been said about the negative aspects of British colonialism, it cannot be denied that wherever the empire found itself, it worked untiringly to better the population to the degree it knew how. And the British heritage, the heritage of the West, is one of learning, law, and charity, seeds planted by Christianity. It is a legacy of freedom that flowers throughout the world on every continent among all races and is no longer unique to the Western world, but characteristic of the "Anglosphere."

Jessica considered her words. There was, and remained today, a thin but necessary line between Church and State. Yet if credit were not given to the Western tradition, if the next generation were not taught the ideals of democracy and free speech, American culture could lose the benefits of their precious tradition of liberty and law. That would be a tragedy indeed.

Jessica took a break and checked the headlines: *Police investigate rape in People's Park. Boy attacked by mountain lion released. Student accused of sexual assault. Body found in parking lot. Free speech protests in Hong Kong, police intervene. Fire Trail suspect still at large . . .* She would call Officer Gan in the morning. It had been over a week since the murder. They must have something by now. She thought of the girl, so innocent, probably a victim not only of a crazed man from People's Park, but a victim of a deviant and twisted pop culture, a culture that denied our innate signals of fear. Would there be other victims like her? And how soon?

Jessica shivered as she began rereading her paper before making her supper.

* * *

Immersed in her reading, Jessica was startled by the ringing of her phone. Of the many ringtones offered, she had chosen the old fashioned one, the landline ring she recalled growing up. She wanted it to sound like a phone, not a buzzer or a pop song. She had considered the chimes, but concluded they were not serious enough, even foreign sounding to her ear.

She recognized the caller identification. "Detective Gan?"

"Good evening, Ms. Thierry. I just wanted to update you on the Fire Trail case. There have been sitings of the suspect based on the sketch, in the hills, near the trail."

Jessica drew in her breath and began to recite her control list.

"You there, Ms. Thierry?"

Jessica said in a low voice, "Yes, Detective Gan."

"Did you hear what I said?"

"I heard you. Sitings." She placed her hand over her heart as if she could calm its rapid beating.

"Are you okay?"

"I'm sorry, detective, you said there have been sitings near the trail. That's good, right? You're getting close to capturing him?"

"We hope so."

"Thanks for letting me know."

"Of course. And Ms. Thierry—"

"Is there more?"

"There appears to have been a campfire on the grounds of Comerford House."

Jessica stood and began pacing the room, the phone held tight against her ear. She peered out the vertical window alongside the door. All was calm in the shadows.

"Ms. Thierry, are you there?"

"Sorry, detective. I'm here. Is Comerford safe? Father Nate and Anna and the staff?"

"They're safe, but use caution coming and going. I've alerted them to the situation."

"It's my fault." Jessica suddenly saw the danger, the madness, she had ushered into their serene world.

"It's not your fault, Ms. Thierry. No, I assure you, it is certainly, most definitely, not your fault. The fault lies with the criminal on the loose, and no one else, except for the police. It's not your fault in any way."

Jessica was only slightly reassured.

Detective Gan's tone was confident. "Just be careful. Don't walk alone. Lock your doors. Be alert. Use common sense. Keep your phone close by. And I'll have a patrol car check on Comerford House from time to time."

"Thanks, Detective Gan. I will."

As Jessica ended the call, she began to shake. She lowered herself slowly onto her torn couch. Then came the tears, in gushes, torrents of salty tears. Just as quickly, they subsided. Still gripping the couch, she relaxed her fingers and wiped her eyes with the back of her hand, found a tissue and blew her nose. She breathed deeply, reciting her control list. She moved to the counter and returned to her paper.

Eighteen

Civilization

Shortly before noon on the following Saturday, Father Nate heated pea soup in his kitchen. When the soup simmered, he found two mugs, poured each three-quarters full, and placed them on a tray with a bowl of Anna's whole-wheat croutons. As he worked, Jellylorum the tabby rubbed against Father Nate's pants, covering the black cloth with white hair. Father Nate glanced down. He wasn't so worried about the hair as he was about stumbling over the cat.

"Careful, Jelly, don't trip me." The cat's weight and quick movements demanded his attention as he added two glasses of milk to the tray, a straw, and paper napkins. He wished Brenda was there for all three meals, but he would manage lunch without her, since life wasn't perfect. He climbed the stairs to Nicholas' bedroom, on the lookout for Jellylorum zigzagging in front of him, and trying to avoid hitting the mechanical chair on the railing.

With the tabby close to his shins, Father Nate maneuvered through the doorway and placed the tray on a table near his brother's chair. Nicholas was working at his computer, the keyboard and screen within reach on the desk. A shorthand, their own style of texting, had enhanced their communication over the last six months.

Nicholas turned toward his brother as he pulled up an oak chair, an aging straight-back found in the storage room of the main house. Anna had donated a red cushion, which Father Nate tied to the back spindles, but which Jellylorum or Coricocat untied with a swift bat-and-pull of a claw. Coricocat, the tortoiseshell, did not appear a threat, for she lay on Nicholas' lap and beneath the keyboard, purring loudly. She appeared to enjoy the warmth and the light tapping.

"Lunchtime." Father Nate angled Nicholas' chair toward the window with a partial view of the city and the bay, slightly obscured by the pitched eaves and chimneys of Comerford House. The fog was burning off and a weak sun shimmered through a mist that hugged the skyline. He opened the window, and a cool breeze freshened the room. A distant siren wailed. He closed it again, fearing his brother would chill.

Nicholas typed. "Thank you."

"How's the book coming?" Father Nate settled into the chair, within arm's reach of both the tray and Nicholas.

"Good," his brother typed.

Father Nate blessed the food, blessed Nicholas, and kissed his forehead. "Hungry?"

Nicholas gave a slight nod, barely recognizable.

His brother spooned the thick green liquid into Nicholas' mouth, and Nicholas swallowed, working his muscles with concentration. Coricocat squealed and jumped off his lap to a safer place on the sofa. Nicholas' hands lay anchored on the keyboard. He typed, "Delicious."

Father Nate smiled, sipping from his own mug.

As he fed Nicholas, he asked, "What's the current crisis?" He knew that there was always a current crisis when Nicholas was writing a book, and this book was no different, perhaps even more crisis-ridden. The working title was *The Question of Civilization*, and the purpose was to consider the subject's definition, roots, and present state in the world. Nicholas began the project when he was healthy and planned to finish it before he died. Father Nate considered it good therapy, although he wasn't too optimistic as to its completion.

Nicholas typed. "Definition a problem."

Father Nate rubbed his chin. "I thought you had that part done." He had assumed it was the first part—definitions.

"Saved for last."

"Oh."

"Ideas?"

"You're the genius." Father Nate grinned.

"Ha! ☺"

"How about a definition I read recently. I think it was Aristotle: 'The purpose of politics is not to make living together possible, but to make living well possible.' Substitute civilization for politics."

"More."

"More detail?"

"Too broad."

"How about Francis Fukuyama? Aren't you reading his new book?" Father Nate had seen it on the computer screen recently.

Nicholas typed quickly: "Humans biologically favor family; government redirects these impulses to the common good; the modern state does this through law and democracy; the purpose of politics is to make living together possible."

"Seems rather bleak," Father Nate said. "We do need more. What about human rights? Freedom? Speech? Worship? Charity? Pursuit of happiness?"

"Keeping out the jungle."

Father Nate nodded. "Define civilization by what it's not."

"Yes."

"So, the jungle, the uncivil, the wild, the un-tame, the bestial, the animal, pure instinct. Selfish survival. Un-control. Anarchy. These things are *not* civilization?"

"Go on." Nicholas was making notes. "A sentence."

Father Nate considered. "Here's a try: Civilization is a society in which the common good is desired and advanced, but individual life and liberty protected; in which the natural world is controlled, but cultivated and cared for; in which respectful debate is encouraged and slander discouraged; in which social charity is promoted, yet private property protected; in which the rule of law and representative government ensures all of the above."

Nicholas typed: "And opposite to barbaric."

"We return to Fukuyama. The instinct to protect family, while good, is overridden by a common good, a desire to live in peace and not succumb to tribal warfare."

"Yes."

"Why say The *Question* of Civilization?"

Nicholas typed: "The twentieth century believed the 'civilized' man bad and the 'natural' man good. Ideas from the Enlightenment, Rousseau . . . the noble savage. Wicked imperialism, colonialism, etc."

Father Nate nodded. "I understand."

"We must return to classic definitions. Or we will collapse, either from within or without. We will become barbaric, just like the decapitators."

Father Nate, in that moment, knew that Nicholas' book had to be written. Timing and history and faith were distilled into that one moment, and as he gathered the lunch things, he said more intensely than he had intended, "Finish the book. Our world needs it."

Nicholas looked at him gratefully.

The priest kissed his brother on the forehead. "Back to work," he said, touching his shoulder tenderly. "No slouching. No excuses."

He returned Coricocat to her favorite lap and, balancing the tray, stepped down the stairs without tripping over Jellylorum or scraping against the lift, another miracle.

Nineteen
Ellie

As Father Nate successfully maneuvered down the stairs that Saturday, Jessica parked in the upper lot and followed the path to Comerford House, around the side and up to the front porch. The door was closed, as she had expected, for it was not yet opening time, but it was unlocked, and that was surprising.

She entered the foyer in search of Anna. As she turned toward the music room she heard a female voice.

"Come on, Zachary, I know you want to be with me. I can tell. You know you do."

Jessica stepped to the door and opened it.

Zachary and the girl were on the piano bench. When Zachary saw Jessica, he jumped up, glaring at the girl. "Ms. Sarton, you need to go."

The girl stood and faced Jessica.

Jessica frowned, her eyes moving from the low-slung short-shorts, to her deep cleavage, to her smirking smile and mischievous, triumphant eyes. Her black hair fell straight around her face. Her fingernails, long and dark purple, rested on her hips. A tulip had been tattooed above one breast. She stared at Jessica with an expression of contempt mingled with annoyance.

Jessica glanced at Zachary's beet-red face. "Sorry to interrupt," she said quickly, studying a spot in the distance, backing slowly through the doorway. "I was looking for Anna." She crossed the foyer to the stairs.

"Jessica!" Zachary called after her.

The tears that rushed to the surface were disturbing, and Jessica wiped them with the back of her hand as she climbed upstairs to the children's library. She pulled herself together, straightening her cuffs and jacket, and dusting her slacks. She entered the library.

Anna glanced up from books stacked alongside a desktop computer. "Jessica, glad you're here. Can you help me until the first tour starts? This is the stack we're keeping. This is the stack I'm researching. Could you make index cards for the keepers? Title, author, publisher, like the sample one there." Anna scrutinized her. "What's wrong, my dear?"

"Nothing."

Anna nodded. "Well, okay, thanks for being here on time. I appreciate your help."

Behind Anna's words Jessica heard concern coupled with a fear of intruding. "I'm sorry, Anna, but I'm fine, really, I am." Yet she couldn't erase the girl's face, her cleavage, her long bare legs. Did it make it better or worse that Zachary was embarrassed? And why should she, Jessica, care? And what happened to her control list? She could not recall one phrase, one word, as she strained to hear sounds from the room below.

She concentrated on the task before her. The children's library was a friendly room, with picture books displayed on a circular child-sized table as though the stuffed animals in the tiny chairs were listening with great interest. Yellow café curtains hung from shiny brass rods in the two windows; the chairs had been lacquered red and white, the table blue. Pine shelves held more books, waiting to be chosen by small eager hands. Jessica pulled out a chair between Raggedy Ann and Winnie-the-Pooh.

Anna was chatting about the pageant protest that morning and how hecklers had been arrested by the police, and did free speech protect hecklers, but Anna and her team thought their own cause was right and just, and children shouldn't be made into child stars like that, paraded around and wearing provocative clothing, little bras and such . . . look what happened to JonBenet Ramsay! Anna then seemed to be talking about Facebook and child porn. "Where were the Internet police?" she asked, shaking her head.

Jessica mumbled assent, then tried with perplexing difficulty to copy titles and authors onto the cards in her usually neat printing, which, for some reason, grew shakier and shakier and nearly unreadable.

"I'm hoping to bring back Story Time now that I have you to help me," Anna said, on to another subject. "We discontinued it over the summer, but I do miss it. Seems like Saturdays would be best, don't you think? Jessica? What do you think about Saturdays for Story Time? We used to do it Wednesdays but I think Saturdays better."

Jessica was listening for sounds in the music room. She didn't catch the question. "Sorry?" she said, realizing she hadn't comprehended most of the words she had heard.

"What's wrong, Jessica? I can tell something is wrong!"

More tears welled up, and Jessica feared she was losing all control.

Anna sat next to her and put an arm around her. "It's okay, it's okay. You can cry. You don't have to explain." She handed Jessica a tissue.

Jessica dabbed her eyes and blew her nose with the tissue. She stood. "Thank you, Anna, I must be coming down with something. I have a bad headache. Will you excuse me? I'll just freshen up in the powder room and get ready for the tour."

"Of course, not to worry. You go ahead. I completely understand. Oh, and Jessica, I nearly forgot the good news—"

"Good news?"

"The Foundation approved your application! Isn't that wonderful?"

Jessica managed a weak smile. "That's great. Thanks, Anna." As Jessica reached the doorway, Zachary loomed before her. "Excuse me," Jessica mumbled, "I need to get ready—"

"But I want to explain." His hands were on his hips and he sounded miserable.

Jessica fixed her eyes on the hall carpet. "No explanations necessary." She took the stairs as fast as she dared, barely touching the banister with her fingertips, and made it to the foyer and the safety of the powder room.

The gilt-framed mirror was kind; her eyes were pinched, her nose red, but her face did not betray her confused and twisted feelings as she feared it would. She splashed cold water on her cheeks and rearranged the strands of hair around her face. She repositioned a pin firmly in the French braid. She sat on a green silk-covered stool and studied her history cards. At two o'clock she stepped boldly into the foyer and took her place at the foot of the stairs, holding the lantern bag with her materials. Zachary stood at the front door, welcoming visitors and pointing to Jessica's gathering place.

She smiled, hoping her quivering upper lip wasn't apparent. "Welcome to Comerford House."

* * *

From time to time, as Jessica spoke of the history of the house, its inhabitants, and the early years of Berkeley, she glanced at the edges of her group, watching for Zachary, but he didn't appear, although Anna remained by her side. Jessica was glad for the older woman's comforting presence, especially as they moved into the music room. The girl was gone and there was no sign of Zachary. Jessica involved herself in the Comerford story and the McKinnons and, to a degree, was successful in lessening the odd pain caused by seeing the girl at the piano. She began to breathe deeply and feel in control again.

When she finished the tour in the kitchen, and the last question was answered to the best of her ability with Anna's additions, she collapsed in a chair in the nook and stared at the roses in the center of the table. Anna busied herself making tea, chatting about the group and the tour and how well Jessica had done. All around her words, like a lacy ribbon, Anna's unsaid questions curled.

Jessica's gaze moved from the flowers to the chapel beyond the lawns and the light refracting on the upper leaves of the eucalyptus trees. Mesmerized by Anna's gentle voice and the beauty of the view through the windows, she was unexpectedly at rest.

"Ahem." Zachary appeared in her line of sight.

Jessica awoke from her dream and blinked. There he was, standing tall in front of the French doors, his brow pulled together. His long fingers held a bouquet of giant sunflowers, which he offered awkwardly. He wore blue jeans, and a white polo under a brown corduroy jacket, clothes she hadn't noticed before in the music room when all she had seen was the girl. He was especially handsome in the brown corduroy, she decided if she was honest with herself.

"A peace offering," Zachary said.

Jessica stood and accepted the flowers. "You don't need to do this."

Anna had disappeared, mumbling about butter in the pantry.

"I do need to do this. I don't like misconceptions, misunderstandings, errors in thinking that one person might have about another person. Ellie Sarton is a student in one of my classes. She stalks me. It's a story I was hoping I wouldn't ever have to tell you. It wasn't part of my plan. I want things to be open . . . er . . . honest . . . between us. We're friends, right?"

Jessica eyed him skeptically. "I see . . . yes, we're friends. You have a plan?"

"Are you staying for tea?"

"I need to get back." The conversation, while making her more at ease in some inexplicable way, was also making her uncomfortable, as though a boundary had been crossed, and she couldn't identify it.

Anna now stood in the pantry doorway. "I couldn't help but overhear," she said to her son. "Is that Ellie person bothering you again?"

"She's shown up in another class. And again today at Comerford. I shouldn't have let her in, I suppose. I didn't want a confrontation and thought I could talk sense into her. Same thing as before."

"What can you do about it? She's stalking you! Isn't that illegal? You better get some advice from other faculty or even an attorney. Maybe Father Nate knows someone?"

"Are you in trouble?" Jessica asked.

"Stay for tea, please, Jessica," Anna said. "I made whole-wheat zucchini bread, and Zachary can make sure you get home safely."

Zachary nodded.

Jessica sat back down, weary, the bloody body of the girl on the Fire Trail flashing in her memory. "I heard from Detective Gan about the campfire on the property."

"I heard about it too," Zachary said. "We'll make sure you are safe."

Anna took charge of the sunflowers and found a vase, filled it from the tap, and arranged the bouquet with studied care. "They don't know it was him for sure. I'm certain they'll catch him. So you're staying for tea, then, and Zachary will see you home."

Jessica smiled. "Thanks, I think I will. I could use a break among friends." The table in the nook, the kitchen with the shiny utensils arrayed in ceramic pitchers and the copper pans hanging from the ceiling, the garden outside growing dim in the shade between hillside and house, the stone steeple merging into the trees—all of these things wrapped Jessica in a serene safety, almost a permanence. She wasn't sure why, perhaps it was the simple friendship of Anna and her son, or the thought of seeing Father Nate again. She wanted to linger; she wanted the moment to last a little longer.

Zachary looked relieved. "Good."

"So what's the story about the student?" Jessica said, biting her lip, and wishing she had waited for him to explain on his own.

Zachary rose to help his mother. "She was in one of my classes last year and threatened me with a sexual harassment charge if I didn't adjust her grade, give her the grade she believed she deserved. She said she needed at least a B or her self-esteem would be harmed. She seriously said that. At first I thought she was joking."

"Ha!" Anna said. "Self-esteem, hogwash. She should work hard like everyone else if she's so worried about her precious self-esteem."

"What did you do?" Jessica asked Zachary, watching him move from counter to table with long strides as he arranged settings for four. She turned toward Anna. "Can I help you?"

"No, you stay put," Anna said.

"I held my ground," Zachary said. "I didn't give in, and I waited for her to make good on her threat."

"Which she didn't do," Anna added. "You can't give in to threats."

"I thought it was over," he explained, "but now she's resurfaced." He took a seat, and his eyes beseeched Jessica to understand.

Jessica believed him. "That's terrible."

"But enough of this," Zachary said. "How about that walk we talked about?" He clearly wanted to take her mind off of the student predator.

"Maybe, I'll have to see."

"It would be good for you," Anna said.

"I *have* missed walking the trail." Her feet on the soft earth, the pull of her muscles uphill and down, but even more, the smells of the trees and the mist and the sun, the breezes stirring it all up . . . the moments when she would stare out over the bay to the city and dream. The Fire Trail walks were like mini retreats from real life. They gave her time for reflection, to consider all that was going on, away from the Internet, the phone, the current demands, whatever they were.

"And here comes Father Nate," Zachary said, getting up to open the French doors. "Just in time."

"In time?" Father Nate asked, stepping inside.

"For grace," said Anna, beaming.

Twenty
Friendship

On Thursday afternoon, September 18th, over two weeks since the murder, Zachary parked his car at the trailhead, got out, and stretched. He was early. He checked the path for any sign of strangers. He would be alert as they walked. He would protect her.

Jessica had not arrived, and as he watched for her, he recalled his productive week since Saturday at Comerford.

She had insisted on driving herself home, saying that she was fine, and Zachary inferred she needed to prove to herself the truth of her statement. Nevertheless, with her reluctant permission, he had followed in his own car. He had kept watch as she parked and entered her studio. The light came on, and all appeared well when she waved from the doorway. As he left he was glad they had exchanged phone numbers. He would keep his cell phone within easy reach and fully charged.

Ms. Sarton had not returned to class. What a relief that this last crisis was seemingly over. Jessica seeing Ellie Sarton with him at the piano mortified Zachary again and again. There was Jessica, in the doorway, looking shocked and angry. And yet, the very shock and anger he saw in those wide eyes, that tense frown and pulled brow, gave him hope. Did this mean that she cared about him? Or was he jumping to conclusions?

After Jessica left the music room, and he heard her steps on the stairs, he made short work of Ms. Sarton, making it clear that she must leave at once, that her presence was inappropriate, and that if this happened again he would report her to the campus authorities. Her laughter increased his concern, and he knew she knew that the Office for the Prevention of Harassment would favor her version over his, so she saw him as bluffing. She held the cards. She had the power to rob him of his good name, destroy his career. Zachary could see this; he would have to play it out as best he could.

But far more important was Jessica, explaining to Jessica, winning Jessica's favor and friendship, if not her love. He had fallen behind in the courtship saga he had written in his head. Browning and Darcy had had no such problems, to be sure. Did Borodin? He thought not. Perhaps Beethoven, with his fabled illicit love, his "immortal beloved," might come close in desperation and complexity.

Now, waiting at the trailhead, Zachary watched for her, elated that she had stayed for tea on Saturday, had accepted his peace offerings of words and flowers. She appeared to believe him and must trust him enough to return to the Fire Trail with its horrific memories. She wanted to be friends, he knew, and friendship was foundational. Things could develop later, he told himself. Father Nate often said, *God writes straight with crooked lines*. Maybe this was just a crooked line that would be written straight later.

Now that he thought of Father Nate, he recalled other things he said, such as, *All is grace.* Zachary wondered about that from time to time, it being so simplistic, and yet, now in the tangled web of his love and fear and worry, in the complicated weave of his heart and soul and mind, the simple phrase was soothing and optimistic. It helped. In the end, Zachary thought, Father Nate meant that God was good, that he loved them, and that all would be well in the end. Zachary wanted to believe this, and the desire to believe had been strengthening since he had rediscovered Jessica, had re-found love.

Zachary heard a car coming up the road. *Jessica.* He straightened his hoodie and adjusted his glasses. He stood ready and waiting, waiting for grace.

* * *

"Hi," she said, smiling. "Am I late?"

"I'm early," he said, entranced by her smile. Zachary took a mental snapshot of Jessica, one to file in their courtship album. She wore a high-collared madras shirt of blues and purples that opened loosely over a white tee and jeans. A small canvas backpack hung from one shoulder. Her sandy hair had been pulled through a Cal

Bears cap and swung as she walked. A few strands fell around her face, touching the freckles. He recalled that she had once worn large glasses and now wore wire rims.

"Nice day to walk," she said.

Zachary glanced at her as their feet fell into an even pace up the path. "Perfect. Not too warm, not too cold." Silly thing to say, he thought, really reaching. "How was your week?" he added hopefully.

"Good. I made significant progress on the paper, pulling together my sources. It's been fascinating reading about the nuns in Berkeley. Who would have guessed?"

Zachary laughed. "It's not the usual Berkeley history we hear about, that's for sure."

"How about *your* week?" Her tone was shaded with concern, and Zachary guessed she was asking about Ellie Sarton.

"The good news is that Ms. Sarton has not returned to class. At least, I think it's good news."

The path parted low growth, shaded by silvery-green bay laurels, and curved gently past mossy oaks with limbs that curled in the mist. Zachary could feel the cool damp, not unpleasant, cosseting them in a soft fresh-smelling cocoon, nearly a rainforest.

"There are many troubled people around, aren't there?" She tilted her head and squinted at him, tossing her ponytail. She glanced into the vegetation and around the path.

"I've been watching, too."

"I'm still nervous about being here. It's been over two weeks, but still—"

"Of course you're nervous. You went through a terrible ordeal." Zachary recalled Laurie's offer. "Do you feel safe at home? A friend of mine—Laurie who owns the bookstore where I work—said she had an extra room if you needed it."

Jessica turned toward him, her eyes full of gratitude. "That's so nice of her. But I'm fine for now. The police come by regularly."

"I'm relieved. There are, as you said, many troubled people in the world. I tend to be trusting, and then a student like Ms. Sarton comes along."

"I used to be trusting, but family experience has made me less trusting."

"I'm sorry." Should he ask about her family or was that being too inquisitive, too direct? Yet she had brought it up.

They walked in silence, their words dancing in a minuet, moving in, then away, following a delicate rhythm, not wanting to lace their histories too tightly, but looking for moments when the lace might be loosened, a moment to share that would reveal who they really were.

"I like your mom," Jessica said, glancing at him with curiosity.

"She's a saint . . . She's been terribly hurt."

"Has she? I'm sorry. Sometimes suffering helps us understand our world."

"You think so?"

"Sometimes."

"My dad left my mom two years ago," Zachary blurted.

Jessica stopped and turned toward him. "I'm so sorry. How painful for you and your mother."

They were nearing an overlook and Zachary slipped his hands in his pockets, a comforting position when he fell into a reverie. He stepped out to the scrubby point and sat on a wooden bench. It was windy here, but the breeze felt good for he had worked up a sweat. Jessica joined him, and they watched the bank of fog settle between hills and sky.

"She's still hurting, I'm sure," he said, "so I try to be as supportive as possible. I'm all she has, at least in terms of family in the area."

"Do you have brothers or sisters?"

Zachary shook his head. "No, wish I did. I'm not sure why they didn't have more children. I think Mom wanted more. I had the impression it just never happened."

"She's a great mom. A great cook."

Zachary smiled with appreciation. "She is, always has been. She stayed home when I was growing up. She loves cooking. She was always clipping recipes from magazines. And she loves children. She assisted at the local preschool."

"Sounds like she's been a mom to many children."

"That's true. She still cooks too, but not like before. She was a little overweight. Dad and I were heavy as well, but we lost the pounds and she didn't, not until recently."

"I can't imagine you overweight."

"I was heavy, that's for sure. I got bullied for it in school."

"How awful."

"I changed schools and that helped. Then Dad enrolled me in tennis and we worked out together, and things turned around. But Mom kept the weight on. She thinks that's why he left her."

"Doesn't seem like a good enough reason."

"No. But then I can't think of many good enough reasons." And his father was surfing the Internet for porn, Zachary thought. How could he do that? He couldn't tell that to Jessica. He added, "Divorce hurts everyone."

Jessica studied him. "You're a good man, Zachary Aguilar."

Zachary felt the heat rush to his cheeks. "Thank you. And you," he said, glancing at her with a bold tenderness, "are a lovely lady, Miss Jessica."

Jessica smiled and turned to the panorama spread before them. She grew silent, and Zachary feared he had been too forward. "How about your folks?" he ventured. "Are they still together? Divorce seems so common these days. Like it's the accepted thing to do."

Jessica's face paled. She shook her head. She drew in a deep breath, and in that moment Zachary knew he had hit a raw nerve, one he had tried to avoid hitting if at all possible, probably a wound deeper than his own family break-up.

"My father died three years ago."

"I shouldn't have asked."

"It's okay, Zachary." She patted his leg in a gesture of peace. "You had no way of knowing. It was sudden. An aneurism in his sleep. I often lay awake at night debating if a sudden death is better than a slow one. But then with a long illness you can prepare yourself. Others around you can be prepared. His passing left a huge gap in my life. And my mom's life too."

"It must have been a shock."

"It was. My folks were in love, never fell out of love. We kids were kind of second and third and fourth string in their lives."

Zachary was entranced by her wistful green eyes, her gaze lost in the peripheries of fog and sky. There were specks of gold in the green. Did that mean they were hazel? "I think I know what you mean about the long illness." He was thinking of Dr. Casparian, his suffering, his years to prepare for death. "But then, I don't suppose we have much choice in the matter, do we?"

"Only if you believe suicide is okay. For me it doesn't seem right, although I haven't really worked out the logic. Just a feeling I have. Life is so precious."

"It's like trespassing where you shouldn't go, or throwing out a great gift as though you don't appreciate it." Zachary wanted to lighten the subject and asked, "You have brothers and sisters?"

Jessica inhaled slowly, creating an unendingly tense moment. Zachary feared something more was coming, more pain. He waited.

"Sure do," she exhaled.

The way she said those two words confirmed that the change of subject was not going to lighten anything. But he was already there and couldn't avoid the follow-up question. "Brothers?" he asked nervously.

"Sisters. Twins. That's another story." She stood, straightened her cuffs, re-shouldered her bag, and turned toward the trail. "We'd better get going."

"Right, it's getting late."

They headed up the path, looping back into a pine forest, the ground covered by low glistening greenery. A bird cawed and something scuttled across the path. They walked without speaking for a time as though feeling their way, treading lightly, listening to the pad of their feet and the beat of their hearts. Treetops rustled and Zachary glimpsed a flock of black birds flying in formation beyond the upper leaves.

"Samantha died of an overdose . . . and drowning, this time of year, second year in college. 2009. She was nineteen."

Zachary groaned. "You've had a rough time."

"They found her body in a reflecting pool on campus."

Zachary waited, silent.

"Ashley survived her childhood, amazingly enough, and is currently in rehab somewhere in the Napa Valley."

Jessica's words, mumbled to the dirt trail, were full of bitterness, and Zachary guessed she had forcibly distanced herself from her sisters long ago, barricaded them out of her life. But bitterness didn't suit Jessica.

"I'm not like them, either of them, and I'm not going to be like them," she said.

With that promise spoken, Zachary understood a key piece of his new friend. He saw her determination, her holding things together so that they would not fall apart, her hunger to learn from her sisters' mistakes, her fight for her own survival.

"Actually," Jessica said, her tone lighter, "I've learned a lot from it all. At least I think I have. We went to family therapy when the twins first got into drugs, and the therapist, Dr. Stein, gave me a theory of emotion and control that I've found useful. Then I discovered the Fidelity Society."

"The Fidelity Society?" Zachary, grateful that she had moved into less painful territory, would stay with this subject and see where it led. The name sounded familiar.

"It's a group on campus that supports chastity outside of marriage. They promote discussion about family and marriage, and they host interesting speakers."

"How did this group help you with your sisters?" Zachary hadn't quite connected the dots, and he felt at ease enough to ask.

"They gave me my list of controls."

"Ah." Should he continue, he asked himself.

She glanced at him, and her eyes were full of teasing humor. "It's okay, I don't mind explaining. The group has given me the strength to talk about it. Essentially the Fidelity meetings have helped me understand that I deserve respect as a woman, that I can control my life if I want to, that I can live a life of beauty." She hesitated, as though waiting for his reaction to one of his favorite words.

"Beauty? That's the kind of life I'd like to live. One of beauty, truth, and goodness." There was a society devoted to this? It was too good, too beautiful, to be true.

Jessica came to a stop, and having scanned the area in all directions, sat on a log beside the trail. Zachary joined her. She pulled an index card from her bag. As she spoke she glanced at it.

"Discipline, self-control, delayed gratification; systems of safety and sanity; respect for the body, sex, mind, time; love as commitment and mutual sacrifice. That's a summary. I keep this to refer to. The ideas have helped me make sense of my life, and I need to have order in my world after the twins, after my father dying." She handed him the card. "You can have this if you like. I have others."

"Thanks," he said, taking it and studying the fine print. "I understand. I'm impressed with the list."

Develop discipline and self-control (practice delayed gratification).

Develop systems of safety and sanity (diet, housing, routines, course work leading to clear goals, no waste).

Respect my body (dress, behavior, what am I communicating?).

Respect my mind (read discerningly; choose movies thoughtfully; limit social media).

Respect time and use it wisely (work ethic).

Respect love as commitment and mutual sacrifice (no shortcuts).

Respect sex as meant for childbearing and family (sex within marriage only).

Zachary exhaled. "This is terrific. I've never seen anything spelled out like this. Brave, actually."

Jessica stood and shouldered her pack. "Fidelity helped a lot. I don't feel as alone as I once did. You're welcome to come to Sunday's meeting if you like."

Zachary was certain that another great step forward had been made with Jessica. He would go to any meeting with her, but this one sounded intriguing. "I'd love to go. It's piqued my interest, to say the least, taking control of your life and creating something beautiful with it, something good and true."

She considered him with gratitude, tilting her head and squinting. "Thanks, Zachary. It's pretty useful stuff."

They padded through the forest, meeting a wider firebreak trail, and looping to another lookout. Jessica stopped and stared into the distance. "This is where I was standing, just before."

Zachary knew immediately what she meant. He stood silently beside her. The fog was evaporating over the city, and he could see the towers of the Golden Gate Bridge emerge. The sun was low and thin, trying to shed its last light on the dying day. "Are you okay?" He touched her shoulder.

"I'm okay. Thanks for doing this. Thanks for being here," she said, her voice hoarse, nearly choking.

"That's what friends are for." He studied the path, eyeing the deeper shadows on either side.

She glanced at him, then studied the trail as well, as though searching for any signs of movement, pulling herself together. "Okay, I'm ready. Let's face the place where I saw him." She turned, and they descended the Fire Trail through the pines. "Her body was in there," she said, pointing to a dark area of low brush. "I was standing here, when he blocked the path." Shivering, she wrapped her arms around herself.

Zachary held her shoulders and gently turned her to face him. Carefully, he slipped his arms around her and he felt hers rest lightly around him. For a brief moment, their hearts beat together, their cheeks touched, and he inhaled a faint aroma of lemon in her hair. Then they stepped back.

"That's what friends are for," Zachary repeated, waiting to see if she turned toward the place where she had found the girl's body. When she didn't move in that direction, he looked toward the trailhead. "Let's go. You've faced your fear. Now it's really over."

She nodded and, without looking back, they headed down the hill to their cars.

* * *

Zachary followed Jessica to her studio on Arch, then drove down Hearst to his room on Short Street, as dusk absorbed the last of the day. He repeated his lines so far:

> How do I love thee? Let me count the ways.
> I love thee to the depth and breadth and height
> My soul can reach, when feeling out of sight
> For the ends of being and ideal grace.

I love thee to the level of every day's
Most quiet need, by sun and candle-light.
I love thee freely, as men strive for right.
I love thee purely, as they turn from praise.

The lines had nearly burst from him today, but he had controlled himself. Instead they paced and circled through his thoughts, so that now he was gratified to let them breathe. And as he finished the second stanza, he knew he had made the right decision to not recite love poetry to a girl who wasn't ready. She would be, one day, but not yet. He repeated the last two lines and realized that if he wanted to love her purely as men turn from praise, that is, humbly and without thought of self, he would wait until she was ready. Then, to be sure, he would be loving her freely, just as men strive for right.

Zachary parked near his bungalow and read the next two lines from the leather volume he had placed in the glove compartment:

I love thee with the passion put to use
In my old griefs, and with my childhood's faith.

Ah, passion put to use. A curious phrase, Zachary thought as Short Street slipped into night. He could see the BART station at the end of the street sending commuters to their homes, to their children, to their dreams, each person carrying a universe within, of differing age, gender, and race. Zachary watched them through the car window, as the street lamps flickered on, bathing the street in a surreal half-light. As he watched, he considered his old griefs and his childhood faith.

How Elizabeth Barrett Browning captured his own heart at this moment in his life. Was that the power of poetry? To touch a twin heart across time, leaping across centuries? Zachary's old griefs—the school bullies, his father leaving—would count as his old passions, to be sure. Could those griefs now be absorbed by his new passion, his newfound love?

He had lost his childhood faith, such as it was, the bits that his grandmother had taught him, but had he lost all faith in God? He didn't think so, but he wasn't sure. And perhaps his faith could still be found, as though it had been put away in a drawer and ignored, then forgotten. After all, EBB doesn't say she *lost* her faith, only that her childhood's faith was (more) passionate. In the next lines, she implies she still believes in God:

> I love thee with a love I seemed to lose
> With my lost saints. I love thee with the breath,
> Smiles, tears, of all my life; and, if God choose,
> I shall but love thee better after death.

Her saints were lost. But God was still there, governing the lovers' afterlife.

One thing he knew, and EBB knew as well, that love and God and saints and passion were all intertwined, like stained glass, where color and form merged with light and leaded borders. So wherever these things lived, Zachary wanted to live too.

And a piece of glimmering emerald had been added to his own stained glass story, his own life sonnet, this most promising afternoon. He knew so much more about Jessica than he had known before, and all of this revelation shone a light on the mystery of her heart. As they walked the Fire Trail a boundary had been removed, a fence had come down.

Zachary locked the car and followed the narrow path to his front door, then took the stairs two at a time, waving to the Zimmermans watching TV. He had a lot of work to do. He needed to make the most of his time, so that he could make essential, pivotal, life-changing time for Jessica. And he would see her on Sunday at ten-thirty, only four days away, an eternity but a hopeful one.

Twenty-One
Freedom

Thursday afternoon, as Jessica and Zachary walked the Fire Trail, Anna helped Father Nate prepare tea in his cottage. The countertop TV was on low volume, and somewhere in the unacknowledged background of her hearing, Anna absorbed the daily crime reports: *Guns and drugs seized by CHP in Berkeley. Business burglarized on College Ave. Home burglarized on Dana St. Two vehicles stolen on Jefferson Ave. Fire Trail murder still unsolved . . .*

As they waited for the water to boil, Father Nate set out two Cal Bear mugs and spoons, a bowl of sweetener packets, a pitcher of milk, and paper towel napkins on a wooden tray. Anna added a plate of red seedless grapes surrounded by cubes of Monterey Jack cheese. Knowing Father Nate appreciated her breads, or at least said he did, she had added a basket of her raisin-walnut muffins (wheat germ and lots of nuts) which she would leave for Father Nate and Nicholas for the weekend. The steam whistled from the spout, and Anna poured the water over sweet-spice tea bags in the shiny blue mugs.

Father Nate turned off the TV and opened the back door so that Anna could carry the tray to a low table on the porch. They settled into wicker rockers, the cats milling around their feet, all present except for Coricocat, the tortoiseshell who, Anna guessed, was happy on Nicholas' lap upstairs. She wondered how Nicholas managed to work, with his limited motor movement and the cat in his lap.

Sleek black Quaxo jumped to the deck railing and sat alert, his green eyes squeezing shut from time to time in sweet companionship. Princess Bombalurina circled Father Nate, then curled on top of the toe of his shoe, where, with serious attention and great energy she bathed her short gray hair. Big red Jellylorum spotted a sparrow flitting through the juniper and bolted to the foot of the steps, ready to pounce. His tail twitched and his jaw chattered. Anna called to him softly, hoping to distract him from the bird, but he ignored her. The long-hair Munkastrap moved to the sheepskin pad under the table, and settled in for a nap, curling into a furry white ball.

Father Nate said grace, and eyed Anna quizzically. "How's your exercise program coming along, now that you have your assistant?" He reached for a muffin.

"I've been using the time to work in the children's library." There were so many books to consider; so many to cull. Time disappeared as she worked, reading reviews, searching the Internet. "I'm keeping records as to my reasons for denying certain books after that free speech article about my library last year." It wasn't her library, Anna often reminded herself, but she thought of it as hers, like a growing child needing healthy nourishment.

Father Nate tore open a sweetener packet and held it over his cup of steaming liquid, watching the sugar stream down. "Good," he said thoughtfully. He stirred his tea and bit into a muffin, savoring it. "It would seem obvious that children's books should be censored, at least to a degree. Why that blogger wrote that piece is beyond me."

The priest's affirmation soothed Anna. "It's common sense really."

"Common sense for the common good. What has happened to the sense of doing things for the good of the commons?" Father Nate stared at the shadowy trees, lost in thought.

To remove any lingering false guilt, Anna added, "Of course, for the most part, I support free speech. There are lots of words I find offensive, but I believe people have the right to say and write them."

Father Nate's smile was heartwarming. "I can tell you one thing, at this moment I must speak freely about these muffins. I think you've outdone yourself, my dear! But there's a secret ingredient I can't quite figure out."

Anna beamed. "Not telling." She had added a few pine nuts, but it wouldn't be a secret if she told him, now would it?

"But getting back to free speech," he said, eyeing her seriously, as though, having lightened the conversation, he could now add weight and leave his legacy of ideas in her safekeeping. "First Amendment rights are vital to our country."

"That's the one about free speech?" Anna glanced up as a seagull landed in an upper branch of a pine tree, flapped his wings, and soared off.

"Even more than free speech. The First Amendment prohibits the establishment of a state religion, but allows for freedom of religion, speech, press, peaceful assembly, and the right to petition the government with grievances. It was added in 1791 to curtail federal power and is part of our Bill of Rights."

"I suppose the religious part is the part you're worried about?"

Father Nate nodded, his eyes narrowing. "You can read my mind. They merge together, of course, but lately the issue over so-called hate speech—when opinions are deemed to cause simple offense—is threatening to close down debate. A journalist was sued recently for challenging a speaker's claims that global warming was manmade. The journalist will probably win the case, but his time and money have been stolen. The case should have been thrown out as a frivolous lawsuit, but the courts have become politicized."

"And the example will discourage others from challenging anyone's facts in public."

"Debate is silenced." Father Nate pulled a chunk off a second muffin, added a cube of cheese, and popped it in his mouth.

"Wasn't Cal's commencement speaker cancelled because of things he said?" Anna recalled he had made public anti-Islamist comments and student groups had objected.

"He was a stand-up comedian, not suitable to speak at such an occasion."

"That wasn't the reason they gave for cancelling."

Father Nate grew thoughtful, set down the remainder of his muffin and tapped his fingers together. "The administration has been inconsistent, to be sure. They should have invited a serious speaker for the ceremony, not one who uses foul language and is often disrespectful. I've heard they've re-invited him, which I think is inappropriate because *he* is inappropriate."

They sat companionably, pondering the words and phrases that gave life to their thoughts, and to Anna the rustle of the eucalyptus and the caw of a crow were like punctuation marks. Jellylorum had given up on the bird but remained on guard, and Munkastrap stared at her from under the table, her purr rumbling, her paws pushing rhythmically back and forth into the sheepskin. Anna breathed deeply, glad for the priest to talk to, glad for the smells of the forest and the creaky old wood of the deck, glad for the cats. She scooped up Munkastrap and stroked her white fur, enjoying her thunderous purr.

"The commencement issue," Father Nate said, "wasn't like other free speech issues, such as Salmon Rushdie's book labeled blasphemous by an imam who sentenced him to a jihad death."

Anna recalled the crisis. She had feared for the man's life. "What happened to him?"

"He's still living, in retreat, hiding. His literary world distanced themselves from him, setting an example."

"Like the journalist taken to court over the global warming lawsuit?"

"Indeed. Fear is contagious, threatening speech even more. There's Theo Van Gogh, murdered for his film disrespectful of the Quran."

"And the Danish cartoons." Anna recalled the uproar. Images of Muhammad were not allowed in Islam.

"Which caused riots in Denmark and the Middle East."

"Silencing more speech." Anna felt a chill as she said the words, as if events were speeding out of control. Would they be living in a police state tomorrow? A world that outlawed any and all controversy?

Father Nate sipped his tea. "I don't like the satire and ridicule and the disrespect. I wish folks would censor themselves, be *mannerly*. We are on the edges of the jungle when we cannot be civil on our own volition. But allowing the freedom to be uncivil is more important than enforcing civility and denying freedom. So we must use our freedom wisely. If we don't police ourselves, others will police us. Without moral parameters, a kind of natural law, if you will, tyranny will silence us."

"The borders of the jungle," Anna said, combining a grape with a cube of cheese, "like those books I reject."

Father Nate rocked slowly, the chair squeaking. Quaxo, seeing a sparrow flit from a bush, jumped off the railing and darted after it, unsuccessful. Father Nate laced his fingers over his chest, closing his eyes. "It seems that the more we give in to our passions without considering others, the more we deny love. The more we deny love, the more we become barbaric. Each time we lose self-control, we invite the bestial into our lives and our culture." He tapped the arm of the rocker. "I'm particularly worried about free assembly on campus."

"How so?"

"The Supreme Court ruled in 2010 in *Christian Legal Society* vs. *Martinez* that Hastings Law School, part of the University of California, could *require* student groups to allow members of any belief or lifestyle. Other campuses have followed suit by expelling Christian organizations that don't comply. This is troubling."

"It isn't logical. The membership of a group should reflect the beliefs of the group." Otherwise, Anna thought, why have the group at all? There was no point.

Father Nate nodded. "They see it as similar to the gender issue—not allowing all-male or all-female clubs."

Anna pulled her shawl about her. "Will this affect Comerford?"

"Not yet, at least that I can see. Although all private foundations should be concerned about this kind of state regulation, since law builds upon law. Any aspect of the law might be relevant in the future, might even close institutions, both religious and secular."

"And speaking of closing, what's the latest about Comerford House?" The house had become like family to her, a family bridging time. She scratched Munkastrap's chin and rubbed her tummy. Like many long-hairs, she liked her tummy rubbed.

"I think they will hold on as long as they can."

She patted his arm. "No need to borrow trouble, as my mother used to say."

"Today's trouble is sufficient." Dusk was settling in, stealing through the forest and around the cottage. Father Nate glanced at his watch. "Forgot the time. I'll ring the bell, then come back for Nicholas."

"I'll do the dishes."

"Many thanks, Anna."

Father Nate dusted off his pants, descended the porch steps, and headed to the chapel as a chatter of caw-caws filled the trees high above.

Anna set Munkastrap down gently. She gathered the tea things, and as she stepped into the kitchen, she heard the bell tolling through the deepening mist. It sounded mournful, she thought, as though death were near.

Twenty-Two
Earthquake

On that same Thursday evening, in her basement studio, Jessica sliced plump zucchini and chopped red bell peppers, placing them in a wooden salad bowl. It was dark outside, nearly eight, but she didn't notice as she reflected on the Fire Trail walk with Zachary. The walk had been invigorating, and it was good to be in the hills once again. And, she knew, the walk had been a healing tonic. It was as though that frightening chapter in her life were over. She hoped that she could now begin a new and better one.

She reached in the fridge for a head of romaine, washed the long green leaves with greater care than usual, tore them into pieces, and dropped them into the bowl. She added quartered tomatoes, and finally, two four-minute eggs pulled out of boiling water, cracked and scooped. A slow drizzle of olive oil, a sprinkle of balsamic vinegar, and she was ready to toast the nine-grain slices. As the bread toasted, she thought how the preparation of such a meal had become an evening ritual for her. It was a ceremony that relaxed her mind and body, as she reached for familiar utensils and beloved vegetables, and washed and chopped and assembled. Some evenings she poured a glass of chianti, but tonight she wanted to make progress on her paper. She wanted a clear head.

She set her dinner on the counter and opened her laptop. The usual news reports ran across her screen: *Guns, drugs seized during arrests in Berkeley. Two vehicles stolen on Jefferson Avenue. College Avenue business burglarized. Dana Street home burglarized. Assault and battery at Addison and McGee.* (Wasn't that near the old Presentation High buildings, her Fidelity location?) Then, her eyes narrowed: *Fire Trail murderer still at large.*

Shivering, Jessica made sure the front door was bolted. She peered out the window into the deepening dark. Should she relocate? She didn't want distractions; she needed to stay focused. She forced her fear into dormancy, at least for the evening.

She checked her phone messages: one from Shelley, one from her mother. Shelley said that she should be home next week, and her mother wanted to see how she was doing. Jessica dialed her mother, let her know about the job, and confirmed October's cemetery meeting. Her mother sounded relieved, but as usual, distant as though playing a part.

Determined to stay focused, Jessica opened her Word document.

Growth

> *The Presentation convents and schools were established in four locations: Sonoma, San Jose, San Francisco, and Berkeley. In 1888 the four convents amalgamated under one constitution. Sister Mary Rose Forest, PVBM, writes:*

> *From a group of two stalwart pioneers they had increased to seventy-five sisters engaged in teaching over 1400 children in four convent schools. The tiny acorn had grown into a sturdy tree, and widespread were its branches.* [9]

> *In 1904 the sisters celebrated the fiftieth anniversary of their arrival in San Francisco, little suspecting the disaster to come.*

Earthquake and Fire

> *At 5:12 in the dawn of Wednesday, April 18, 1906, three days after Easter Sunday, a 7.8 earthquake jolted San Francisco. The North Beach convent saw minor damage, mostly broken statuary, but fires erupted downtown and spread rapidly in the next twenty-four hours; water conduits had been damaged, so there was no water to put out the fires.*

> *When flames threatened their block on Thursday the sisters evacuated. They said goodbye to their beloved convent and school and walked to the ferry terminal, carrying heavy bags of records, chalices, vestments, and clothing. They passed the burned-down Embarcadero wharf, making their way, with the help of guards, to ferries that took them to St.*

Joseph's Convent in Berkeley. By Thursday evening North Beach was destroyed by fire. Sister Mary Rose Forest writes:

> *The Powell Street convent stood in this valley between Russian and Telegraph Hills, which became an inferno of flame on Friday morning. It was about half past eleven o'clock when the convent caught fire. At twelve noon the bell, which for fifty years had rung the midday Angelus, fell from its tower. Soon the famous old convent was only a smoldering ruin.*
>
> *By Saturday morning, April 21, the fire had reached the waterfront. There, after consuming Meiggs' wharf, so long a familiar San Francisco landmark, it died out. The holocaust of the great City of St. Francis was ended!*[10]

The Sisters of the Presentation returned to San Francisco's North Beach neighborhood to help refugees. They handed out groceries, clothing, and bedding at a relief center on Telegraph Hill. They visited the poor, the sick, the confused, living in tents, bringing them comfort. Refugee children "ran wild" and soon the sisters organized a school.

Some of the sisters worked in Oakland and Berkeley. Tens of thousands destitute and frightened people fled the fire in San Francisco and arrived in the East Bay. Relief centers were set up in Fruitvale in Oakland, at St. Joseph Convent, and at St. Joseph Church in Berkeley, helping twelve hundred homeless with food, clothing, and supplies. Because clothing was desperately needed, a sewing center run by the sisters stitched clothes from donated material:

> *Eighty sisters worked busily all day. Sewing machines hummed and nimble fingers plied needles and thread as the nun-seamstresses turned bolts of material . . . into piles of new garments . . . over 150 women and children had*

been clothed by the Berkeley convent . . . the Ladies' Aid Society served as many as 1500 meals a day . . .[11]

The sisters taught children at refugee camps at Adams Point on the northern shore of Lake Merritt in Oakland and Dimond Canyon Camp in East Oakland. They ran a "refuge for unclaimed children," for those children who had been abandoned, orphaned, or whose parents had been unable to reconnect with them. Many children were reunited with their parents. Others were welcomed by St. Joseph Orphanage in South San Francisco.

Serving Berkeley

The influx of families into East Bay communities after 1906 propelled development, and St. Joseph's parish grew. The schools joined to become St. Joseph's Elementary School, and in 1964 St. Joseph's Presentation Academy was renamed Presentation High School. Since many students came from outside the local parish, the school was now maintained by the Presentation Sisters.

When the Bay Area Rapid Transit (BART) came to Berkeley in 1973, St. Joseph's parish community diminished. As local historian Dianne Walker writes:

> St. Joseph's Parish, at one time comprising all of Berkeley, slowly shrank as more parishes in Berkeley were carved out of its original territory. When BART took out sixteen blocks of the few remaining blocks in the Parish, the life of the Parish—including local Parish children attending the schools—was greatly affected. The sense of community, which had gradually frayed as people aged and their children moved into the eastern suburbs, eventually tore. Old-timers, the "Golden Friends," meet for mass daily, but the

Sisters are now gone and their schools and students with them.[12]

Nano Nagle, the Foundress of the Sisters of the Presentation, said, "If I can be of service anywhere in the globe for the saving of souls, I would gladly go."[13] *Today her sisters walk in her footsteps, albeit with a lesser presence in Berkeley. They now work in schools, hospitals, and parishes throughout the world. They provide literacy programs for immigrants. They serve prisons, retreat centers, and foreign missions. The sisters have gone anywhere to serve, having given Berkeley a good start.*

Jessica was struck by how BART influenced the neighborhood and how transportation systems affected, for good or ill, the community's life. The Central Pacific Railroad came to Shattuck Avenue and University Avenue in 1878, infusing life into early Berkeley and St. Joseph's parish to the west. BART arrived nearly one hundred years later and dispersed the historic parish, causing the parish to suffer, schools to close and families to scatter.

The decline in religious institutions in Berkeley posed a question that Jessica probably could never definitively answer: Was there a connection between local crime and the decreasing role of religion? This question led to her thesis about the positive influence of Christian churches, both Protestant and Catholic, upon the state's citizenry in terms of public safety, education, hospitals, and charitable organizations. To Jessica, there seemed to be substantial circumstantial evidence to support her claim, but probably no proof.

But how many historical claims were provable? How many were merely supported by circumstantial evidence giving rise to reasonable deduction? There was a gray area of interpretation, to be sure, and each historian had to arrive at their own conclusions. She would search for as many facts as possible to support her theory, to total the substantial circumstances and create a significant sum.

One thing for sure, the Presentation Sisters carried their lanterns into the dark of early Berkeley, lighting a path for the next generation, for they taught children not only reading, writing, and arithmetic, but critical thinking and right from wrong. They gave them a foundation that would help them understand their dangerous world, even tame it. And the danger, Jessica concluded, had returned, like a wolf set free.

* * *

As Jessica saved the document file to her laptop, she considered when she might visit the attic archives at Comerford. She wanted to scan or photograph Beatrice's letters, perhaps Friday, Saturday, and Sunday before or after work. She would ask Anna tomorrow. She recalled seeing a printer-scanner on the desk in the children's library next to Anna's computer screen. Could it be moved upstairs to the attic and hooked to her own laptop? Zachary might be able to help on Sunday if necessary.

Zachary. She appreciated his friendship, but she would be on her guard; she didn't want more than friendship. She needed to complete her degree and enter the job market. At times when she thought of her meager resources, a slow panic rose and her chest tightened. Her sisters had not fared well; would she end up like them?

Perhaps she looked forward a little too much to Sunday's Fidelity meeting with Zachary, for she was beginning to trust him. They were meeting at 10:30 at Ohlone Park near Sacramento Street, and walking to St. Joseph's from there. She wondered what his reaction would be to the no-nonsense, blunt speakers, but since she wanted to find out more about *his* character, she would have to be honest with him about *her* character. This might be a step toward that goal. The worst that could happen was that he would run away, writing her off as a prude or crazy or both. And it might be good to have him do the running now, rather than later. It was a kind of test, she thought, and, having analyzed the problem and tucked it into a corner of her mind, she felt better, more in control.

Jessica slept deeply that night, dreaming of Nano Nagle in Ireland, the woman with the lantern who visited the sick and the poor, of the nuns and the earthquake and the fire, of the ferries and the schools and the children, of a high school turned into a pink stucco block of townhouses called University Terrace.

Twenty-Three
Beauty

On the following Sunday, Zachary arrived at Ohlone Park thirty minutes early. He sat on a bench and pulled out his EBB sonnet, wondering if always arriving ahead of time was a blessing or a curse, and would Jessica think him too eager and too pressuring?

He recited the lines he had memorized, watching people walk their dogs and push strollers through the grass this sunny Sunday morning. Why had he left his apartment so soon when the park was only two blocks away? He knew why, of course. She might be early too. Also, time was lengthening in his room and he wanted to shrink it. He needed to get out, to feel the sun on his skin, to stretch his legs.

He tried the sonnet on for size, sculpting his memory:

> How do I love thee? Let me count the ways.
> I love thee to the depth and breadth and height
> My soul can reach, when feeling out of sight
> For the ends of being and ideal grace.
> I love thee to the level of every day's
> Most quiet need, by sun and candle-light.
> I love thee freely, as men strive for right.
> I love thee purely, as they turn from praise.
> I love thee with the passion put to use
> In my old griefs, and with my childhood's faith.

So far so good. He opened the book and read the last lines:

> I love thee with a love I seemed to lose
> With my lost saints. I love thee with the breath,
> Smiles, tears, of all my life; and, if God choose,
> I shall but love thee better after death.

He thought he liked "the breath,/Smiles, tears, of all my life" the best.

As he repeated the words, he glanced up Hearst toward the campus and the hills, the direction she would be coming from. It was encouraging she had invited him to this Fidelity meeting. He recalled Thursday's Fire Trail walk with satisfaction, reliving those moments of closeness—the comfortable, even pace they kept, as though they were a natural couple, the confided stories of childhood, although painful. She opened her heart; he opened his.

He even shared the obesity and the bullying, recollections he hadn't shared with anyone, and Jessica, dear sweet Jessica, had put him at ease. But how he had flinched when he saw he had opened her own memory wounds—her father and sisters—as though he were a surgeon with a scalpel and had the right. He didn't foresee where the conversation was leading. He had felt ambushed, not by her, but by the words tumbling along. And then the tone changed and the threatened crisis was averted with her delicate comment about the preciousness of life. The comment itself had been precious; she was precious.

And to think there was such a group as the Fidelity Society, a group dedicated to living lives of beauty. This was something he understood deeply.

He had been fortunate, Zachary thought, to have discovered beauty. Truth and goodness hid behind it most of the time (but not always, he had come to realize), or perhaps they were facets of the same jewel, a kind of trinity. Three facets holding a central heart, love. Maybe he would try writing a poem about that someday, when he had more time, later, after his doctorate, after his marriage to Jessica, when he was settled into a true, good, beautiful life of love.

Jessica had faced her fear on the Fire Trail, and he, Zachary, had helped her. In their short embrace, those seconds in which he could feel her heart beating and her light touch with her arms and the tips of her fingers barely touching his back, time stood still. It was, he realized, a friends' moment, not a lovers' moment, but she was there, she was close. Her hair smelled of lemon and her shirt was softer and thinner than he had thought it would be. He could feel her shoulder blades for a brief second. He would tread the next hours and days and weeks carefully. He wanted to progress, not regress like that moment in the music room.

Zachary slipped on his earbuds and tapped his music app on his phone. His most recent beauty-discovery soon began, the second movement of Vivaldi's Oboe Concerto in C. He glanced up the Ohlone Parkway. No Jessica yet, but it was only ten-twenty. As the music poured into his ears, his shoulders relaxed. He allowed his gaze to leave Hearst and drift to the partially overcast skies. The sun slipped in and out, and the leaves refracted the light as they danced in the breeze. The Vivaldi piece reminded him of water, light dancing on water, and Zachary imagined Vivaldi's Venice.

He had seen photos and Googled YouTube videos. The city glowed and glimmered softly, all muted golds and pale light and old stone, and he imagined the sun dancing on the water much as it now refracted from the leaves above him. The water, he thought, must lap the stone facades, then splash with greater strength as a gondola furrowed the canal. It was saltwater: Was there a smell of the sea? Were there seagulls? Here in Berkeley, not far from the ocean, white gulls sometimes soared the skies. Like those birds in flight, the music soared into his soul, and Zachary sailed a gondola in Venice. His sleek craft divided the waters, splashing diamond wakes in the sunlight. Did Elizabeth Barrett Browning know this beauty?

She visited Venice in June, 1851, with her two-year-old, her husband Robert, and her ladies' maid, Lily Wilson. In a letter, EBB described the canals as "silver trails of water up between all that gorgeous colour and carving." It was an image Zachary would not forget, and when he listened to Vivaldi he thought of those silver trails running between the golden stone palazzos. And Vivaldi's oboe solos caught the forward movement of the water, pulsing through Venice. Zachary closed his eyes. He was there.

A rustle disturbed the air, and Zachary knew, from the lemony fragrance, that Jessica was near. "Thinking of beauty?" she asked. "What are you listening to? Must be beautiful."

Zachary opened his eyes and grinned. He could feel the heat again rising to his cheeks. "Vivaldi." He pulled the earbuds off and handed them to her, watching her slip them over her delicate ears. He noticed a freckle on a lobe. He watched her face, waiting for the certain moment of joy.

She raised her brows in awe. "This is . . . remarkable." Her head was nodding to the rhythm of the oboe, to the movement of the oars on the water.

"It reminds me of Venice," Zachary said. "Vivaldi was Venetian."

"Incredible . . . it just ended. Thanks. Could you write down the name for me?"

She wore her Comerford clothes, but had added a pink scarf to the white blouse and gray jacket. The scarf must have been made of a soft fabric, and it was long and lacy, looping her neck and falling over the tucks of the blouse. Her hair was up again, as she had done on other Comerford days, and the breeze played with the wavy strands that framed her freckles. Zachary hoped he had captured the details to keep in his courtship album.

"We'd better head to the meeting," she said. "Fidelity starts at eleven, and it's ten-thirty already. We want to get seats. They've been filling the room lately." They crossed Hearst and walked through a historic residential neighborhood of old trees and bungalows, along McGee Avenue. "I didn't realize that Vivaldi was from Venice."

Zachary shifted his pack to the other shoulder. He had brought his sheet music in case he went to Comerford House after working at Laurie's. He had added a snack and water, and a lined pad to take notes. "Vivaldi was born there in 1678. In fact an earthquake hit the city on the morning of his birth. He was given an emergency baptism and his mother dedicated him to God to become a priest. He was called 'the red priest' because of his hair."

"Why, you're a historian, Zachary Aguilar."

Zachary smiled. "The stories of the artists intrigue me. What kind of a life produces beauty like that? I think about that sometimes, especially when some artists weren't particularly good or true, qualities I'd like to associate with beauty." He glanced at her for her reaction.

She nodded. "How true." They laughed.

Encouraged by her laughter, Zachary added, "But Antonio Vivaldi seems to have been good and true, and it's sad he died unknown, a pauper. He was sickly—asthmatic, they think—so instead of parish work, he was assigned to a local orphanage to teach the girls violin. Most of his pieces were written for the orphans."

Jessica turned toward him. "Really? That's a good story."

"They were children of wealthy Venetians and their mistresses. It is said the girls lived in luxury, and the school became known all over Europe for their angelic performances."

"I can imagine."

"I was touched, you know, by his life. He was sickly and did so much for Venice, not to mention the orphans. He died poor and unknown. He's only become popular since the mid-twentieth century, thanks to Alfredo Casella who revived his works."

"Have you been to Venice?"

"No, but Venice has always fascinated me. Elizabeth Barrett Browning called it a city in the sea. She said the canals were silver trails of water."

"Silver trails. Lovely. Did she live in Venice? She was English, wasn't she?"

"She was English and visited Venice. And her story is poignant, just as touching as Vivaldi's story. She lived in the early nineteenth century and eloped with Robert Browning, a fellow writer, in 1846. Her *Sonnets from the Portuguese*, probably her most famous collection of poetry, was composed the year they met in secret."

"Charming! Why did she call it *from the Portuguese*?"

"That's curious too. After they married, Robert Browning wanted to publish her collection, saying they were the best love sonnets since Shakespeare, but she objected, saying they were too personal. So she agreed to his idea, that is, to pretend they were merely translations of newly discovered Portuguese sonnets."

Jessica laughed. "I like her already. Sensitive and sweet."

Just like you, Zachary thought. Feeling brave, he added, "I'm actually memorizing one of her poems."

"Nice. One of the sonnets?"

"Exactly. I find memorization helps me understand in a different way, with both head and heart, I guess."

"I can see that."

They walked in silence for a moment and Zachary thought that Jessica might be mulling over the love story and holding it close. Then she added, almost to herself, "I'll have to find a copy of her sonnets."

"It's all online now. But I'll find a copy for you at Laurie's, if you like."

"Thanks, Zachary, but you don't have to—"

"I'd like to."

"So let me guess. They eloped to Venice."

"You're close. They married secretly in London, honeymooned in Paris, and settled in Florence—the Casa Guidi—where they lived until her death fifteen years later. She was frail from a genetic disease, and the warmer climate was thought to be good for her."

"I've heard of the love story, but not the details. She visited Venice from Florence?"

"They spent a month there in 1851—they had a two-year old son by then—and she described the time in her letters."

"Letters! The nineteenth century is a treasure trove of letters. I've been reading the letters of the Presentation Sisters. Some of their correspondence is at Comerford House. Your mother showed them to me yesterday."

Zachary nodded. "Those letters are valuable primary sources, great for historians. Really fascinating. Almost turned me toward history rather than literature when I realized what was available, and much of it going online, public domain. Project Gutenberg has put all of Barrett-Browning's work online. It's remarkable."

Jessica glanced at him with a tilt of her head and slightly lowered lids. "They interweave don't they? One informs the other. History and literature. Especially literature that was written in the past, not just set in the past."

"Well said. It all forms a whole."

They crossed University Avenue and continued to Addison. Soon the twin-towered St. Joseph's Church appeared, shaded by old oaks beginning to change color. "This was Father's Nate's parish church once. He was on staff and lived nearby."

"Really? It's part of my research."

"Was this the area you spoke of, the historic settlement of Berkeley? Something to do with the Presentation Sisters?"

She nodded, pausing on the corner to consider the white facade. She took a photo, then led him along the other side of the street. "See these pink stucco condos? This is University Terrace. They occupy the land of the old convent and high school."

"So the high school is gone? Seems sad."

"It *is* sad. BART arrived, taking over part of the neighborhood parish, so many families relocated. The school and convent sold its property to Cal, but the parish church remained. In fact, Ohlone Greenway runs above the BART underground line. It's called People's Park Annex because the neighborhood fought to turn the land into a park."

"My street ends at the BART station." Zachary guessed his house was within the parish boundaries and just missed being destroyed by the transit system. "Father Nate said I should visit the church since I seek transcendence and beauty. Have you ever been inside?"

"No, I haven't. I'm not much of a churchgoer but they say going to church makes people happy, protects against depression. I liked Evensong at Comerford Chapel."

"I'm glad. I like it too. It makes me feel at peace, and you could say that protects against depression."

"Want to peek in? We have a few minutes, but not much more."

They climbed steps to the entrance and passed through the narthex. A mass was in progress, and they watched from the back. The ethereal vaulted space was lined with colorful stained glass. A priest in a white robe faced the altar, his back to his people, chanting, his arms raised in praise. The congregation of men and women and children sang in response.

"What language is that?" Zachary whispered. "Arabic?"

"It's Eritrean," Jessica replied softly. "They're refugees who escaped the Islamic wars in Africa. I read about them online. The language is close to Aramaic, the language of Jesus' time."

"I've never heard it before." Zachary listened to the fervent singing, a blend of East and West. He was thankful for America, who had welcomed these suffering people. "Wasn't it Eritrean Catholics who were beheaded on the shoreline?"

"Yes."

They listened for a few moments, then left quietly.

Zachary read a schedule outside the church. "They have English and Spanish masses too."

"Reflecting the community," Jessica said. "It's nearly eleven. We'd better get a seat for the lecture. Follow me."

Twenty-Four
Marriage

They found seats in the back. Zachary read the banner: *Fidelity over infidelity, selflessness over selfishness, honor over dishonor, truth over lies, restraint over indulgence.* It was a functional room, with a podium and speakers' table.

Nervous whispering added to an air of expectancy. It was as if, Zachary considered, the audience wanted to be filled with something good. And, in a way, a compelling lecture promised this, the feeding of the mind and possibly the soul, but ideally sustenance for both. As he pulled out his lined pad and pen, he recalled the ethereal singing in the church, and briefly asked himself if the soul could be fed without God. Did he believe in the soul?

As he asked the question, he grew keenly aware of Jessica sitting alongside him, of the faint aroma of her lemony hair. In his side vision he could see she was tilting her head in concentration as though memorizing the banner. A stack of brochures was coming down the row. She took one and handed the rest to him, which he passed along.

He opened the shiny trifold. It detailed the lecture series, and he noticed that today a Dr. Susan Jacobs was speaking on the topic, "What Is Marriage?" As Zachary thought of his parents and how marriage so often ended in divorce, he appreciated that Dr. Jacobs had taken on this unfashionable subject. But she might make a few enemies in the room.

For most folks, it was accepted to live together, unmarried. It was accepted to have children without marriage, for marriage had been deemed harmful. Zachary found it curious that gays desired marriage, when straights had nearly destroyed the institution. As he considered these opposites, he watched an attractive brunette, her hair falling gently to her shoulders, remove the microphone from its stand and walk to the head of the central aisle, like a talk-show host. She surveyed the room, her eyes making contact wherever she could, smiled, and tapped the mic.

"Welcome," she said, "to the Fidelity Society, a place where refugees from the sexual revolution can gather without fear of speaking their mind, without fear of the speech police."

There was a ripple of laughter, lightening the audience's mood, and Zachary thought her soft humor had done the trick, setting folks at ease, sort of.

"At our last meeting we talked about love, falling in love, the definition of love, how to find the perfect mate. We claimed that these college years are the golden ones in which to search, the best years to look for Mr. or Ms. Right. So, let's say you've found Mr. or Ms. Right, what comes next? The song, 'First comes love, then comes marriage, then comes a baby in a baby carriage' is a pretty good answer. It was true when it was written, and I am here to tell you today it's just as true now. And just as desirable, in that order."

The sudden quiet was awkward, and Zachary shifted uneasily in his chair. Babies were not something one talked about. Not everyone wanted babies. Certainly no one wanted them now, not in the college years, and some didn't want them ever. It was an option, no more than that, like choosing an entrée off a menu or a class from a course catalog. Zachary glanced at Jessica, who was leaning forward, as though not wanting to miss a single word.

"So what is marriage? And what is the big debate all about? There are basically two views of marriage, the *conjugal* view and the *revisionist* view.

Zachary wrote: *Two views of marriage, conjugal and revisionist.*

"The conjugal view is the traditional one, the view that has been fundamental to law and society, celebrated in literature and art. It says that marriage comprises a spiritual, emotional, and physical bond which becomes embodied in a third person, a child. Such marriage is called sacramental by religions because the child is literally a union of two human beings, a union created in love, albeit we do not always live up to love's ideals. Nevertheless, ideals are foundational, imperative to a free people, and this is why governments support and have supported the conjugal view of marriage."

Zachary was stunned by the image of a child being the embodiment of two others, his parents. And out of love. To be sure, as she said, it was an ideal, but what was life worth, without ideals?

"It is this ideal—to create a healthy, responsible, educated electorate—that the state desires. And this is the only reason the state is interested—or should be interested—in such a union. Without the rearing of children who will care for the aging populace, to move the nation forward, the nation will die. These children, they say, will be the nation's workforce and military defense. All other unions, those that do not represent this civic goal, should be made contractually without oversight from the state."

It seemed reasonable to Zachary that the state should have an interest in something before making laws about it. No one had ever pointed this out to him about marriage.

"This is not to say that a childless marriage is not a marriage, for we are in the realm of policy to encourage goals for the majority, policy that defines the ideal aimed for. This is something government needs to acknowledge, so vital is the conjugal version of marriage to the nation's existence. In fact the legal name for sexual union is *the generative act*, creating, generating the next generation to work and fight for the nation. The state is not interested in our pleasure, but in what we produce for the good of the commons, the common good."

Zachary thought this sounded cold but most likely right and true. And he desired to know what was right and true.

"Now the *revisionist* version of marriage claims that any union between two people, or even three, or four, or any number, regardless of gender, should be called marriage. All that is necessary is sexual union and emotional bonding. The problem with this view is that it is so broad that it can be expanded indefinitely. The state is not or should not be interested in these unions for they are not vital to the nation's future; they do not produce children in a nurturing environment. The line between friendship and such unions is vague, and this vagueness has nearly destroyed friendship."

Zachary wondered if she was going to speak about polygamy. He had heard there were court cases going forward in that regard.

"And so the conjugal version is held as an ideal for society to thrive, to give birth to a productive generation. Studies show that children of such unions do indeed thrive, fewer become delinquent, more lead productive lives, than those raised by other unions. The state is, or should be, interested in carefully defining marriage in this way."

Dr. Jacobs studied the room. "So what happens in a marriage ceremony, and why do we have these ceremonies at all? Is it merely a time to celebrate love and have a good party?"

Glances of nervous recognition were exchanged, and Zachary feared the speaker was sounding too judgmental.

"Sound familiar? Why is it that as marriage becomes less and less about commitment, weddings become grander. The reason? Folks do what they feel like at the time. If they think they are in love, they celebrate. If they think they have fallen out of love, they find someone else to love, and start over. One must be true to oneself, they say, be uninhibited, emancipated, liberated, forgetting commitment, abandoning spouse and children for greener grass, greater self-fulfillment. Certainly such individuals looking out for number one admit no duty to the state to raise children as a stabilizing good in society."

Zachary winced. Dr. Jacobs had perfectly described his father. As he shifted in his chair, Jessica glanced at him, her eyes sympathetic. Now she knew his story, Zachary realized. She knew about his parents and their divorce.

The speaker continued, reaching her full stride. "We are a culture of self, and marriage has been torn apart by our cult of self-esteem and personal needs. We no longer pray to a God outside ourselves. We no longer pray for others. We meditate . . . on what? On ourselves, our inner gods. We mock those institutions that teach us how to truly love: our churches and temples. In order to be happy, our culture says, we must throw out self-discipline, follow our feelings, laud informality over formality, level the playing field by homogenizing society, making everyone the same. Just so, we throw out the formal marriage ceremony, with its vows and discipline. We want no constraints. We want to be free. We delight in irreverence, but at what cost?"

Zachary glanced around the room. They were listening, listening as though some inner suspicion had been validated. He too heard the ring of truth in Dr. Jacobs' words, however unfashionable those words were.

"Religion calls the marriage ceremony a *solemnization*. Sounds serious, because it is and should be. Let's look at the true nature of the traditional ceremony. First the ceremony is public: There must be legal witnesses. The witnesses represent society. And what are they witnessing to, with signatures, on papers to be registered with the state? They are witnesses to the vows between a man and a woman. In a conjugal marriage, the bride and groom promise fidelity for life. They promise to honor, love, and give themselves to one another with their bodies, hearts, and minds. They consummate the marriage, an act of interest to the state, *because it is a generative act, a life-giving act,* and may produce children. Conjugal marriage between one man and one woman provides the best possible setting for the raising of children, the nation's next generation. Statistics prove this."

A scream erupted from the back of the room and Zachary turned to see several young men shouting obscenities and making rude gestures. A police officer restrained them, and Dr. Jacobs addressed the hecklers. "There will be a time for comments and questions later, thank you."

They pulled away from the officer, and Zachary could see there was one leader and two followers. The leader headed up the aisle toward the speaker, raising his fist. Zachary was ready to tackle him, but the officer subdued the man and led him from the room. His two followers took seats in the back.

Dr. Jacobs continued, her tone measured and serious, as though she had been chosen to save society from falling over a precipice. "We must think carefully and prudently before whittling marriage to the bone, before we destroy it with redefinition. To protect children, to produce a responsible and law-abiding generation, marriage *must* be permanent and sexually exclusive. Each person gives all to the other and commits for a lifetime. This is the deal, the *ideal*. And ideals form good society. Ideals should not be based on fashion, feelings, or fads."

Zachary felt Jessica's gaze and his eyes met hers. "I agree," he whispered.

Jessica smiled. "Me too."

Dr. Jacobs' tone had become subdued, as though she were entering an even more sensitive and complex area of thought. "Many say we should not impose our values on one another. They say there should be no taboos. But in the end this is what societies do by definition, one way or another. They foster the good and shame the bad. *And the good and the bad are defined by what protects and furthers the life of the society, the nation.* Taboos will always exist, but taboos are ephemeral. Today the most obvious and powerful taboos are generated by the left and called political correctness. What we need to support as educated voters are taboos that are *good for us as a free nation.*

Zachary was struck by the profundity of Dr. Jacobs' comments.

"Totalitarian states save people from their choices; they stifle creativity and free speech. They control both mind and body. These states are the ultimate taboo enforcers. But as a free people, we must guard against redefinitions of traditional roles that were established for good reason. And marriage is one of them. Conjugal marriage, in the end, is a pillar that supports our free institutions and secures our future as a free people. Marriage is not something to trifle with; we do so at our peril."

Zachary glanced at Jessica. She scribbled on her notepad, then looked up with an intensity that surprised him. He too was struck forcibly by what he had heard. Conjugal marriage was perfect, ideal, transcendent. The great romantic poets wrote about this kind of love, this kind of union, and how every man—and woman—deeply desired such happiness. Dr. Jacobs merely confirmed all that he had read and admired.

The speaker concluded her lecture. A few in the audience had slipped out the back doors, bored or upset, but most had stayed. The attendees remaining applauded enthusiastically. All that the speaker had extolled, Zachary knew, today's culture abhorred. Generations had been raised with opposite beliefs. It was to be expected that not everyone could accept her words.

But Zachary, armed with Shakespeare, John Donne, Browning, and even Vivaldi, Beethoven, and Borodin, knew such ideals kept the fabric of their world from tearing. And Zachary feared the fabric was doing just that. He could see the rips, the unraveling of the weave of history and culture. Where was beauty in this, where was truth, where was goodness? Something was terribly wrong. And Dr. Jacobs was absolutely, courageously, right.

Jessica laid her hand on his shoulder. "What do you think?" she whispered.

"Thanks for inviting me. This is excellent, absolutely excellent."

Jessica grinned. "Good. They'll have a break, then small groups, and Q & A. But I need to get to Comerford House for the tour."

"And I need to work a few hours at Laurie's."

Twenty-Five
The Sacristy

When Zachary realized that Jessica had driven to St. Joseph's and walked to Ohlone Park just to walk back with him, he was sure he'd made a great leap forward in their romance, that she would care enough, or simply enjoy his company enough, to do such a thing. After the lecture, he gladly accepted a ride to Laurie's.

As they drove up Dwight Way, passing People's Park, Jessica slowed down and gazed at the food truck distributing meals to the homeless. "The murderer may have come from there. He may still be there. It's been eighteen days since I found the body and at times it feels like yesterday."

Zachary hesitated, not sure what to say that would be helpful. "Don't forget Laurie offered you a room if you like."

Jessica narrowed her eyes thoughtfully and tilted her head, glancing at him. "That's nice of her, but I'm okay. Detective Gan has been watching out for me, and Shelley is due home soon. I need to work on my dissertation in familiar surroundings."

"Let me know if you change your mind?"

Jessica idled the car in front of the bookstore. "I will, and . . . thanks, Zachary."

"My pleasure, Miss Jessica," he said, getting out and waving from the curb. He watched her wave back, then drive into the distance.

* * *

Zachary entered the shop, greeted by the jangle of bells.

"Good morning, Zachary." Laurie beamed her bright smile, but her eyes showed concern. "How are you? How's Jessica? Any news?"

"The police haven't found the suspect, but there've been sightings. They think the murder was random, that the murderer was waiting on the trail for a girl coming by alone."

Laurie shook her head, her face full of sadness. She stared out the window, seeming to forget Zachary.

"What should I work on first, Laurie?" He didn't like to see her sad. It wasn't like her.

"I'm sorry, Zachary. Violence like this reminds me of earlier days, earlier friends. The present is a better place to be. If you could finish shelving books in History, then work on the cards again, that would be helpful."

Zachary headed toward Literature.

"Other way, Zachary," Laurie said, pointing.

"I know, but I want to find that copy of Elizabeth Barrett Browning's *Sonnets from the Portuguese* if it's still there and we didn't price it too high . . . for a friend."

Laurie laughed and clapped her hands with delight. "If we don't have it, I'll find one, and we can negotiate something, I'm sure."

He was glad to have made Laurie laugh and turned toward History to begin shelving.

A little before three, he said goodbye to Laurie, shouldered his pack, and began his walk up the hill toward Comerford House. He hoped to arrive in time to see Jessica finish her tour. He didn't think that at this stage in their friendship she would mind.

* * *

Zachary could hear Jessica in Comerford's kitchen, ending the tour and explaining about the shop, the chapel, and the upstairs rooms. As the visitors dispersed, she saw him standing in the doorway.

"How long have you been there?" she asked suspiciously, but sounded pleased as well.

202

"Just arrived. Thought I might practice the piano a bit and maybe help you out . . . if you needed any help, that is."

She joined him in the foyer, pausing at the foot of the stairs. "Thanks. Actually I could use some help."

He followed her up the stairs, sliding his hand along the smooth bannister. "You're working on Beatrice's letters?" The Beethoven piece could wait.

She nodded. "I'm scanning them into the computer, to save for reference. I already did the floor plans and maps. Your mother and Father Nate set it up for me in the attic."

"You could include the letters in your dissertation."

"I was thinking about that."

"They would be a good addition." This was a promising development. Working together. Side by side. An excellent turn of events, Zachary thought, as she climbed ahead of him, in her charcoal slacks and gray jacket, her pleated white blouse, her pink scarf, her hair pulled into its French braid so naturally.

Jessica took a seat at a massive oak desk and turned on a computer. A stack of yellowing sheets with delicate cursive lettering lay next to a printer-scanner. Zachary slipped on the rubber gloves Jessica handed him, then laid the letters, one by one, on the screen and gently closed the lid. She ran the scanner program on the computer, saving each document, and reset for the next one. They developed a routine, and Zachary looked from time to time through the western window out to the city and the bay, over the pines and eucalyptus, out and over Berkeley. The mist swirled and lifted, as the sun emerged and submerged. He placed another letter on the screen and closed the heavy lid. As they worked, they chatted.

"So, Zachary, what do you think you'll do with your degree? Teach?"

"Probably. But I can do steamfitting, if I have to." He grinned. "Although I'd rather teach."

"I'd like to teach. The more I study history the more I see its importance to an undergraduate degree."

"How so?" Zachary had taken history courses, but he didn't recall any that were required, just subjects chosen from a substantial catalogue.

Jessica grew thoughtful, seeming to consider the best answer. "It helps answer the important question, 'What is the good life?' And now the question isn't even asked. They've dropped Western Civilization requirements, core classes in the Humanities, in most universities."

"Cal doesn't require Western Civ, as I recall."

"My advisor," Jessica said, as she reset the scanner program, "says the Western Civ core curriculum—the one he was required to take in the sixties—was called a *liberal* education, but liberal means something else, nearly the opposite, today. He said a liberal education back then taught him how to think critically, communicate clearly, debate opposite points of view, and solve complex problems."

"I can see that. English would be part of that too." Zachary reached for another letter, placing it carefully on the screen. "How to write and speak teaches one how to think logically. And we learn by reading other writers, good ones."

"History, especially our own cultural history, teaches us where we have gone wrong, so we won't repeat mistakes," Jessica said thoughtfully, "and where we have gone right, so we can repeat our successes." She laughed. "I sound like an advertisement."

The light in the room had lessened, and through the small window Zachary could see the sun disappear behind the fogbank. "But it's true what you say. Even if students don't major in these things, say they go into engineering, a top field now, it would seem that they should still take Western Civ as part of their college education." A damp breeze slipped in through the western window, swirled about them, and sailed out the eastern window up and into the hills.

Jessica paused, examining one of the letters. "Look at this drawing. Curious. What do you think?"

He held it up to the light. "It's a rough sketch of an early floor plan."

"Beatrice is writing to one of the sisters, saying she has saved her legacy in a vault in the sacristy. This is a drawing of the old sacristy."

"I didn't know there was a sacristy, old or new." He studied it closely. "It's carved out of the hillside, slightly north of the chapel."

"What happened to it?"

"It must have been buried over the years by earth movement—earthquakes, slides." He considered the drawing for a moment. "My mother said that Father Nate found a key behind the altar. Do you think that back wall might show us something?"

"Let's look."

Zachary checked the time. "Evensong starts in an hour. We might have time before the singers arrive."

They closed down the computer and scanner. They locked the windows and put away the archived letters in their protective wrap, setting them gently in a drawer of an antique armoire. Zachary picked up a flashlight in the kitchen, and they crossed the lawn to the chapel.

* * *

The evening sun shone from the west, lighting up the chapel door and the stained glass window above. Zachary followed Jessica inside. They walked up the central aisle to the altar. Light filtered through the stained glass, flickering red and green and gold on the altar's white linen.

"Where did Father Nate find the key?" Jessica asked.

"Mom said in the wall behind the altar in a crevice formed by the Napa earthquake."

Jessica tilted her head and squinted. "If the room slid sideways and downward when the earth caved in, the entrance might have lined up with this back wall, so that the sacristy shifted to a place behind and below the chapel."

"Let me take a look." Zachary parted the altar's linen panels. He crawled inside. He explored the back wall and soon found a deep crevice. With gentle pressure a portion of the wall fell away from him.

He could hear Jessica behind him. "Can you see anything?"

He peered through the opening. "A room of some sort. Could be the sacristy. Come see."

Zachary crawled through and then helped Jessica.

The space was partially caved in, the hillside claiming it with fresh soil and debris from the recent earthquake, Zachary guessed.

"Nothing here," Zachary said. "The former owners must have cleared anything belonging to the sacristy."

Jessica examined the earth and stone walls. "You're right. Whatever was here is gone. I wonder where the legacy mentioned in the letter was kept."

"Nothing here now. But we need to tell Father Nate about this."

"Wait, what's that there? Looks like a niche of some kind."

Zachary shone his light on the space. There appeared to be a metal box in the niche, a foot square. Jessica worked the lid open. She slipped her hand inside and pulled out a dark velvet pouch. She glanced at Zachary, her eyes wide. "Should we open it?"

Zachary nodded. Time stopped as they stared at the bag, lit by the beam from his flashlight.

As Jessica worked her fingers into the drawstring, loosening it, the velvet partially disintegrated, falling to the floor. The rest remained in her palm and she raised her hand to Zachary, toward the beam of light.

"Coins of some kind," Zachary said.

"Maybe old Irish coins?"

They heard voices above, probably from the upper parking lot. "The singers," Zachary said.

Jessica slipped the bag of coins into her pocket. Zachary helped her through the opening and they emerged from under the altar. By the time the Comerford Singers arrived, Zachary and Jessica were gone and, Zachary hoped, the altar appeared untouched.

They met Father Nate on the porch as he reached for the bell rope and told him about the sacristy. They showed him the bits of the velvet purse and the coins.

"Really?" He stared at the coins in Jessica's palm. He rubbed his chin, then clasped his hands as though in prayer. "Amazing. These might be valuable. Shall I take them to a safe place? After I ring the bell?"

"Please do," Jessica said, giving the treasure to the priest.

"God worked through you, my dear. This is a miracle you can tell to your children." He slipped the coins into his shirt pocket as the last of the pouch fell through his fingers. "I wonder what this means for Comerford. I'll call the Foundation Chairman tomorrow. We need an evaluation. The past may save the present after all." He chuckled and glanced up to the heavens.

The organ prelude had begun, and the notes slipped out the door as the priest pulled the rope and the bell chimed over the city of Berkeley. The singers were gathering for the procession.

"Coming to Evensong?" Zachary asked Jessica.

She tilted her head. "Seems appropriate."

"I think so too." As they stepped inside, he asked, "Want to walk the trail again sometime?"

"Thought you'd never ask," Jessica replied, laughing as they took seats in a pew.

Twenty-Six
Truth

Three weeks after the murder, Father Nate Casparian led his small congregation on his monthly prayer walk through Berkeley. Like the robe he wore, he had donned this discipline to pray for the community of Berkeley on the last Wednesday of each month, following Evening Prayer.

He handed a satchel of prayer cards and flyers to an assistant to distribute, then set out in his thick-soled walkers. Another student carried a bag of paper lanterns. A third student handed him a long pole bearing a white banner, then rang the chapel bell, sending seven mournful notes through the mist hovering over Berkeley. The ringing faded as it reached the bay, silenced long before reaching San Francisco. The sun was nearing the horizon, weakly piercing the fog, but would not fully set for another hour.

Father Nate hoisted his banner high, the pole resting on his hip. Large black letters announced:

BERKELEY PRAYER WALK
Join us in prayer
for Berkeley,
for peace,
for redemption,
for love.

Armed with his prayers, his love, his ministering angels, and the fierce breath of the Holy Spirit blowing him forward, he descended the stairs to Warring Avenue, leading his people toward Bancroft, the southern border of campus. About thirty of his congregation followed, students he knew and students he didn't know, and they added their voices to the prayers and the singing: *Our Father who art in heaven, hallowed be thy name . . .*

As Father Nate prayed his own silent prayers behind the public verbal prayer, or perhaps deeply within it, he observed people along the way. He saw faces of suffering and desire, of fear and determination, of deep anxiety and inner pain, and he offered them up to the Lord's mercy and love. He saw folks most likely homeless and hungry, and he offered them up to the Lord's mercy and love. He wasn't sure if they appreciated the simple offering-up to the Lord, so he handed them dollar bills, or coupons to the local hostel and soup kitchen, or invitations to Comerford Chapel.

At Sproul Plaza, home to the sixties' Free Speech protests, he entered the campus, soon stepping past the campanile as bells rang six-thirty. More students joined him, some for the entertainment and attention, saying a few prayers, then disappearing when bored. A few bystanders laughed and pointed fingers and hecklers hurled abuse.

Father Nate raised his hood, covering his scarred face as best he could, and the black-robed figure carrying the pole with the white banner might have reminded some of the Grim Reaper or Father Time, but this did not bother the old priest. As dusk began to fall the acolytes lit their candles, watching for others who might take part. They prayed the Our Father, the Glory Be, and the Hail Mary, and more souls took part, received their cards and candles, and the singing pulled them up the path toward Strawberry Creek, into the heart of the university. They held their flames high as they sang, lighting up the encroaching dark.

Father Nate led his people past libraries and theaters, laboratories and lecture halls, skirting the fabled Faculty Club sleeping in the shadows, passing the esteemed spaces of scholarship, debate, and learning. These classrooms, he knew, nurtured America's future, the next generation, and he prayed that God would reveal himself to each student and protect them from all evil. He prayed for the faculty, today's and tomorrow's, for Jessica and for Zachary, and Anna as well, that they acquire and teach discernment, recognize truth and lies, and have a vision of God. He prayed for Nicholas, who had valiantly fought the good fight here on this campus.

They crossed Strawberry Creek and, as Moses parted the Red Sea, Father Nate parted a crowd of gaping students who lined the path, enjoying the different drama, wishing to take part, but not knowing why. Some had seen the old priest and his group before, one of many Berkeley theatricals. This haunting medieval procession was simply one more.

As he padded along in his thick-soled trainers, and as his assistants passed out candles and cards, leading the songs and prayers, Father Nate prayed for his community. He prayed for love, that each student, in his or her course of study would learn how to love, would learn love's true definition, one accepted throughout time. Loving, he knew, was not looking out for oneself, but looking out for the other. Loving, he knew, required judgment, suffering, and sacrifice. The priest prayed for true love for these students, that they would find the genuine goodness, wholeness, and happiness of God's love. For this was love in truth; this was Almighty God's plan for us, how we were meant to love and be loved. This was how Almighty God loved us. This was the beatific vision, the vision of God and man, for Father Nate knew St. Maximus was right when he said that virtue comes from union with God and not the other way around. Goodness was the fruit of such union, the inevitable and intrinsic, the natural result.

Father Nate prayed that each student would recognize the truth of God. He prayed that good would win over evil in their hearts, that light would shine in the dark corners. For Father Nate, being unfashionable, unfamiliar with politically correct opinion, believed in good and evil. He had known evil in the stories his father and grandfather had told of Armenia. Knowledge of evil had led his brother to study history, to illuminate and explain the past, to understand how any society could allow such darkness to breed in the guise of goodness. For evil always named itself good. It hid in the shadows, away from the light that would reveal its true name and nature.

And then, decades after the Armenian genocide, the cancer of Hitler's racism nearly devoured Germany. There, too, evil hid behind words and slogans and lies, slaughtering its own people. And today, evil hid within Islam, bleeding into civilized worlds in the name of Allah, the God of Abraham. More lies, Father Nate thought, more deceit. And the young became the victims, their earnest and open hearts searching for God in a secularized, unbelieving world. They did not understand who they were following, his real name; they became the sacrifice as they sacrificed innocents to the lord of darkness. Their hearts were empty, and their hearts needed filling.

So Father Nate prayed that the one true God of Abraham and Sarah, Isaac and Rebecca, and yes, Ishmael and Hagar, would fill their hearts with himself, with his glory, with his true light and his true plan for them. He prayed that God would lead them out of themselves, that he would lead them to love others, to care for others, to build, not destroy.

For, Father Nate knew, this God of Abraham had built the West, had inspired the art and architecture and literature of millennia, had led mankind toward life, liberty, and the pursuit of happiness. This was the God of beauty, truth, and love. So many lived in a desert, and Father Nate prayed that they would find the oasis promised by his God of love and would no longer thirst. They simply needed to ask the way, to look to his son, to light and life, to union with God the Father.

The banner weighed heavily, and the priest's arms cramped in pain. He shifted the weight by laying the pole on his shoulder, and an observer later commented he brought to mind a medieval mendicant carrying a cross.

More comfortable now, Father Nate prayed to his God, the Creator of the World, the God who became man and walked among his creation. As the priest prayed, he saw once again the truth hidden by modernity's lies, that if you don't practice self-discipline, you will be disciplined by others. He saw that if you don't protect freedom, you will cease to be free. Nathaniel Casparian understood in a lucid flash that if you do not grow in love toward the light, you will grow in hate toward the dark, that if you do not embrace life, you will embrace death, and rot will consume you. There was no middle ground, no compromise, no being lukewarm.

Nathaniel Casparian could see it all, could feel truth's texture, see its colors, hear its music, as he plodded along the cement sidewalk, carrying his banner, like Aaron with Moses' staff, weighing heavier with each step. But as he stepped, he didn't see a deep crack in the pavement. He tripped. He fell to the ground, the banner with him.

Younger hands grasped him gently, slowly righting him. Younger hands held the banner high and led the way. The priest was grateful, and in his thanksgiving and love, he wept, the tears streaming down his scarred cheeks and falling onto his robe. Now he paid more attention to his stepping, and in the twilight, he followed the white banner, leaning on his young friends, leading his procession up Hearst to Gayley, and up the stairs toward Comerford House and the stone chapel.

Soon the chapel was lit by a myriad of paper lanterns held high. Father Nate intoned a blessing and a closing prayer, and his flock dispersed, peacefully and silently into the dark, down the hill to their homes.

* * *

Jellylorum the tabby and Quaxo the black shorthair met the priest on the porch of the cottage and bounded inside when he entered. He was relieved to see Anna in the kitchen, heating soup. "You waited. How kind," he said. Anna had become like a daughter, an adult child given to him in his old age.

Her face was open and honest. "Of course, dear friend. I'm making sure you get your supper. I fed the cats, but these two have been scratching to get in and I don't know why. I heard about the fall you took. Are you okay?"

He nodded, and observed the cats who now rubbed his legs, whimpering. "Hey, what's up? It's okay, I'm home now. Let's sit for a bit."

Suddenly deeply tired, he collapsed in his easy chair, the cats at his feet. The parlor was small, more of an alcove adjacent to the kitchen, but it was cozy and he had always thought of it as his retreat from the world. In a way the chapel was that too, but here, in the domestic warmth of the cottage, it was a different kind of retreat, made for mortals, not immortals. That wasn't to say that God wasn't here—sometimes Father Nate was certain that the Almighty was nearby as he fed the cats, or even in his morning prayers as he boiled water for tea—but the chapel was more heavenly directed, and the cottage was, well, more earthy, with the occasional angel flitting over the sink rather than in full chorus over the altar.

Anna brought him his bowl of steaming soup and a saucer of toast, and joined him with a similar tray on the couch opposite. She had lit the fire, a sweet touch since he didn't always remember how comforting it was to have a fire burning in the grate and didn't take the time. After grace they spooned the carrots and rigatoni and beans that swirled in the clear aromatic broth.

Anna handed him a tub of grated parmesan and a paper napkin, set down her bowl, and sighed. "So, Father, why go on these perilous walks at your age?"

"It's what I do."

"It's what you do, but—"

"I know, I took a spill. It happens. We fall, we get up, we go on. It's life."

Anna smiled a smile that held all of her mothering years, and Father Nate watched her expression with interest. He could see that the words had brought back Zachary's childhood, or perhaps her own, and maybe even her teaching the children in the preschool. The words had pulled from her history a key pillar, foundational to growing up: facing failure and moving on. Was this taught today?

He wasn't so sure. Was this a part of conserving and cultivating the good of the past? It should be.

"Yes," she said tenderly, "we get up and go on. It's how I was raised. It's how I raised Zachary. No self-pity. No excuses. No wallowing." She looked at him knowingly, perhaps accusingly, and added, "No false martyrdoms."

Father Nate tapped his nose. "A key Christian concept. A key Judaic concept. A key component of the idea of progress that we try to improve the lot of the community, the state, the nation. We move forward. We work to improve ourselves. 'Be ye perfect,' our Lord said. And he explained the commandments given to Moses. He gave us the Beatitudes." The priest grew quiet.

"And he didn't run away from suffering," Anna said.

Father Nate nodded. "He didn't invite suffering, but he didn't run away. But you were thinking of something else."

"It troubles me," Anna said, "that drugs are given to children today to treat sadness. Children aren't always encouraged to pick themselves up after they fall, to carry on as you say."

"These drugs are treating legitimate disorders, right?" Father Nate read the papers, listened to the news. But he deferred to Anna on this one. She had more experience with children and education.

"But many are drugged way too quickly. I was suspicious this was happening. A friend refused to give drugs to her son, although the school recommended them. She called it the pathologization of life, medicating our feelings. There are studies showing that many children grow up not knowing how to deal with negative emotions. They feel sad and they need to feel happy. They fail or don't do well on an exam, and they need to boost their self-esteem. So they take a pill."

"Really?" The priest leaned forward. He had not heard of this, and it explained a good deal about teens and young adults he had known in the last few decades. Quick to take offense. Quick to make demands through protests and sit-ins. Quick to drop out of even trying, because trying meant possible failure, and failure wasn't an option. "I know what you mean, now that I think about it. The Church provides ways to deal with human emotions, ways to face the human condition, ways to understand who we are and are meant to be, ways to face failure. Probably the most valuable teaching is the virtue of humility and danger of pride, as was taught by cultures going back to Greece, back to Abraham."

"But many have lapsed away from faith and the Church. What's to be done?"

"I'm not sure, Anna, not sure at all. All I know is that goodness comes from God." He considered her words as he finished his soup. It was as Anna carried the bowls into the kitchen that Father Nate added, "You know, my dear, to my knowledge moral life comes from religion. When we lose religion in the public square—or the university quad as it were—we lose our moral compass."

"So you carry your banner through campus, keeping religion in the public square, the university quad."

"I try." Father Nate followed with the trays, set them on the counter by the sink, and turned on the faucet. He squirted liquid soap into the hot water and dropped the bowls into the rising suds. "We can only do what God tells us. The rest is up to him . . . with the aid of our prayers."

"He seems to be helping us out with recent events," Anna said. "The old sacristy, the coins. Who would have guessed?"

The priest raised his brows and chuckled. "Who would have guessed indeed? Miracles are everywhere and all around us. The coins will take time to evaluate, and an archaeological team from the university is coming in to prop up the back walls. Comerford might be saved after all."

The cats were whimpering again and running from the door to Father Nate and back. "What's wrong, my dears?" Father Nate asked.

"They want to go out." Anna opened the door, but Quaxo and Jellylorum stayed in the doorway, looking at Anna, then at Father Nate. "Something's not right. Let's see if they'll show us."

Nate shook his head. "It's unlike them to be afraid like this. The others, but not these two." With mounting concern, he grabbed the baseball bat he kept in the closet.

"I'll go with you," Anna said.

"You stay here." With those words, Father Nate stepped onto the path, following the cats toward the chapel.

Twenty-Seven
The Fire Trail

About the time that Father Nate was saying Evening Prayer, Jessica was lacing her shoes, preparing to meet Zachary at the trailhead at six, to catch the sunset at seven from one of the panoramic lookouts.

She was exuberant and wanted to share her exuberance with her new friend. She had emerged from her advisor meeting earlier that day with a clear approval of her work and a pathway to the completion of her dissertation. The scanned letters of Beatrice, unpublished primary documents, weighed heavily in her favor. Dr. Barnes was also interested in the discovery of the old sacristy and the coins, saying she should document the find in her paper. She would be seeing Zachary soon, so everything was lining up perfectly. How good it was to have a friend like Zachary with whom she could share such good news.

Jessica had spent the better part of Monday, Tuesday, and Wednesday immersed in her manuscript, working the correspondence into her document to support her thesis. As she detailed the relationships between Beatrice and the Presentation Sisters who had been her teachers, between Beatrice and the clergy who had become a part of her family, she had turned off her phone and had taken breaks only to eat and sleep.

She stepped out the door, locking it behind her, and checked her voicemail. It was Zachary: "Listen, Jessica, I'm really sorry. I can't make our walk today. Hope you get this message in time. Ms. Sarton—that girl—is at the Student Health Clinic. She was assaulted at a frat party last night. She's asking for me, so I need to check on her." There was a pause and she could feel his anguish. "Oh, please understand! I'll call soon and let you know what's happening. We can reschedule."

Jessica considered what to do. She was disappointed, but she would see Zachary soon enough. Should she feel angry about Ellie

Sarton? She thought not. She trusted Zachary. Should she go on the walk anyway? Did she feel strong enough? Of course she did. There had been no recent sightings of the murderer, no evidence of his returning to the grounds of Comerford House.

A nagging fear remained in the back of her mind, but she ignored it. Her shoes were laced, her phone and pepper spray in her pocket. Officer Gan's number was in her phone. Her bag was packed with water, walnuts, and her mini-flashlight, but she would be safely back before dark. She was ready, and while the vague anxiety would not leave, she chose to listen to the voice of her world, that she could ignore such warnings, that she could be strong and independent, a true modern woman. She phoned Zachary and got voicemail.

"Hi, Zachary—Just wanted you to know I'm going on the walk myself. It's okay. It'll be good for me. I'll call when I get back. No worries."

Armed with her residual elation and the firm belief that her life was moving in a new and successful direction, she headed to her car. Soon she maneuvered into a parking space at the trailhead. She checked her phone one more time, and seeing that the battery was low, turned it off and slipped it in her pack. She could turn it on later if needed.

The Fire Trail beckoned her, leading peacefully into the forest. She locked the car and slipped her pack over her shoulder. She could do this. She needed to do this. Even without Zachary . . . especially without Zachary. She would climb above the fog and see the sun drop between San Francisco's towers, *on her own.*

* * *

Jessica followed the soft dirt path into the forest of straight pines. The evening light shafted through the trees at a low angle, and soon the shadows deepened. She walked with a purpose and yet with a relaxed stride, as though the walking itself would unravel the many thoughts running through her head.

While not seeing herself as religious, she was impressed by the fortitude and goodness of the Presentation Sisters. Their faithful care and devotion to the children of Berkeley—including Beatrice McKinnon—were exemplary, self-sacrificing. Would her own life have been different, would the twins' lives have been different, if they had attended parochial schools? She envied Beatrice, her education and her role models, not only in her mother but in the sisters who taught her. She admired their lives of integrity which, she intuited, came from their faith and their Church.

Jessica's childhood had been a chaotic one, in spite of her parents' loving marriage. Their love probably was the one lodestar in Jessica's life, and now as she traipsed the path between giant eucalyptus trees she considered the power of committed love. Did she want to experience such a love? Was it too risky? Her mother had been hurt by such love. So had Anna.

As her shoes padded the damp trail, she thought how she had loved Ashley and Samantha, but they had abandoned her. Even her mother had allowed her grief to overshadow her, so that she could only move within that somber sphere, rarely listening to the outside world, rarely focusing on her youngest daughter. In a way, Jessica felt abandoned by her mother as well.

Jessica could see how Anna had grown dear. It was as though unseen angels ministered to her at this time in her life. Did angels even exist? Many traditions included angels in their histories. This was a kind of evidence, wasn't it?

Jessica arrived at the first vista point. San Francisco was buried in the fog, but the sun burned behind the bank, emanating a silvery mist. She was high above, watching over it, as though she could reign for a time and control the fate of her world. The great Pacific Ocean spread west from the other side of San Francisco, rolling on to Hawaii and Australia and Asia. She stood on the edge of her hemisphere, on the borders of her world. She would carry this moment in her heart; she, like the Amazons of old, would protect her culture from harm, she would choose the good and reject the bad. She would teach the next generation to do the same, through the study of history.

Jessica sipped from her water bottle and returned to the trail. She had a ways to go, with one more panorama point. She would come home refreshed, ready to work. As the trail widened between the trees, her thoughts returned to Zachary. He had become a friend, possibly too quickly. Did they have a future? What kind of a future would it be?

She found him attractive and had begun to trust him. Was it true, as Dr. Jacobs said in the lecture, that college was the best time to find a soul mate? Did she want a soul mate? Did she want a husband? Did she want children? The Fidelity Society had planted these questions in her mind. She guessed that in other times and other families, parents planted these questions or the culture planted these questions, but Jessica, now twenty-two, had never considered them. Her life had been about what she was not, and where she didn't want to go. It was about not becoming what she feared, the body at the bottom of a pool, the addict in rehab, the mother of aborted babies.

She was not going to be like the twins; she needed financial security; she needed safety. She could not afford to waste a moment of her days and weeks and years. But in all of this ruthless goal-setting, she had not considered a husband and children. Fidelity had planted pleasant seeds. *Marriage. Family.* In many ways marriage and family sounded far more secure than anything else, but was this merely an illusion, simply illogical? Marriage and children were attractive: to love and be loved, to share your life with another, as her mother had done; to raise children sensibly, understanding the perils of modernity, choosing the good and rejecting the bad, as she would try to do.

222

Zachary. He stirred something within her. Was it love? She loved his ingenuousness, his honesty, his delight in beauty, poetry, music. But was he a useless poet? He worked hard, had his feet planted firmly on the ground. He worried about money just as she did, had no college loans. She could see where their friendship might lead, and if nothing else, she could say that Zachary had opened her heart to the possibility of such a future, one with marriage and family. For that she was grateful.

She reached the last vista point where she rested, sipping her water and munching a few nuts. She inhaled the fresh air and looked out to the submerged, unseen bay. The sun was setting, light had lessened, and the last rays rimmed the dark fogbank with fire. Dense mist swirled between the hills. Jessica shivered. She decided she had better get back before dark set in.

* * *

He stood where he had stood before, as though waiting for her, hitching his pants and staring with the same glassy eyes. She braced herself, reached for her pepper spray, and tried to slip by. He grabbed her arm and waved a knife, slashing through her sleeve.

Her hand was on the spray and, in spite of the pain and the blood seeping through her shirt, she held the spray high and pushed the nozzle. It missed direct contact with his face but surprised him and he paused, startled. She tried again, and the spray found his eyes.

Howling, he released her, dropped the knife, and covered his face. She ran downhill toward the parking lot, clutching her arm. She could hear him behind her. She made it to her car, but her fingers shook and she fumbled with her keys. As he closed in, she darted into the forest to the Fire Trail loop running above Comerford House. He followed, screaming and cursing.

In the growing dark she tripped on a root and caught herself, scratched by brambles. She ran, ignoring her bleeding arm, dodging boulders and branches, pausing only to hear the thrashing footsteps behind her.

She saw a light. The chapel. Was it open? Could she hide there? She descended the stone steps. The lamp glimmered over the door. It was unlocked and she entered the dim space, ran up the central aisle to a pew near the altar, crouched low, scared to breathe. Her pack was gone, along with her phone. She must have dropped it on the trail.

It was not long before he entered.

He stood in the doorway and grunted. Squinting from the spray, his eyes searched the interior, and in the dim light Jessica could see his glistening black hair and ghostly face. He held his knife like an old warrior seeking battle.

Jessica knew she was only partially hidden. She waited for his next move. She glanced around the chapel, up to the loft. Could she hide there? How? Where were the stairs? Then she saw him climb to the loft, finding passage through a side door. She knew he would soon spot her. She turned to the altar and crawled under the linen drapings. Peeking through the panels, she saw him peer over the loft railing, his hand raising the knife as if to curse God.

"You can't get away," he screamed. "God can't help you."

Her arm throbbed and, faint and woozy, she twisted her bloody sleeve around the wound, applying pressure. She crouched in the narrow space, turning toward the opening in the back wall. She had no light and the cavern, the old sacristy, was dark. She hesitated.

The man stumbled wildly down the loft stairs, shouting, and Jessica thought he must have been high on drink or drugs. Then she recognized Father Nate's voice, "What's going on here?" She heard cats squeal and hiss, then the crazed man curse again.

The priest cried out in shock and pain.

Jessica peered through the drapings. Father Nate lay in the doorway, holding his side. The man turned toward her, his eyes bright. Slowly, with horrifying deliberation, he stepped up the central aisle toward the altar.

Jessica worked her way through the opening in the back wall, legs first, sliding forward slowly on her back, landing on the cavern floor. Something crumbled behind her, dusting her with soil and pebbles, and she feared that the opening had closed, or worse, an avalanche had been triggered. She stared into the dark, trembling and holding her bleeding arm, afraid to move, listening for any sound.

Twenty-Eight
Rescue

Watching Father Nate hurry after the cats, Anna decided this was one time she should ignore his advice. She grabbed a carving knife from the kitchen and found a flashlight in a drawer. She took a deep breath, made sure her phone was on and ready, and said a quick prayer to the God she wasn't sure existed.

She followed Father Nate along the path to the chapel, keeping her distance in the shadows. She wouldn't use the flashlight unless absolutely necessary, for while it was dark, residual light came from the cottage behind and the chapel ahead. For the time being, darkness was her ally. But what could all the fracas be about? And what happened to the cats?

She saw Father Nate enter the chapel and heard his cry as he fell. The cats screeched and a tall form of a man appeared in the doorway. He cursed, his hand on his cheek as though scratched. She was ready to defend the fallen Father Nate and bind wounds with whatever she could find or help him back to the cottage out of harm's way, when she saw the man turn and walk into the chapel. She wondered what he was doing there. Probably stealing the candlesticks. They shouldn't leave candlesticks out like that. Or could he be the Fire Trail suspect? The one who had camped up the hill. She pulled her wits about her.

Anna tapped 911. "Comerford House," she gasped, "the chapel. Crazy man. Father Nate hurt. Oh, please come!"

Anna knew she needed time, time to stall this madman until the police arrived. She crept up the steps to the porch where the baseball bat had dropped, then crouched next to Father Nate.

"Get away," he whispered. "Run!"

"Let me help you get up." She set down the flashlight and knife and slipped an arm around his hefty form. "Can you walk?"

"Anna, go!"

"Not without you."

"I'm too heavy."

"You have to help me. You can do it. One, two, three . . ." He heaved himself upward and she pulled him to a standing position. They stumbled into the dark cover of the forest. She looked back. The crazed man had returned to the chapel porch, silent now, staring with his glassy eyes. The cats had bounded up the path toward the cottage.

Anna helped Father Nate toward the bushes and into a shallow ravine. Under cover of leafy branches, they huddled, and she tried to pray, simple prayers, asking for help. The priest's blood had oozed through his shirt and onto hers. She took off her cardigan and tried to stanch the wound, which was, she feared, near his ribs, close to his heart. She peeked through the branches. The man had left the chapel and was thrashing through the woods, whacking the brush with the baseball bat and waving Anna's carving knife.

A searchlight shone from the upper lot, and Anna heard footsteps. Father Nate was too weak to move now. He was bleeding a lot, and Anna feared for him. He was not young; his heart could not bear this.

The thrashing stopped and Anna waited, listening, watching the searchlight roam. Finally she heard footsteps and two officers emerged through the dark, heading for the chapel.

"Over here," she said hoarsely. "And be quick." She waited for the baseball bat to crash down upon them but instead saw the welcome sight of uniforms. "He's lost a lot of blood. Help us!"

Twenty-Nine
Lost

"She's in here," the aide said.

Zachary entered a room partitioned by floor-length curtains. A nurse was taking her patient's temperature and writing on a clipboard.

Ellie Sarton lay on a hospital bed, her head slightly raised. Her face was pale and swollen, one eye black-and-blue, her cheek bandaged. "Thanks for coming," she said weakly.

"Are you all right, Ms. Sarton?"

"I guess not."

The nurse turned to him and said, "She'll be all right. It takes time. They roughed her up a little, poor thing."

Zachary sat on a nearby chair and leaned forward, feeling compassion for the young woman who had threatened him. "Do you want to tell me about it?"

"I passed out at a fraternity party and woke up here. I don't remember, but they say I was . . . raped. I have no family, no one to call, so I asked them to call you. It was good of you to come, Mr. Aguilar."

"You sound different." Was this the same Ellie Sarton?

"I wanted to tell you that I'm sorry, say it to your face."

Zachary believed her. He nodded, waiting. "Thank you." The words were barely formed, barely uttered.

She tried to push herself up on her elbows. "I've caused a lot of trouble for you over the last year, and I'm really sorry."

"You certainly have," he said, "but now maybe you can make some changes in your life?"

"I hope so. I'm going back to church."

"Church? Really?"

"Presbyterian. My hometown church. They have one here in Berkeley and they have support groups I can join. The nurse was telling me about them. Sounds nice right now."

"You need friends. That would be good."

"And I'm dropping your class."

"That's for the best."

"Can you forgive me?"

Zachary held her hand, so cold and weak, between his hands. "I forgive you, Ms. Sarton. Now get well."

Ellie managed a thin smile. "Thanks. I'll try."

* * *

Leaving the clinic and pondering these events with both relief and concern, Zachary answered his phone. His mother sounded distraught, panicky, tears choking her words.

"Calm down, Mom. I can't understand you."

"Father Nate was stabbed in the chapel, and they're taking him to Emergency."

"Stabbed? How is he?" Zachary opened his car door and slipped behind the wheel.

"We don't know. He's lost a lot of blood. I'm going with the ambulance."

"Who attacked him?"

"A crazy man, on drugs I think, probably a robber. He got away, but the cats scratched him I'm guessing, at least I sure hope they did. He was heading toward the Fire Trail."

"The Fire Trail?" Zachary checked his watch. Nearly eight-thirty. Even if she hiked the trail, Jessica would be home by now. But his growing unease alarmed him. "Listen, let me know how he is, okay? I've got to touch base with Jessica."

"Isn't she with you? I thought you were going on a walk today."

"Had to cancel. Gotta go, Mom. Need to find her."

"You think he's the man she saw on the trail? The one who killed that poor girl?"

"Could be."

"I'm getting in the ambulance . . . they're ready. Love you, Son."

"Love you too, Mom."

Zachary listened to Jessica's phone message. His heart racing, he called her. It rang and rang and finally went to voicemail. "Jessica, call me. Need to know you're okay. The murder suspect may be near the Fire Trail. Stay in your studio, lock everything. Call me when you get this, okay?"

Should he drive to her house and check? It wasn't far. She should be back by now.

Zachary parked on Arch Street and ran down through the ivy. He pounded on the door. No answer. He peered through the window panel. Darkness.

Where was she? Why didn't she answer her phone? With an increasing, sickening ache in the pit of his stomach, he raced to his car and drove as fast as he dared to Comerford, grateful he had keys to the house and the chapel.

* * *

Zachary parked in the upper lot next to a police car. He grabbed his large flashlight from the trunk and bounded down the path to the chapel. The door was unlocked and he rushed inside.

He shone the beam of light up the central aisle. He gasped. A stream of blood trailed up the aisle to a front pew where a pool formed. Was this Father Nate's blood? Was he standing here by the altar when he was attacked? When he tried to get away, was this his blood in the aisle, as he headed for the front door?

Zachary locked the chapel behind him and checked his phone as he crossed the lawn to the house. He called Jessica and left another message. He unlocked the French doors and entered the deserted kitchen. He stepped into the front foyer.

A police officer appeared. "Who are you? What are you doing here?"

The officer held Jessica's pack.

Zachary reached for it. "That's Jessica's. Where did you find it? Where is she? Is she all right? Tell me, tell me!" He wanted to grab the man and shake the information out of him.

"Calm down, young man. We don't know where Ms. Thierry is. We found this bag in the woods. She's the young lady who reported the Fire Trail murder a few weeks ago. Do you know anything, where she might be?" He rested one hand on his holstered gun. The other hand gripped the pack.

"She's my friend. Where did you find that bag?"

The officer removed his hand from the gun, set the pack between his feet, and took out a pad and pencil. "Who are you again? And what are you doing here?" he asked, his tone less threatening.

His knees weak, Zachary lowered himself to a bench along the wall. He tried to piece together what had happened. "Jessica saw the murderer, and she saw the girl he murdered. But aren't you looking for the man who hurt Father Nate?" He rubbed his temples. "My mother called–"

"Your mother? You must be Zachary Aguilar, then? She mentioned you. Do you have ID?"

"I do." Zachary pulled out his driver's license. "Where did you find that pack?" *Precious minutes were disappearing. Jessica was in danger.*

The officer exhaled deeply, seeming to trust Zachary for the moment. "On the trail."

"The Fire Trail?"

"The stretch above the house."

Where was she? Something must have happened to her that she would lose her pack like that, and was that blood on her bag? Zachary stood.

"Are you looking for her? Why aren't you looking for her? What happened to the attacker?"

"We haven't found him yet. I shouldn't worry at this point. There's probably an explanation for Ms. Thierry's whereabouts. When did you last see her?"

"Sunday."

"Or speak with her?"

"Sunday. I left a voicemail this afternoon to cancel our walk on the Fire Trail. But she went anyway—she left me a message saying she was going alone." *Dear God . . . what was going on?*

"You cancelled? Why?"

"I needed to check on someone at the Student Health Clinic," Zachary replied.

"Perhaps you should come down to the station and answer a few questions while I write up this report."

"But we need to find Jessica!"

"Maybe" the officer began, pausing, "you can come down later. Stay close by, okay? Don't go into the forest, at least not tonight."

"There's blood in the chapel. Did you check it? Is it Father Nate's? It might be the man you're looking for—"

"We took a sample."

Zachary's phone rang. His mother. As he answered, the officer let himself out the front door, giving Zachary a short salute with one hand and holding Jessica's bag with the other.

"They think Father Nate's going to be okay," Anna said, sounding relieved but exhausted. "Can you come get me?"

Thirty
Hope

As Jessica's eyes slowly adjusted to the dark, vague forms of wall and crevice and rock emerged. She recalled a slight opening in the chamber's ceiling, but the sun had gone down and it was dark. She ran her fingers over her throbbing arm, over her shirt caked with blood. She was woozy and cold and thirsty, her throat parched, her lips dry. She tried to swallow. She pulled her jacket around her.

Her breathing grew more and more shallow in the thin air. The cold seeped into her bones. It was unlikely that she would be found. Would she die here? What was it like to die?

Groggy and achingly cold, she shivered, closed her eyes, and drifted into a deep sleep.

* * *

The Lady of the Lantern came to her. Was she in Heaven?

The lady's eyes were large and she was young, younger than Jessica imagined from her photos. She wore the costume of her day, headscarf and cape, long skirt and apron, but Jessica could not identify the colors. She wanted to name them and tried, for they were beautiful, glowing with a rainbow iridescence, like a prism seen in a drop of shimmering water or in a tumbling stream. Jessica decided, in an odd dream-mood of needing to understand her visitor by her clothing, that because all the colors of the spectrum were in the fabric, she could not see any one color. They say that is what light is, she considered, as if she were outside her body watching herself.

"You are not supposed to be here," Nano said, holding her lantern up to Jessica's face. "Who are you? They should not have sent me here without instructions." Her voice lilted, moving in and out of melody.

Jessica stared at the woman, not knowing what to say.

"Can you not speak? Are you not human? You look to be human, a girl maybe, although those clothes . . . one cannot be sure, when a woman dresses as a man."

Gathering her weakening will, Jessica tried to speak, but her mouth couldn't form the words. Somehow Nano knew her intent: "I came through the chapel. I'm hurt. Am I dying? Am I dead? Are you real?"

Nano shook her head at such silliness. "Too many questions for such a young lady. But let me see your arm, my lass . . . yes, it needs dressing. You are hurt, just as you say." She removed her cloak and wrapped it around Jessica. "You are not dying . . . not yet, but maybe soon . . . time is a deceiver, is it not? I thought I had time, but then the time was gone. Poof! Now, let me see, there was another question that you asked of me. Yes, I am real. But not real like you. Real like in Heaven, so actually, more real." She laughed at her own words, tossing her head and rolling her eyes in enviable joy, and her laughter echoed like a harp plucked in the stone chamber.

"But why have you come to me? To take me to Heaven?" Jessica was sure, perfectly sure, that death would be delightful if she had a friend like this to show her the way. "Are we going there? Soon? Can I come with you . . . please?"

"Ah, it is clear to me now, why I am sent. To give you hope. It was my specialty once." She held up her lantern and examined the room. "Yes, Beatrice loved my good Presentation Sisters. Beatrice sent me, it is all coming clear, clear as the day after a storm in my dear Ireland. And Our Lady sent me, too, naturally, since she is in charge of such visits. Beatrice didn't say why, just go. She said she had no time to explain. I laughed because we have lots of time in Heaven. But she meant you and your time, of course, which, you might say, is a wee bit different."

"Can you help me?"

"I can only give you hope, which is a precious and wonderful gift. Listen to me now. Listen carefully. You must wait. You must stay awake. You must believe and you must have faith. It is all true, you know."

"What is all true?" Disappointed she wasn't going to Heaven right away, Jessica was happy to live in the vision of this beautiful lady.

Nano smiled, and an expression passed over her face as if she were listening to someone else. "I must go. You will live, my little one, you will live to tell the story of my Presentation Sisters. Stay awake. Stay faithful. Be a good girl, now." She set the lantern down alongside Jessica.

Jessica felt a slap on her cheek and she awoke, touching the place with her palm. What was that, a dream, a vision, or both? She tried to hold on to the beautiful lady with the lantern, but the vision faded with each minute. All she knew was that someone she loved, and who loved her, ordered her to stay awake. And she left behind her lantern and cape.

Thirty-One
Found

It was nearly eleven that evening when Zachary dropped his mother off at the Elmwood house. He assured her that Father Nate would be all right, for the doctors and nurses had said so and it was true and his wound was cleansed and dressed. The priest was being kept for observation, considering his age and ordeal.

Zachary promised his mother that he would return to Father Nate's cottage, feed the cats, look in on Nicholas, and spend the night there. Brenda would come in the morning at seven.

Zachary moved through those hours, numb. Where was Jessica? She must be in trouble. Dear God, how could he find her? Was it too late? The bloody backpack was not encouraging. The crazed murderer in the woods added to his fears. Everything in him said to search the Fire Trail for any other signs, but in the dark, with the man out there? What could he do? What could he do *now*?

Nicholas was sound asleep when Zachary tiptoed up the stairs and checked on him. Zachary fed the cats and comforted Quaxo and Jellylorum. As he sat in Father Nate's chair and stroked their backs, scratching behind their ears, he imagined they knew the answers to his questions. Their eyes seemed all-knowing, and their heads angled in a perplexing, tantalizing way. "What is it? Can you find her?" he asked.

* * *

Zachary dozed, Jellylorum stretched heavily over his ankles and Quaxo curled on his lap. He woke at first light, his legs numb, his feet cramping from the weight of the tabby. He thought he might have had a strange dream, an encouraging dream, of a woman with a lantern, but he couldn't recall anything else.

But as he made coffee, the evening's events came to him forcibly, and he was relieved to see the confident face of Brenda at the door. He explained Father Nate's ordeal, and she agreed to return at midday to give Nicholas lunch. "You do what you need to do, young man," she said, shaking her finger, with the tone of a woman having raised children, grandchildren, and more.

Zachary headed for the chapel. In the morning light he could see better, before the forensics team arrived. He would be careful not to touch or disturb anything, but in this moment of quiet he wanted to reconstruct the scene. He prayed, if you could call it a prayer, that love would lead him to her. He was certain that the murderer, Father Nate's ordeal, and the chapel itself, all had something to do with Jessica's disappearance.

As Zachary entered the dim space, he contemplated the pews where he, Nicholas, and his mother had so often sung together, where he had known transcendence and beauty, and even a lovely peace, again and again.

Oddly, the pewter candlesticks remained on the altar, unstolen.

He examined the aisle. The bloody stream had dried to a reddish brown. It ran along the smoothly worn stone to the front pew. Was it the priest's blood? Zachary had asked Father Nate at the hospital what had happened, and he had said he was attacked on the porch. He said nothing of walking up the aisle, dripping blood, but rather, that Anna had rescued him on the front steps. He said the man resembled the police sketch, but he couldn't be sure in the dim light.

Whose blood was this?

If it was Jessica's, what did that mean? Did the murderer kidnap her, take her into the forest? Should he search the Fire Trail? But the police had searched already and would again today. Father Nate hadn't mentioned Jessica at all. He hadn't seen her. His mother said that when they were hiding in the bushes, they could hear the man thrashing about with the bat, not something the man would be doing if Jessica had been with him.

Zachary wanted to tear out his hair. He wanted to scream. But instead he would try Pascal's famous wager, to bet on God's existence in spite of his own wavering belief. He knelt in a pew and folded his hands. He bowed his head. "If you exist, God, please help me, please help Jessica, and cure our unbelief." It was the best he could do, and the prayer did, after all, calm his panic, giving him a clearer head.

As his eye refocused on the altar, he had an idea.

Zachary stepped up the aisle and parted the altar hangings. He crawled inside and ran his hands over the back wall. The opening had closed. Had it caved in? He heard a voice behind him. "Wait, Son, what are you doing?" One of the officers.

"In here!" Zachary shouted. "She's in here, I'm sure! Jessica!" he screamed.

The men pulled the altar away from the wall. In the better light, Zachary could see the wall space behind the altar was loosely packed rubble. He began digging with his hands.

An officer grabbed a candlestick and rammed the base into the rock pile, then followed with his heal, again and again. The rocks gave way and they dug out an opening.

Zachary pulled himself through. "Jessica? You in here?"

A rustle, a moan.

The officer shone a light into the dark chamber.

She lay in a rumpled heap, wrapped in a dark cape with a rusty lantern in her lap. She opened her eyes and blinked in the bright light.

"Zachary? I tried to stay awake. I tried. Just like she told me to."

"It's okay. You're going to be all right. You're safe now." Zachary set the lantern aside, lifted her in his arms, and maneuvered her through the opening where officers helped her to the other side.

241

They called an ambulance, checked Jessica's vital signs, and made her as comfortable as possible, wrapped in the cape and leaning against Zachary in a pew. Zachary stared at the altar. He folded his hands, closed his eyes, and murmured, "Thank you."

* * *

"Mom?" Jessica awoke to see her mother sitting in a chair by her hospital bed.

"You're awake! Thank heavens. My poor baby." She reached to stroke Jessica's hand.

Jessica smiled weakly, her mouth still parched. An IV was attached to her wrist.

"I'm sorry, Mom, to trouble you like this." She hated to see her mother so upset. "I'll be okay."

Ashley peered through the doorway. "Can I come in?" She carried a pink azalea plant wrapped in gold foil and set it on a nearby table.

"Ashley? You're here too?"

Her sister moved closer to their mother, and laid her hand on the blanket over Jessica's legs.

Her mother smoothed Jessica's hair away from her eyes and felt her forehead with the back of her palm. It was a gesture Jessica recalled from childhood.

"What day is it? How long have I been sleeping?"

"It's Friday afternoon," her mother said. "I came yesterday as soon as I heard. I've been watching and waiting for you to wake up."

"I must have worried you."

"We both were worried." She glanced at Ashley. "But now so relieved."

"I'm out of rehab, Sis. This time for real."

242

"Good." Jessica had heard this before. "I'm glad."

"She's coming home," their mother added, "to live with me."

"What happened to Billy?"

"We broke up."

"I'm sorry."

"For the best." Ashley tossed her long auburn hair defiantly and stared into the distance.

"I need to close my eyes again. I'm sorry . . ." Jessica listened to her mother and her sister and the nurse whisper together, then light footsteps, then the curtain closed gently, the rings jangling lightly on the metal rod, as she drifted into a dreamless sleep.

Thirty-Two
Music

Wednesday evening, a week after Jessica's ordeal and four weeks after the murder, the Comerford Chamber Music Society concluded their concert as the last notes hung in the air for three silent beats. The musicians stood and bowed, Zachary included, and Jessica applauded with the others who filled the music room. In his formal coat and tails, she thought he was most handsome. She could see his pride, though it wasn't obvious, and his eyes met hers with a delight she had not noticed before. Was that love? That she could see his secret delight?

Brenda, alongside Dr. Casparian, clapped vigorously for both of them as he nodded his appreciation as best he could. The applause lessened, and she wheeled him toward the reception in the salon across the foyer.

Jessica reflected on the week. She had come a long way since then, since hearing Zachary's voice and waking to his arms around her in the chapel. She had mumbled something she could not recall. There was an ambulance and an IV and nurses and doctors. They kept her at the hospital for twenty-four hours, rehydrating and stabilizing her. Her wound was deep and healing slowly. She changed the dressings twice a day, keeping it dry and clean.

Shelley had returned, worried but challenged by events. And slowly, each day, Jessica regained her strength, encouraged by Zachary's half hour of conversation each afternoon. He was a good friend. Her mother had visited, and Jessica insisted that she was going to be fine. They spoke of Ashley and of weaving their family together again.

Now, as the room cleared, Zachary came to her, followed by a beautiful black woman, the conductor, a Dr. Warner, according to the program.

"I want you to meet someone," Zachary said. "Laurie Warner, may I present my good friend, Jessica Thierry."

245

Jessica looked into the woman's bright eyes, and she recognized a kindred soul. She sensed that Laurie Warner had suffered but had used the suffering for good. Jessica grinned and took the proffered hand in hers. "I'm honored to meet you," she said, meaning every word. "The concert was incredible."

"Thank you. I'm honored to meet you too, Miss Jessica," Laurie said, winking at Zachary. "I've heard a good deal about you, I must warn you, from this charming young man who works in my store. But also my dear friend Anna goes on and on about you, not to mention our Father Nate, my old parish priest." Laurie considered Zachary with pride, as though the boy were her own. "He's not a bad pianist either . . . in a pinch." She grinned.

Zachary blushed and Jessica laughed. "So you're not only the conductor of the Chamber Music Society but the Laurie of Laurie's Fine Books?" She loved connecting the dots. Sometimes the world shrank to human size; sometimes one could hold it in the palm of one's hand and imagine one day understanding it. This was one of those sweet moments.

"I am the very same. Now, Miss Jessica, I heard about your recent ordeal. Are you recovered?" She narrowed her eyes in concern.

"I'm better, thank you." Jessica glanced at her wrapped arm, then remembered the offer of a room. "And thank you for saying I could stay with you. That was generous of you."

"It was my pleasure. Now don't overdo things, just let friends help you." She glanced meaningfully at Zachary. "I'm so glad to finally meet you, Miss Jessica, but I'd better join the others. Stop by the store sometime. I might be able to help you with your history project."

Jessica nodded. "Thanks—Zachary told you about my dissertation?"

"Anna too. Everyone is thrilled with the subject. I loved Presentation High."

Jessica started. "You went to Presentation High?"

"I did, and St. Joseph's Church, where I still attend from time to time. Would you like to interview me for your dissertation? I might have some old yearbooks, photos, newsletters, that sort of thing."

"My mom's idea," Zachary added, "and a good one, don't you think?"

"I'd love to interview you," Jessica said.

"There are other alumnae in the area. Come to our next reunion." Her face lit up. "And I'll connect you with the sisters. They still teach and do good works all over the world."

Jessica nodded with appreciation. "That would be perfect. Thank you so much."

"I'd better join the reception." Laurie crossed the room and looked back. "Are you coming? Having a little wine and cheese?"

"In a minute," Zachary said, as they watched her leave. He turned to Jessica. "How did you like the concert?"

"It was beautiful. You played perfectly."

Zachary shook his head. "Lots of mistakes, but it was such an honor to play with the CCMS."

"You were a last-minute substitute?"

He nodded. "Probably won't happen again, not after this."

"Why?"

"Didn't you hear the missed beats?"

"I didn't hear anything that wasn't perfect. You played beautifully . . . you really did." Her voice, once controlled and smooth, began to tremble, something the doctor said would go away with time.

"What's wrong?"

"I'm still a little shaky. Zachary, I keep thinking about him. Nightmares. It was four weeks ago today that I saw him—and the body—on the Fire Trail. It was only last week that he suddenly reappeared."

His brow pulled together and he touched her shoulder tenderly. "I know."

With a slight halt in her step, Jessica walked to the open windows and gazed over the forest, the city, and the bay spread under the dark sky.

"He's gone. He can't hurt you," Zachary whispered, close behind her.

"Detective Gan told me." She barely mouthed the words. "In spite of all he did, I feel bad for him . . . that he lived such a life and died such a death."

The flag still flew, not yet taken down for the day. The stars and stripes rippled in the breeze, lit by the porch light.

Zachary put his arm around her gently, avoiding her wound. "The officer had to shoot him when he found him in the woods. The man rushed him with a knife."

"I suppose the officer had to defend himself, but –"

"The man had choices."

"You think that he really had choices in his life?"

"No one forced him to get high on speed. No one forced him to lie in wait on the Fire Trail for a lone runner."

"I guess not. It was a random attack, wasn't it? Verona Bradley just happened to be the one coming by."

"It could have been any lone woman on the trail at that time."

"But this last time . . . I came across him . . ." She shuddered. "That wasn't by chance was it?"

"He was watching for you, just as you feared."

"But tried to deny."

"We all want to deny painful realities. You saw him at the murder scene. You could identify him."

"Who was he?"

"Detective Gan said he was wanted for other crimes in other states. People's Park was his latest landing place. He was an addict and a dealer and went where he could negotiate his stash. The police were watching him, but didn't have enough evidence to charge him. He went by the name Zebediah the Great, but I haven't learned his real name."

"It's sad that he never found help."

"Life can be sad. But I'm learning that life is both sad and joyous and all the degrees in between. The dark and the light. But we can choose to move toward the light, toward civility, as Dr. Casparian would say, and toward God, as Father Nate would say. And we can still care about those who don't make that choice. That, perhaps, is the key to the civilized world."

Jessica considered his words, then said, "I like Laurie. She's a civilized person."

Zachary grinned. "She's amazing. She has lots of stories to tell, and maybe she'll share them one day. I could see she liked you, and she's a good judge of character. Can see right through people. That reminds me, I have something for you, something Laurie found for me, since she sold the last copy." Zachary felt in his satchel and pulled out a slim black volume. He handed it to her. "A promise is a promise."

Jessica examined the book, *Sonnets from the Portuguese*. "Elizabeth Barrett Browning, your poet! How wonderful. Thank you, Zachary."

"My great pleasure. One day I shall recite one of the sonnets for you, if you like. I'm not ready yet."

It was Jessica's turn to feel the heat rise to her cheeks. "I'd like that."

Zachary paused, then said, "Are you feeling up to joining the reception?"

Light chatter drifted across the foyer from the parlor opposite. "I'm not sure."

At that moment Father Nate, leaning on a cane, Anna at his side, entered the room.

"He's home," Zachary said. He helped Father Nate into a chair.

"I'm glad to see you, my son."

Jessica could hear the love in his words. He was weak, but he had the old fire in his eyes and she was grateful.

"I wasn't sure if I would see anyone again," he said, "at least on this good earth. Looks like I have more work to do after all."

Anna smiled. "I brought him home today and we've been watching him carefully. I'm glad they kept him for awhile after that infection set in."

Jessica could see her relief. "All clear now?" She couldn't imagine Comerford House without Father Nate.

"If he takes his antibiotics." Anna waved her finger at the priest.

"And Miss Jessica, you look like you survived your ordeal, so my prayers were answered. It was a terrible and frightening time for all of us. We were so worried about you."

"I'm much better, thank you, Father Nate," Jessica replied. "And I'm glad you're all right."

"Thanks be to God you're on the mend. And I'll be all right, right enough anyway." With a glance at Zachary he added, "Miss Jessica, did you enjoy the concert? We were listening from the foyer. They set up extra seats, since the room was packed. I thought it was magnificent." He steepled his fingers, nodding. "Especially the pianist."

"Thanks, Father," Zachary said, "I did my best but—"

"You were excellent, no apologies." Father Nate's eyes traveled to each of them in turn, as though assessing them at this moment in their lives.

And in that moment, in her weakness from her ordeal, Jessica's heart opened to this new family given her, as though reborn. She, like Father Nate, now considered each of them in turn, and was thankful, simply for their friendship, their ease with one another.

Father Nate pulled himself out of the chair and took Anna's arm. "Shall we join the party, my dear? I never liked sherry much, but the tea is calling me. I could use a nice hot cup of tea."

Anna patted his hand. "Father, you haven't told them the news about Comerford House."

Jessica waited, expectant.

Father Nate beamed. "Looks like we have another miracle. The coins are valuable artifacts, as well as the cape and the lantern, all dating to the eighteenth century. There is some consternation that the cape survived all the years. At any rate, the Foundation Board is optimistic about Comerford staying open with these recent finds."

A distant fragment of a memory, full of sweetness, color, and longing, nudged the edges of Jessica's consciousness. She searched and searched but couldn't retrieve it. "I'm so glad Comerford House will stay open," she said, happy to see Father Nate happy, and relieved to see Anna's relief.

"Me too," Zachary said.

The pair stepped across the room, the priest's gait slower than before, as though it hurt to move. Jessica guessed his chest was still bandaged under his shirt. She touched her own bandaged arm and thought of her mother and her visit to the hospital. Their monthly meeting at the cemetery was scheduled for ten in the morning. Ashley was supposed to join them.

"Zachary, I've gotten to know and like your mother—she's become my mentor and friend. Would you like to meet *my* mother and my sister?" Jessica surprised herself as the words burst out unplanned.

"I'd like that," Zachary said. "I'd like that very much."

"I join her at Queen of Heaven Cemetery in Lafayette the first Thursday of each month. Ashley might come too."

"To visit your father's grave?"

"And Samantha's."

"Of course. I'd be honored."

"Thank you."

"I've been thinking," Zachary said, hesitantly. "I believe that God showed me where you were hidden. He answered my prayer."

Jessica noticed a new tone in Zachary's voice, one of security and certainty and thankfulness. "Really? You prayed?"

"Would you like to go to St. Joseph's one day, for a real service? The white vaults and the light and the stained glass and . . . the singing. It was beautiful. It was transcendent."

Jessica nodded. "I'd like that." She recalled the chanting, the adoration and worship, but also the certainty, the sanity, the sense of safety. "Maybe Laurie will be there. Let's ask Father Nate and your mom. They might like to come too. St. Joseph's was his parish, as I recall."

"He still goes occasionally to a weekday Mass or an early Sunday Mass."

They fell into a comfortable silence, and Jessica eyed the piano. "Play it for me, Zachary." She turned toward him, half teasing, half serious.

"Play what? The Beethoven concerto? You just heard it."

"I know, but play it like you played it that day."

"When I opened the door and there you were?" He bowed from the waist. "I'd be happy to."

Zachary walked to the grand piano and sat on the bench; she sat alongside. He counted the beats and began to play. As the notes gathered and soared, and as they formed rivers and streams, cascading through the open window into the forest and over

Berkeley and the bay beyond, Jessica placed her hand lightly on his to feel the music's beauty through his fingers.

And as she did, as her hand joined his, she entered his world, and he entered hers. He turned and gazed at her with his deep brown eyes, and she wondered what he saw. She hoped he saw beauty. She hoped he saw eternity, for in that moment she knew they had stepped outside of time, and for such a friend, or perhaps for someone more than a friend, she was truly grateful. Confidence took root in her heart, safety seemed within reach, and she thought she might be on the edge of love.

If she could enter that country of civility and sanity, of ordered passion, even with just one other, she might keep the uncivil and the insane out. She and Zachary could draw a border around such a country. They could create their own Fire Trail.

Author's Notes

The histories in this work are true, to the best of my research, including the histories of Berkeley, the Presentation Sisters, and the Comerfords. The McKinnon family is fictitious, as is their historic house and the present-day characters in this story. The news reports come from reports either on the day mentioned in September of 2014 or within a few weeks.

More information about the Presentation Sisters can be found at www.presentationsisterssf.org. A delightful video recounting their history in California, produced in commemoration of their 160th anniversary in 2014, may be found on the site.

In 2013, Pope Francis declared Nano Nagle, foundress of the Presentation Sisters, as *Venerable*, a Servant of God, "heroic in virtue," a person of sanctity, proposed for beatification and canonization as a saint.

The Fidelity Society is loosely based on the Anscombe Society, begun at Princeton, and the Love and Fidelity Network which links such university groups.

The music pieces mentioned can be accessed through YouTube and are indeed exquisitely beautiful.

I have taken a few topographical liberties with Berkeley streets and campus routes, but have tried to keep their essence intact.

The Fire Trail looping through the Berkeley hills remains a popular trail for joggers, walkers, and hikers of all ages, particularly recommended to enjoy with a friend.

About the Author

CHRISTINE SUNDERLAND, deeply concerned with America's cultural collapse, the decline in civil order, and threats to freedom of speech and religion, is the author of five award-winning novels: *Pilgrimage, Offerings, Inheritance, Hana-lani,* and *The Magdalene Mystery.*

She holds a BA in English Literature from San Francisco State University, *Summa Cum Laude.* She serves as Project Manager for the Berkeley Center for Western Civilization (www.WesternCivCenter.org) and Managing Editor for the American Church Union (www.AmericanChurchUnion.com). She writes a weekly blog on faith and culture, and contributes to American Christian Fiction Writers, The Christian Post, Liberty Island Magazine, and CatholicFiction.net. Visit Christine at www.ChristineSunderland.com. She lives in the San Francisco Bay Area with her husband and two incredible cats.

Endnotes for Jessica's Dissertation

[1] Many of the hospitals, social work institutions, and schools in the Bay Area today were founded by Roman Catholic nuns who arrived in San Francisco in the 1850s and 1860s.

[2] Forest, Sister Mary Rose, PBVM, *With Hearts of Oak, The story of the Sisters of the Presentation of the Blessed Virgin Mary in California 1854-1907* (San Francisco: Sisters of the Presentation of the Blessed Virgin Mary, 2004), 2.

[3] Ibid., 23.

[4] Ibid., 99-100, *Oakland Evening Tribune*, July 1, 1878.

[5] Ibid., 102, *History of Alameda County, California Including Is Geology, Topography, Soil, and Productions; Together with a Full and Particular Record of the Spanish Grants*, 799.

[6] Ibid., 103.

[7] Sandweiss, Eric, *Historical and Cultural Review: Presentation High School, Berkeley, California* (University of California, Office of Property Development: 1990).

[8] Stadtman, Verne, ed. (1967). *The Centennial Record of the University of California*. Regents of the University of California, p. 114. Centennial Record of the University of California.

[9] *With Hearts of Oak*, 123.

[10] Ibid., 140.

[11] Ibid., 145.

[12] From a private history written by Dianne Walker, University Terrace, Berkeley.

[13] Sister Stephanie Still, PBVM, President, Sisters of the Presentation of the Blessed Virgin Mary.

Printed in Great Britain
by Amazon

76855710R00158